Love . . . From Both Sides

Nick Spalding is an author who, try as he might, can't seem to write anything serious. He's worked in the communications industry his entire life, mainly in media and marketing. As talking rubbish for a living can get tiresome (for anyone other than a politician), he thought he'd have a crack at writing comedy fiction – with an agreeable level of success so far, it has to be said. Nick lives in the south of England with his fiancée. He is approaching his forties with the kind of dread usually associated with a trip to the gallows, suffers from the occasional bout of insomnia, and still thinks Batman is cool. Nick Spalding is one of the top ten bestselling authors in eBook format in 2012. You can find out more about Nick by following him on twitter https://twitter.com/spalding_author or by reading his blog http://spaldings-racket.blogspot.co.uk/

Love . . . From Both Sides

Nick Spalding

CORONET

First published in Great Britain in 2012 by Coronet
An imprint of Hodder & Stoughton
An Hachette UK company

First published in paperback in 2013

6

A CIP catalogue record for this title is available from the British Library

ISBN 978 1 444 76817 6

Typeset in Plantin Light by Palimpsest Book Production Limited,
Falkirk, Stirlingshire

Printed and bound in the UK by
CPI Group (UK) Ltd, Croydon, CR0 4YY

Hodder & Stoughton policy is to use papers that are natural, renewable and
recyclable products and made from wood grown in sustainable forests. The
logging and manufacturing processes are expected to conform to the
environmental regulations of the country of origin.

Hodder & Stoughton Ltd
338 Euston Road
London NW1 3BH

www.hodder.co.uk

Contents

Author's Note

'You should write a book about dating,' my fiancée said to me one evening, while I was putting the finishing touches to my previous book, *Life . . . On A High*.

'I can't,' I told her. 'I've used all the funny stories I know in this book.'

'You're not the only one who's had dating disasters, Spalding,' she pointed out. 'I've got some you could write about. I'm sure your friends have too.'

It turns out she was right. After several wine-soaked conversations with the variety of reprobates I call my friends, I had enough material for a new book. More than enough, in fact.

It looks like finding the love of your life is filled with more pitfalls, pratfalls and problems than I'd imagined. From the stories I've heard over the past few months it's frankly a miracle any relationships get off the ground at all.

Jamie and Laura aren't real people, but the trials and tribulations they go through over the course of this story most certainly are.

This book is dedicated to everyone who's gone through

the hell of dating and tried to keep a smile on their face while doing it. It's also dedicated to the girl that made going through it all *completely* worthwhile for me.

I love you with all my heart, gorgeous girl.

Nick.

Jamie's Blog
Sunday 9 January

Oh God, her breath smells like the gates of hell have opened . . .

This was the first thought that went through my head when I met Isobel outside the local J D Wetherspoon on Thursday night. The second was that I would be killing Jackie the moment I stepped into the office on Monday morning.

'Oh, you should meet my friend Isobel,' the evil, lying harridan had said over the coffee machine a couple of weeks ago. 'She's a lovely girl. I think you two will really get on!'

And like an idiot I'd believed her.

Jackie has a reputation for being sickeningly positive and upbeat about almost everything, so I should have known her assessment of Isobel's character would be *way* off the mark. Jackie would have probably got on quite well with Hitler if he hadn't talked much about that whole Jewish thing, and instead concentrated on celebrity love triangles.

I chose to ignore my gut instincts, however. I've been single for two years now – and in those trying circumstances desperation trumps common sense every time.

Two years . . .

I still can't believe it. It's the longest I've ever been on my own. The number of Asda Meals For One I've bought must run into the thousands. Not that I wanted to date for a long time after Carla, it has to be said. The whole experience with my demonic ex-fiancée convinced me that being Captain Single was the way forward for the first few months after her evil stench had dissipated.

A man can only go so long without the comfort of a good woman by his side, though.

Of course, when I say 'a good woman' I mean one with a heartbeat and no skin diseases, and when I say 'by his side' I mean on top of him and naked. The trauma of the bad break-up with Carla may have put me off dating emotionally and intellectually, but you try telling my stupid penis that.

Frankly, Jackie could have told me Isobel's vagina was like a bear trap and I would still have considered going on a blind date with her.

Despite her being the oral harbinger of the apocalypse, I decide to give Isobel a chance – providing I can find a seat downwind of her.

The horrendous breath is palpable from a good foot away, so the kiss on the cheek by way of greeting is a bad idea: it brings me close to the Gates of Hades. I hold my breath though and escape relatively unscathed.

Isobel isn't entirely unattractive, though her mousey brown hair is scraped back into a ponytail so tight it's acting like a DIY facelift. My eyes start to water in sympathy. Her boobs look quite nice, peeking out as they do from a Wonderbra that's at least a size too small for her. The black blouse she's also elected to wear is too frilly, and the maroon knee-length skirt doesn't do much for her square arse, but it's either an hour in the pub with her or back to my flat for some more lonely masturbation and barbecue flavour Pringles.

I open the pub door with a sigh of resignation and wait for her to go in.

'Fanks very much. Ain't you a gentleman?' Isobel says, her bad breath apparently strong enough to render her unable to pronounce Ts and Hs.

'My pleasure,' I reply, forcing a smile.

I can't help but look at her square arse with a degree of despondency as she walks ahead of me towards the bar. I can't help but feel that its boxy form is in some way symbolic of my complete and utter failure to establish a successful relationship with a woman recently.

'What would you like to drink?' I ask when we get to the rather greasy-looking bar, hoping she'll order a pint of Listerine.

'Double vodka and Red Bull, please mate.'

Good grief.

Five minutes later sees Jamie Newman and his lovely blind date ensconced in one of the ratty-looking booths that run along the back wall of the pub. The table we sit at is largely free of stains, but someone has carved 'Pete wanks the big one' round one edge in elaborate letters, in a feat of whittling that must have taken the best part of an hour to finish.

Some may believe that Thursday is the new Friday, but

none of them are frequenting this place tonight. It's deader than Elvis in here. Breath monster and I are the only customers, save a wizened old man in a green cagoule nursing half a bitter at the bar, and two fat lads of indeterminate age huddled around the fruit machine, inserting their Jobseeker's Allowance into it with an eagerness that represents a real triumph of mindless optimism over cold, hard reality.

'Jacks says you do journalism stuff,' Isobel remarks, swigging her drink and no doubt resisting the urge to belch every time she does.

'Um . . . yes. Kind of.'

I'm actually a freelance public relations consultant and copywriter, currently working with a local newspaper on re-branding their image, but trying to explain the difference to Isobel would require a flip chart and the patience of Job, so I just leave it there.

'Do you enjoy it?'

'Er . . . yeah. I suppose so. I really love to write, and the job certainly gives me a lot of opportunity to do it, so it could be worse.'

'Really?' Isobel sneers. 'I fucking hate writing.'

I'm amazed.

'You gotta worry about all that grandma stuff, haven't you?'

Yes indeed.

Many times I've been hunched over a particularly difficult piece of promotional copy with my grandmother slapping me around the head every time she spots an unnecessary adverb.

'Jackie says you're a hairdresser,' I say, changing the subject.

'That's right. Got my own business, haven't I?'

I bet it's called Curl Up 'N' Dye.

'It's called A Cut Above!'

Damn.

'I'm doin' really well. Loadsa customers these days. Taking a week off next month for some holibobs in Menorca.'

Kill me. Kill me now.

'Aah . . . that's lovely,' I say, taking a large gulp of lukewarm Stella Artois.

'You going on 'oliday anywhere, Jake?'

'Jamie,' I correct her. 'Maybe. I've got some friends in Canada I was thinking of visiting later in the year if I get the chance.'

'Never really thought nothing about Canada,' Isobel says, mangling her double negatives for all she's worth. 'I know they speak French.' She pauses, head cocked to one side. 'Is Canada near France then?'

Oh my, yes. Jackie is going to get it in the neck and no mistake . . .

Speaking of mistakes, I'll freely admit I probably made a big one by having sex with Isobel that night.

However, the above was only the first of *many* large gulps of lukewarm beer I had that evening, in an attempt to arrest the slide into crippling depression. And we all know that too much alcohol can rapidly escalate a situation from quite bad to absolutely dreadful in no time at all.

By the time Isobel is telling me all about how her

5

brother has just been released from jail – having served a six-month stretch for a burglary that '*them bastard coppers fitted him up for*' – I'm halfway through pint number five and her arse is looking a lot less square.

By pint seven I've got my hand on her thigh and she's massaging my genitals under the table. I say massaging . . . *kneading* is more accurate. If Isobel ever wants to trade A Cut Above for a bread shop she already has the skills and technique to a T.

Still, it's making me hard – which just goes to show that when you haven't had sex for two years, having your genitals squeezed like a pound of dough is not necessarily a barrier to sexual excitement.

'Put your hand up my skirt,' she whispers in my ear.

I drunkenly oblige, shoving my arm between Isobel's legs with all the grace and sophistication you'd expect from a man way past the legal limit. I resemble a butcher prepping a Christmas turkey for stuffing.

I manage to get my little finger caught in her suspender, which bends it back painfully and causes me to simultaneously stab her in the vagina with my thumb. This doesn't appear to bother Isobel in the slightest. In fact, she leers at me like a sex offender and moves in for a kiss. One of her hands crushes my testicles in a death grip, while the other one wraps itself around my forearm, keeping my hand exactly where she wants it – hovering over her growler.

I'm very proud to say I don't vomit.

Not even as my nose is assailed by a blast of horror breath emanating from her mouth – now delightfully laced with the aroma of seven double vodka and Red Bulls. Her tongue goes down my throat in an apparent attempt to lick my kidneys. I feel like John Hurt in *Alien*.

After thirty seconds that last two hours, Isobel lets me come up for air and I make every effort not to gag. As far as I'm concerned this is one of the worst things that's ever happened to me, but I look down to find that my battered penis completely disagrees and wants more.

Isobel locks her face round mine again and unzips my fly in an expert piece of multi-tasking that must have come from years of practice. Her long fingernails snake into my trousers and find purchase. What follows is a sensation that only cows getting milked can fully appreciate.

However, this change in tactic and grip allows me to remove my arm from the moist sex cauldron lying underneath her skirt.

I break away from the stomach-churning kiss to grab what's left of my seventh pint – and drain the bastard in one go, trying to fight back tears of shame as I do.

'I want to screw you,' Isobel gurgles into my ear.

Do you really? I hadn't realised . . . what with you pretty much jerking me off in public, and your skirt pulled up high enough for me to see the Poundland thong you're wearing.

'Okay,' I mumble back, deathly afraid I'm about to ejaculate over her hand – thus ruining the hideous plans she no doubt has in store for me back at the flesh palace she calls home.

One short but traumatic taxi ride later I'm surprised to find that the flesh palace is actually a rather neat three-bedroom semi-detached in an area of town where the drug dealers have the good grace to conduct their business indoors.

'Me mam's place,' Isobel explains. 'I'm only livin' here until the divorce is finalised.'

I really am going to kill Jackie.

Isobel's mum is out, thank God. If she's anything like her daughter I'd have found myself being double-teamed into an early grave. The front door is barely closed before Isobel is on her knees and unzipping my trousers again. She whips out my abused penis – which by now is beginning to resemble a caveman's club.

The experience that follows can be accurately recreated by any man who might be reading this. If you're a woman you'll just have to use your imagination. Simply find the nearest Henry hoover, turn it on and stick your John Thomas in the hose. If you can find a yak nearby that's trying to clear a particularly large hairball, you'll get the aural effect as well.

I'm not complaining though. Not out loud, at least. This is the first blow job I've had in two years – since Carla decided her boss was a better prospect for having healthy children and a balanced bank account, and promptly left me. I was surprised about it at the time, but looking back the signs were most definitely there. Especially when it came to bedroom shenanigans. Our sex life had dwindled from the daily double feature when we first met, to a monthly late-night show four years later – one that generally finished with an unsatisfactory climax before the end credits.

Carla could never manage to get both my testicles in

her mouth, it should be noted. Isobel is quite the talented lass. She eventually stops her impression of a performing seal and stands up with a look of such animal aggression in her eyes I regret not telling my loved ones where I was going that evening.

'Upstairs, big boy,' she orders. 'You're gonna eat me.'

I trust she means that she wants me to perform cunnilingus on her – and not that she wants me to engage in cannibalism. I can't be a hundred per cent sure either way, though.

Isobel pulls me up the stairs by my belt, my penis waggling around merrily as we approach her bedroom. On the door is one of those children's name plaques. 'Isobel' is written on it in bubblegum pink and a couple of tutu-clad fairies squat at either end, gormless smiles on their cherubic faces. It hits me that I'm about to have carnal knowledge of a sexually belligerent divorcée in her childhood hideaway.

Once we are in the room, Isobel pulls her skirt down in a flash, her square arse exposed for me to see and (sort of) enjoy. Her blouse is next, revealing those attractive breasts we spoke about earlier.

Focus on the boobs, Jamie, I tell myself. *That'll get you through this.*

Isobel lies on the bed, spreads her legs and pulls her Poundland thong to one side.

'Get to work,' she demands.

Even my penis is starting to have doubts about this whole debacle now and is beginning to lose its happy mood. Still, I've come this far, so I do indeed 'get to work' as best I can.

Thankfully Isobel's lack of hygiene is only an oral issue – otherwise the seven pints I've consumed would probably return for a triumphant encore right about now.

Isobel grabs me by both ears and pulls my head in so hard it's like childbirth in reverse. As I lap like an arthritic dog trying to satisfy Isobel's desires as best I can, I'm painfully aware that I have to insert my currently flaccid penis into her at some point in the very near future.

The scene now looks so pathetic, from an objective point of view it's enough to make a grown man cry: Me squatting on the floor at the side of Isobel's single bed, performing drunk oral sex on her and mindlessly flogging my penis in a last ditch attempt to get it hard enough to penetrate the hairdressing sex fiend; Isobel with her legs locked around my neck, her head thrown back in an orgiastic display of carnal delight.

'Do me now!' she screeches like a hyperactive drill sergeant.

'Okay!' I cry subserviently and stand up, still beating myself off like a man possessed. Luckily I'm just about upstanding enough to enter Isobel's dark domain.

This is like chucking a chipolata up the Blackwall Tunnel.

I don't know who Isobel's soon to be ex-husband is, but there must be horse DNA in his genetic code.

Despite my lack of girth and malfunctioning erectile tissue, Isobel seems to be enjoying herself immensely and starts spouting such filth from her mouth it makes me wish I'd brought a crucifix.

'Oh yes . . . ram that hot pussy, you horny bastard!'

Yes ma'am! Please don't hit me!

'You feel massive!'

I'm pretty sure I don't, love, but thanks for the vote of confidence.

'Bury me, you bastard. Bury me!'

With a stake through your heart and some holy water? No problem!

'Cum all over my face! I want it in my mouth!'

Which might explain the awful breath, I suppose.

All I want to do now is arrive . . . then leave. Nothing would give me greater pleasure than to escape this sexcapade from hell and retreat to the safety and sanctity of my one-bedroom house. In my thirty-one years on this planet, I've never felt so completely helpless.

Isobel suddenly stops bucking and thrashing like a landed turbot and stares me right in the eye. 'I'm done. Pull out and finish over me.'

I once read that the universe is a place of diametric opposites: Good vs evil, light vs darkness, love vs hate and so on and so forth. If there is a place in the universe that is the epitome of love, romance and passion . . . then this woman's bedroom on a Thursday evening in January is surely at the absolute other end.

Isobel opens her gob so wide it's like I'm about to ejaculate into a pedal bin.

With a cheerless grunt I spurt over my blind date, getting some in her eyes. The rest spatters onto her breasts and face, along with what's left of my self esteem. I know I haven't actually just been raped, but I'm definitely in the neighbourhood and looking at the map for directions.

I tuck Jamie Junior back into his hidey-hole and look down at Isobel. All pretence has now left my body, along with my spermatozoa.

'Can I leave now?' I ask forlornly.

Isobel's expression of sexual contentment is replaced by one of disgust.

'Well that's charming, isn't it? I give you a good time and you just want to piss off straight away?'

I start to argue that the only person who's had a good time in this room tonight is her, but can't summon the energy to defend myself and just nod my head in resignation.

Isobel jumps to her feet. 'Get out then!' she screams and thrusts her finger in the direction of the door.

There's still some of my 'product' on her hand, which flicks violently off. It flies across the room and splats onto a badly rendered portrait of Jesus hanging above Isobel's dressing table. If somebody had told me that this evening would end with my semen sliding down the cheek of our Lord and Saviour, I would probably have stayed indoors and played *Gran Turismo*.

Isobel may be a man-hungry lunatic with a sex drive like a malfunctioning Formula One car, but it also transpires she is a religious nut as well.

She lets out a cry of anguish, rushes over to the portrait and starts wiping it with her blouse. It's an oil painting, so Big J's cheek gets smudged badly as she feverishly tries to clean off my man gravy. Isobel starts crying.

'I'm sorry!' I wail, as if I'd actively gone over and knocked one out over Christ's face on purpose.

'Just bloody leave!' Isobel orders, and for once I'm delighted to follow instructions.

'Er . . . bye then!' I offer, along with a half-hearted wave – and exit stage left with great urgency.

Taking the stairs two at a time, I reach ground level in three seconds flat and see Isobel's mother coming in through the front door. Given that *Good evening, madam, I've just penetrated your daughter and mucked up on the son of God* isn't the best way of introducing oneself, I elect to repeat the half-hearted wave, along with a smile bordering on the maniacal.

I decide it's best not to wait around for a response, and am off running down the front path as fast as my little legs can carry me, hoping Izzy's mum hasn't got a good enough look at my face to provide an accurate description to the police.

Unbelievably, I get a text from Isobel the next day:

That woz a weird nite. Ur fun tho. Wanna hook up again? U can have me up the backdoor if u like xxx.

Thus far I have neglected to respond.

Laura's Diary
Wednesday, February 2nd

Dear Mum,

Your daughter is a shameful excuse for a human being. Any redeeming value I may have had was extinguished last night in an act so heinous I may never recover. All I can say by way of explanation is that I did it because I thought I needed to 'get back into the game', as it were – and pleasuring Brian with my hand on our first date seemed the most appropriate method of doing so . . . for some reason.

Quite why I thought giving a twenty-nine-year-old estate agent with a lazy eye a hand job was the best way to reintroduce myself to the dating scene completely eludes me.

It was totally out of character.

You never brought me up to be that kind of girl, after all. Before this I'd not so much as kissed a man before the third date. But there I was, sitting in the passenger seat of his 52 plate Vectra doing my best milkmaid impression, while looking out of the window wondering how I'd arrived at this place in my life.

You know how bad I was after Mike and I split up – but I don't think *I'd* even realised how much of a knock my confidence had taken, until I was staring at Brian's average penis as he went cross-eyed and started to dribble.

I hadn't really wanted the date. Tim had pushed me into it.

'It'll be good for you, Loz,' he told me over his cappuccino with an almond twist. 'Dan tells me Brian is a very nice boy. They go to the gym together. Apparently he's not that well hung, but has a lovely body otherwise.'

'I'm not sure, Tim. Blind dates and I have never agreed with one another. You remember Mr Pants, don't you? I certainly do. I still have nightmares about it.'

'You can't sit around waiting for Mr Right to walk into your life for much longer, miss. That evil thirtieth birthday is looming on the horizon, you know!'

'Yeah, yeah. I know.'

Boy, do I know. I'm afraid a lifetime of watching the wrong movies and reading the wrong magazines has convinced me (like a million other women) that reaching thirty without being part of a successful relationship is worse than contracting leprosy. If only I'd known this, I'd have avoided every single Jennifer Aniston film ever made and read *Caravanning Monthly* instead.

There's a smirk on Tim's face I don't like the look of one bit.

'Dan showed Brian your picture on Facebook,' he said with a twinkle in his eye. 'He really liked the look of you.'

'Oh bloody hell, Tim! You could have warned me. My profile picture is still that one of me dressed as the Bride of Frankenstein from last year's Halloween party.'

'Don't worry. Dan wouldn't have concentrated on that one. I'm sure he went straight to the Goa bikini shots.'

'I'm not so sure they're any better.'

'Please! Those tits of yours look fantastic.'

'Wow. You make me sound so *classy*.'

'Classy doesn't get you dates, Loz. When it comes to straight men, the tits do it every time. Brian *really* wants to meet you.'

I stared out of the Starbucks window in much the same way I'd be looking out of Brian's windscreen a few days later.

'Oh, alright. I suppose it can't hurt.'

'Great, I'll get Dan to give Brian your number. Expect a call!'

That's how the date came about, Mum. You always used to say Tim was a bad influence and would get me into trouble.

I know it's a gigantic cliché for a single girl to have a gay best friend, but Tim has always given me what I thought was good advice in the past – most notably when he talked me out of getting a Robbie Williams tattoo on my arse in the final year of school, and when he ordered me to dump Mitchell The Snorter a scant three weeks before the maniac was arrested for indecent exposure. I never shared your concerns that Tim might lead me astray, so I had to trust him on this blind date thing – for better or for worse.

Five days after my chat with Tim I'm standing in front of the mirror wondering what the hell to wear that might impress an estate agent who isn't well hung, but has a lovely body otherwise.

Deciding is no easy task. I have to wonder at what point somebody has come into my flat and burgled me of every item of evening wear that doesn't make me look like a prostitute at one end of the spectrum, or an Amish grandmother at the other. My wardrobe is full to bursting, but all of it is equally and totally awful. Some strange form of schizophrenia comes over me whenever I go clothes shopping, where a totally different woman inhabits my body and makes purchases – resulting in the owner-ship of piles and piles of crap no-one in her right mind would wear.

I can stand here now and remember picking up the salmon pink playsuit in H&M, thinking it would look nice with my complexion. I can even remember walking up to the counter and paying for it, happy I'd picked up a brilliant bargain. I stare at it now though and it looks like something only a colour-blind, mentally disabled super-hero would don of an evening. I can only stand in front of the mirror with it on for about thirty seconds before becoming heavily nauseous. The colour alone makes me look like the contents of a fishmonger's bin.

I'm thinking this probably isn't the right note to strike on my date with Brian.

My contact with Mr Lovely Body Otherwise had so far amounted to one phone call, conducted at my end in the fruit aisle of Tesco. As I squeezed a few mangos, looking for one that hadn't gone too ripe, my phone rang and I answered it to find Brian on the other end, sounding nervous as hell. After a few standard pleasantries he asked me to a bar in the city called Fluid. It is one of those places usually frequented by men who wear fake Armani suits and drive Porsche Boxsters – accompanied by girls whose knicker elastic automatically loosens at the sight of both. It wasn't a good sign that Brian had picked it as the location of our first date. I would have preferred somewhere quieter that didn't contain several tonnes of chrome and brushed aluminium.

Still, as Tim reminded me, thirty is coming up fast and I'm ripening quicker than the Tesco mangos, so I agreed to meet Brian in Fluid at eight the next evening and hung up. A decision I was wholeheartedly regretting a day later, as I looked in my cupboard with the sure knowledge I had absolutely nothing to wear.

About the only item approximating fashionable was a black cocktail dress I wore once to a birthday party last year. I hadn't put it on since because it's too short and shows off my knobbly knees. I had to wear a pair of tights in order to disguise their horrific, malformed shape. Idly leafing through a coffee-table book a few months ago, I was dismayed to find a photo of the moon's surface that bore more than a little resemblance to them.

Sadly, the only other dress I would have considered wearing for the date was the red one I bought for Mike's pleasure on our third anniversary. It's virtually skin tight and puts my breasts on display like the meat on a butcher's counter. I couldn't be more forward if I wore a T-shirt saying 'This vagina for rent'.

So it was either the black cocktail dress or a phone call to Brian saying that I'd come down with a severe case of 'blowout-itis' and couldn't make it.

Every time I flipped open my ancient Nokia a vision of Tim's disgusted expression floated across my mind, so I pulled on the tights and slipped the dress over my head, allowing myself a small smile as it slid snugly over my hips. This smooth action proved that the chocolate binge from a couple of weeks ago hadn't as yet made its presence felt on my figure. Underwear-wise I went for a pair of plain black hipsters and matching bra. There was no point in putting anything sexy on, as the tights would have ruined the aesthetic completely. They were about as sexy as genital warts.

Besides, lovely body or not, Brian wasn't going to be investigating my lady garden that evening, so what would be the point?

The hair went back in a ponytail as I hadn't had time to wash it, and I also decided to apply make-up sparingly. My entire outfit screamed *I'm not entirely sure about this*, which was fine with me. If Brian turned out to be stimulating in every sense of the word I could break out the lacy thong, fresh dye job and ruby red lipstick the next time I saw him. I keep them all in a drawer at the bottom of my wardrobe marked 'whore-tastic' for such rare eventualities.

Slipping on the wedges I paid way too much for in the House of Fraser sale, I tottered out of my bedroom ready for battle . . .

An hour later I'm already considering a tactical withdrawal. It's not that Brian is necessarily a bad guy – it's just that he could quite easily pass for a new shipment of stock in the wallpaper department at B&Q.

If he were a colour he'd be beige. If he were a country he'd be Switzerland. If he were a member of Take That he'd be Howard. I'm sure he'd be the perfect match for a woman just like him, but as I'm after bright blue, Brazil and Robbie, this date isn't working out too well. Also, the tights are making my ankles sweat, which isn't helping matters.

You know how you always told me to be polite, Mum? This is the first time your advice has backfired. If I wasn't so polite I probably would have held up a hand as Brian started in on a third anecdote about his cricket team, and told him I was leaving before my brain suffered a boredom-related aneurism.

As it was, I just sipped my Pinot Grigio politely and tried to produce a dull smile every time Brian made a joke about googlies and being silly mid-off. I couldn't help but let my mind wander as he explained the finer points of county cricket to me, and started to look around the bar for people having a worse time than me. This is only natural. Misery loves company, as people are often heard to say – usually when they're the ones who are miserable and looking for some back-up.

Fluid is largely full of happy posh idiots this evening, but I do spy one woman sitting next to a fat man in a fake Armani suit who looks like she wants to kill him, then herself. Our eyes lock across the room and in an unspoken moment we feel each other's pain.

I'm on a blind date with someone who thinks it's a good idea to explain the rules of cricket, my expression seems to say.

Really? That's sounds like a fucking honeymoon, love, she

replies, without a word passing between us. *I've been married to this cretin for twelve years and eight belt notches. He's currently telling me how the stock portfolio will see us into our old age. He's blissfully unaware that I'm going to divorce him next week for cheating on me and rob him blind.* Quite how a roll of the eyes and a swift grimace tells me all of this I don't know, but I'm still sure that's what she's thinking.

I sigh and turn back to Brian, who is now telling me how to put a pair of cricket pads on. You may be wondering how I went from this state of affairs to pleasuring Brian in his Vauxhall Vectra, Mum. Well, you know how I came home at three in the morning when I was eighteen and you grounded me because I was completely shitfaced? You remember how you shouted *This is the kind of mess too much alcohol can get you into!* up the stairs while I threw up what felt like all of my internal organs?

The polite sips of Pinot Grigio turn into large swigs as Brian explains how the exhaust manifold cracked on his Vectra last week while he was driving to the monthly meeting of his Dungeons & Dragons clan. Even gulps aren't doing the job when he tells me how fascinating the equity market is at the moment – and I'm wishing the Pinot was mainlined straight into my bloodstream when he describes the great retro seventies wallpaper his mother let him hang in his bedroom last week. My partner in misery has left with her fat husband, so I can't even look to her for silent solace. No, I must now endure Brian and his anecdotes all on my own. While he is dull, the Pinot is unfortunately telling me he's also quite a handsome chap.

The Pinot lies, though. It is wicked, *wicked* stuff – ready and willing to lead a young girl down dark and winding paths to places she shouldn't go.

Brian looks at his watch. 'Wow, getting quite late, Laura. Would you like a lift home?'

Well now, Brian, let's see . . . It's either a lift with you, or a twenty-quid ride in a taxi.

I'm pretty drunk and wearing tights that are making my legs sweat like merry hell, so I'm willing to risk brain death listening to another one of your anecdotes, if it means I can have a free lift that'll get me home quicker.

'Yes please. That'd be lovely,' I tell him and swig the last dregs of my fifth large glass of wine.

I somehow manage to make it to the passenger seat of his Vectra in the virtually deserted car park at the back of Fluid without breaking an ankle on my four-inch wedges.

He climbs in the driver's side and looks at me. It's *that* look. The *I've spent the best part of thirty quid on you tonight and I'm hoping to get something out of it* look.

Now, I could just smile and tell Brian to get driving. He doesn't look the kind of guy who's likely to get fisty with a woman if he doesn't get his own way. The Pinot suggests that I shouldn't do that, however. It suggests I should just sit there and await developments.

Brian leans towards me.

'I had a really nice time tonight,' he says. 'You're easy to talk to.'

I'm quite surprised to hear this, as I have never played cricket, wouldn't know an orc wizard if it bit me on the butt and can't stand the seventies.

'Thanks.'

He leans a bit closer.

Now, as you know, Mum, I've not kissed a man other than Mike for five years. My relationship with him may have exploded into sharp, painful fragments at its conclusion, but I still remember how good the bastard was at making my toes curl whenever he planted his lips on mine. At the time I never dreamed of ever letting another man kiss me again, so I'm rustier than a Scottish weather vane when it comes to this kind of thing.

Had I been sober I would have put a stop to proceedings before they got out of hand, but the Pinot is in control and decides it might be a good idea to let Brian kiss me, just to remember what it feels like. Brian's technique is to purse his lips the way Nan used to when she said goodbye after Christmas lunch, and stab his head forward like a hungry chicken.

I break the kiss before he cracks my head against the passenger window. *Now what?*

'Well,' says Pinot, 'we don't want to kiss him again, do we?'

No, we bloody don't. I don't need bruised lips or a fractured skull.

'So we'd better do something else to satisfy him.'

What do you suggest, oh wine of the Italian vineyards?

'Screwing him is going a bit far.'

Yes . . . yes it is.

'I don't even fancy the prospect of a blow job, what with that neck strain we got from lying funny on the pillow last night.'

True.

'Well . . . you might as well toss him off then, Laura. It's been ages since you've had a penis in your hand and you'd better make sure you still know what you're doing with one before a guy comes along that you actually do want to date.'

The logic is unassailable. I reach my left hand down to the inevitable bulge between Brian's legs and give it a squeeze. He makes a strange noise as I do so: 'Blibble.' Not a sigh, or a moan, or even a sharp intake of breath. Just *blibble*. Weird. I unzip him and pull out what is indeed a very average but otherwise inoffensive penis.

'Oh Laura,' he says under his breath.

Oh brother, I think – and start to rhythmically pump my hand up and down. Unfortunately for me I've met the only Dungeons & Dragons fan in the world that doesn't orgasm the second a woman touches his genitals.

A full five minutes of pumping go by with no indication that Brian is about to arrive at his final destination. I've now started wondering what to buy the next time I'm in Tesco. I can't really think of anything I do want, but am bloody sure I *won't* be buying mangos.

My mind then moves onto work matters. This is par for the course these days. When I used to daydream about owning my own high street chocolate shop, I never thought about how stressful the whole thing would be. In my head I had visions of chatting with happy customers and creating new flavour combinations in the kitchen for them to try – I didn't for one second contemplate the realities of cataloguing profit and loss in an Excel spreadsheet and filling out multiple forms from the bank to obtain yet another loan to stay afloat.

Foremost on my mind as I continue to pump my hand is that I have to get a new order of those popular praline fondants into the shop by the end of the month, and the Green & Black's people will no doubt be on the phone again soon wanting to know if I'm re-ordering the summer selection this year. Running a shop on your own is rather like juggling a set of balls in zero gravity. I wouldn't recommend it to anyone with bad organisational skills.

I remember what I'm doing and look over to see that Brian has gone cross-eyed. A small dribble of saliva runs down his cheek. This is starting to get ridiculous. I'll have sobered up by the time he ejaculates at this rate. Time for some dirty talk.

'I want you to come for me, Brian, *right now*,' I say in a breathy whisper into his left ear. I mean it as well. There are two episodes of *Extreme Makeover* I've got recorded that I'd like to watch before bed.

The breathy thing seems to do the trick (doesn't it always?) and Brian christens my hand and his steering wheel with a shudder, along with another odd blibbling noise. He then says the following: 'Hoocheemumma!'

I don't know what 'hoocheemumma' means. Nor do I wish to.

I know men can say strange things when they climax (the second guy I was with shouted *There's the magic!* every time) but this particular piece of gibberish is on a whole other level. Brian says it in such a deep, throaty

25

voice it's like an African witch doctor is putting a hex on me. I hate to think what he might shout when he orgasms during full sex. Whatever it is, I'm sure it'd give the folk in the next village a good dose of herpes.

A quick clean-up with the (slightly worrying) pack of tissues Brian keeps in his glove box and I'm finally being driven home. I've established that I'm still quite capable of giving a man a hand job – and that I'm now firmly back in the dating scene.

Woo hoo.

I stagger out of Brian's Vectra before he gets the chance to kiss me goodbye.

'Can I see you again?' he shouts out of the window as I round the car, rummaging through my handbag for the front door keys. I look at Brian's expectant face.

'I'll text you,' I lie.

The Pinot has the decency to feel a little ashamed of itself as Brian offers me a happy smile and drives off into the night – a content and sexually satisfied estate agent.

I feel quite awful as I open the front door . . . and finally trip over the high wedges, landing spread-eagled on the carpet, painfully bashing one of my lumpy knees against the staircase.

Yes indeed, Laura McIntyre is back on the dating scene with a vengeance, Mum!

Love and miss you always,

Your shameless and shameful daughter, Laura.

xx

P.S. I've received *seven* texts from Brian since our date, asking in increasingly fraught tones about when the second one is going to be. I haven't worked out how I'm going to let him down yet without coming across as a complete bitch. I might get Tim and Dan to tell him I've come down with a dose of herpes. That should put him off.

Jamie's Blog

Saturday 26 February

There are invariably times in life when you wish you were somebody else. Last night, on my second blind date in as many months, I wish I'd been someone at least seventy-three per cent more physically attractive – with an IQ ten to twenty points higher. Then it might not have felt like punching so far above my weight that I suffered oxygen deprivation.

Annika was a goddess. A blonde, perfect, golden-skinned creature of myth (or Sweden, as they apparently call it these days).

New in town and my cousin Sean's work colleague, she was looking to meet people. Sean thought I'd be the perfect candidate, given that he knew I was horrifically single and would therefore be guaranteed not to have any plans.

'She's stunning, mate,' he told me over the phone.

'Hmmm. Real stunning? Or let's wind up the pathetic single cousin stunning?'

'Honestly . . . drop dead *gorgeous*. You want to get in there before somebody else snaps her up – which they will in about five seconds. Shit, I'd have a pop if I wasn't snowed under with three kids, and Denise didn't give such a good blow job.'

'Well, okay. But if I turn up and she looks like Susan Boyle's uglier sister I'm going to kill you.'

She didn't look like Susan Boyle's uglier sister. In fact, if someone who looks like the less attractive sibling of the warbling Scottish lunatic was at one end of the attractiveness spectrum, then Annika was at the other.

It was ball-achingly terrifying.

Because I didn't entirely trust Sean – I figured he was either winding me up or just had very low standards – I didn't go overboard with my preparations. Also, memories of Isobel the sex fiend were still at the front of my mind, so I was determined to stay sober throughout.

The best way to achieve this was to pick a location that didn't serve alcohol. I dutifully texted the number Sean had given me to arrange a date with Annika in Café Leon, a coffee shop in town that caters for people with too much money and chronic insomnia.

Annika texted back that she was looking forward to meeting me, which was a good start. There have been more occasions than I care to remember when I haven't even got *that* far.

I naturally arrive early and spend ten minutes trying to decide which of the complimentary magazines I should be casually reading when Annika walks in.

FHM and *Loaded* are definitely out. *Empire* will make me look like a movie geek and *Take a Break* will make her think she's meeting a retard. I go for a copy of *GQ* – the magazine that no man actually reads, only buys to impress other people.

It takes me a further five minutes to decide between

sitting on the brown leather sofa near the counter, or at a nearby table. I elect for the table, given that while sitting on the huge sofa might be the more comfortable option, it would make me look like a five-year-old waiting for his dad.

I shoo the waitress away when she comes to grab my order. 'I'm actually waiting for somebody,' I tell her, like she gives a toss.

I sit back, open the *GQ* at a random page, and try to look as interesting and compelling as possible. This largely consists of squinting slightly, putting one finger to my chin and looking upwards thoughtfully. I look less like one of the cultural elite, and more like someone in an optician's waiting room with an emergency appointment.

Annika walks in and I know I'm in *serious* trouble. It appears Sean doesn't have low standards. If anything he shows a marked ability to underestimate physical perfection. I'm not even going to bother trying to give you an accurate description of this girl. Instead, I suggest you spend a constructive ten minutes on the internet Googling *stunning Scandinavian girls* and multiply whatever results you get by ten. That would be Annika's uglier little sister.

You may be wondering why I'm not sounding more positive about this. After all, how lucky am I to be on a date with this goddess? No. *No, no, no.*

I'd have been quite happy if she'd just been a very attractive girl. I have enough self confidence to hold a conversation with a pretty woman, without becoming tongue-tied or making a fool of myself. Hell, I once even bumped into Scarlett Johansson in the lift of a swanky

London hotel and managed to conduct a polite conversation with her while we rode the lift up ten floors. She's not keen on fish, it transpires.

So pretty girls I can cope with. This fucker is *flawless*, though . . .

I always thought being slack-jawed is something only people in bad books and movies suffer from, but it happens in real life too. Annika is wearing a pair of tight black jeans that show off her long, sculpted thighs to full effect. Her honey blonde hair shines with health and light. The black high heels she's wearing make her walk in a way that would instantly kill any man over the age of seventy who got an eyeful of her peachy bottom.

It's a saving grace she's wearing a suede jacket when she walks in, because if I'd caught sight of how amazing her tits look in the pastel blue sweater she's got on, my brain would probably have exploded.

'Hello. Are you Jamie?' she says with a gentle European accent.

No! No, that's not me, oh great and perfect one. How could a sorry sack of horse manure like me ever think he could be on a date with you? I'm sure this Jamie of whom you speak will be here shortly. I'll just go and sit in the corner where I belong and try not to dribble while I stare at you.

'Yes . . . yes, that's me,' I reply, in an octave higher than my usual speaking voice. 'Pleased to meet you!'

'Thanks, you too.'

Annika takes off her jacket and I can't quite suppress the slight moan of excitement that jumps from the back of my throat as she shrugs the thing off. Those are classic 34DDs if I ever saw a pair in my life. I will never be able to look at a blue sweater again without getting a raging hard-on.

'What . . . what would you like to drink a coffee a tea or something else they do very nice muffins in here especially the blueberry ones I quite like the chocolate ones as well though they're really bad for you!'

No, I haven't lost my ability to punctuate dialogue. That's how it came out.

'Um . . .' Annika didn't quite get all that – understandably.

'Sorry!' I tell her as she sits down opposite me. I take a deep breath and try to speak less like I'm off my face on amphetamines. 'What would you like to drink? A coffee?'

'Yes please. I'd like a latte, if that's okay?'

Of course it's okay, you faultless higher life-form. I'd orally molest a badger if you told me to.

'Sure, I'll call the waitress over.'

Now, I am usually a pretty easygoing, self-effacing kind of bloke. Not prone to being bombastic or arrogant. It's just not in my DNA. However, being in the presence of Annika makes me feel more inadequate than an impotent midget with a one-inch penis, so something deep down in my idiot brain decides I have to compensate for this perceived shortfall by acting *big* and *tough*. Maybe if I come across as a commanding, hyper-confident kind of guy I might actually stand a chance of getting through this blind date intact.

In any normal situation I would wait politely until the waitress was drifting past my general vicinity and raise a hesitant hand, calling her over in an equally timid voice. The waitress would fail to hear of course, forcing me to wait another few minutes until she'd finished serving the two goths in the corner.

Today, though, I intend to show Annika my thrusting prowess. I locate the waitress over by the tills, raise one stiff arm skyward, click my fingers three times in sharp staccato fashion and virtually bellow 'WAITRESS!' at her from across the café.

I realise my stupidity as soon as it's out of my mouth. Annika's perfect brow creases in horror as she processes the fact she's on a blind date with Captain Arrogance.

Everyone in the café is looking at me with various levels of disgust – including the waitress, who's probably not used to being ordered around like a newly-recruited army private. She shuffles over, glowering at me.

Annika is now sitting back in her chair with her arms folded. You can already see the excuses to leave formulating behind those glorious blue eyes of hers.

'Aah . . . sorry,' I say meekly to the waitress. 'I've been suffering with a build-up of ear wax recently and it's made me a bit deaf.'

As feeble excuses go, this one is a *cracker*. There's nothing more guaranteed to break the ice with a woman than letting her in on the fact you have a disgusting waxy build-up. The waitress, who couldn't care less about the health of my auditory canals, seems to accept the excuse with fairly good grace though.

From the corner of my eye, I can see Annika peering closely at my left ear. Things are not going well.

'What would you like to drink?' the bored waitress asks.

If pretending to be confident has backfired, maybe coming across as a cosmopolitan kind of guy will do a better job. Annika is European, and as such is no doubt a well-travelled, culturally experienced kind of girl. If I can appeal to that side of her nature it will probably go well for me . . . and what better way to show how cool, relaxed and open to interesting new things I am than ordering an exciting flavour of coffee?

'A latte and a . . .' I peer over at the chalk board above the counter. There's about ten different varieties on offer, none of which I've ever ordered. I usually stick to a bog standard Americano – or if I'm really pushing the boat out I might order a mocha. The list in front of me is replete with flavours I didn't even know existed.

I'm aware that both Annika and the waitress are now staring at me as I squint at the board, trying to decide what coffee to have. In desperation, I decide to combine several: 'A latte and a . . . a . . . skinny mocha cappuccino with a twist of lime, mint and vanilla, please.'

The waitress looks at me like I've just shat in her hand. 'What?'

'Er . . . a skinny . . . er, what did I say? Um . . . a mocha cappuccino with vanilla, lime and some mint. Add another shot of espresso as well. And some more mint.'

She writes this down and offers me one last look of disgust before wending her way back to the counter to give the barista the strangest order he's ever taken. I turn back to Annika, breaking her continuing and horrified examination of my ear hole.

'That's an interesting choice,' she says.

I lean back in my chair, waving a hand in a gesture of indifference that I think makes me look cool, but everybody else thinks makes me look like a screaming homosexual.

'Well I like to try new things, Annika. Life gets really boring otherwise, don't you think?'

'I suppose so.'

Silence descends. It's thicker than Kim Kardashian. *Think of something to say, idiot.*

'Do you like coffee?'

Brilliant.

Here we are sitting in a coffee shop and she's just ordered a latte. The chances of her liking coffee are probably quite high, all things considered.

To Annika's credit, she answers this massively redundant question. 'Yes. I drink it all the time.'

'Really? Instant or ground?'

Bugger me. Is this really the best conversation I can come up with?

'Er . . . instant, I suppose.'

'Excellent. Caff or decaff?'

Why not just ask her if she enjoys watching paint dry and be done with it?

'Caffeinated mostly, though I swap to decaff after 8 p.m.'

'Me too!'

At last! We have something in common!

'Oh. That's . . . that's nice.'

We lapse back into silence. The part of my brain that creates small talk has shut down for the day – citing unsuitable working conditions – and has bunked off for a smoke. What's left is apparently unable to do anything other than stare at Annika's breasts.

I don't want to stare at Annika's breasts, but my subconscious has now dropped into some kind of default setting as a way of protecting itself from this awful date – and boob watching is the way it intends to cope with the situation.

There follows a very uncomfortable three seconds where I know that she knows that I'm staring at her tits. A further two seconds pass as she realises that I know that she knows that I'm staring at her tits.

It takes a Herculean effort to snap out of this enforced default mode and look her in the eyes again.

For God's sake, say something. It doesn't matter what!

I pick up the ratty copy of *GQ* I was flicking through before Annika's arrival.

'I read *GQ*,' I tell her and waggle the magazine at her for added emphasis. 'Do you read *GQ*?'

Yes . . . yes of course she does. She being the perfect audience for a men's lifestyle magazine, you cretin.

'No. I never have.'

'I do. It's great.'

'Okay . . .'

'There's a particularly interesting article in this edition all about . . .' I flick through the mag trying to find a feature. '. . . men addicted to excessive masturbation.'

Oh crap. I stop the words *Have you ever been addicted to excessive masturbation, Annika?* from escaping my traitorous mouth and put the magazine back down. Another period of silence, pregnant with awkwardness, descends.

It's mercifully broken by the waitress, who brings over a latte for Annika, and something resembling nasal discharge for me.

'Here you go,' she says, offering me a smile. It's a speculative smile, as if her and the barista have made a bet on how much I'm going to drink.

Annika picks up her cup. Even she is watching me carefully to see what happens.

I look down at my mug of coffee, which is strong enough to look back with a sneer on its face.

With trepidation, I grasp the warm mug and put it to my lips. I take a sip . . . and immediately wish my taste buds didn't work. It's like someone's blended a packet of Polos into a jar of Nescafé and topped it off with washing-up liquid. My face crumples like a bulldog chewing a thistle. But I can't spit the bastard out, can I? I'm the one who ordered this concoction to appear daring and cosmopolitan, so I'm going to have to drink it.

I force a smile. 'Mmmm. Lovely stuff.'

I keep my lips together as much as possible because there's every chance my teeth have been irrevocably stained green by the minty coffee.

'Is it nice?' Annika asks, in much the same way someone would ask the Elephant Man if it was painful.

'Yes,' I say from between pursed lips. I take another gulp to prove how nice it is. It'll be another four hours before my bowels extensively disagree with me.

The waitress is now looking at me half in horror and half in grudging admiration. She backs away carefully and walks back to the counter, not able to take her eyes off the steaming mug of terror she's just served up. With a final gulp and accompanying grimace, I put down the mug and try to think of something else to talk about.

'So . . . how are you finding the UK?' I ask Annika, hoping to salvage the conversation and move us away from coffee appreciation.

'Oh, it's very nice,' she replies with sincerity.

'That's great. Missing Sweden at all, are you?'

This animates her even more. 'Yes. A lot. Especially my family. Other things too, though.'

'What like? Never been there myself.'

This is better! Now I'm starting to sound like a proper adult.

She looks up. 'Oh, lots of things . . . the clean air, the friendly people . . . the scenery.'

'The porn?' I interject.

'Excuse me?'

Oh shit.

I laugh nervously. 'You know. The er . . . the *porn?* Sweden's famous for it, isn't it?' *Shut up Jamie. Shut your big, stupid mouth.* 'My mate gave me about ten DVDs full of it last year . . . the girls all looked like you.'

Annika is on her feet before the last syllable of that particularly stupid sentence is out of my mouth.

'I think I should be going,' she says, putting on her jacket.

'But . . . but you haven't had your drink yet!' I point out, as if the idea of losing half a latte is enough to keep her in the company of what is apparently a sex-crazed, arrogant maniac who drinks minty coffee.

'That's okay,' she replies. 'You can have it. I'm sure they'll put some lime in it for you if you ask. Goodbye.'

Annika turns to leave and without a backward glance rushes out of the coffee house – and out of my life. Her arse is still majestic. I look round to see the goths trying their hardest not to giggle. My friendly waitress has disappeared under the counter. I can hear snorts of laughter drifting up from it.

I sit at the table, leafing through *GQ* for a further five minutes and reading all about Pete who has to wank himself off at least eight times a day. I feel this is an appropriate amount of time to leave before departing with some semblance of dignity.

I even take a final sip of minty lime coffee before getting to my feet, dropping eight quid in change onto the table (apparently a skinny mocha cappuccino with lime, mint and vanilla is bloody expensive as well as disgusting) and hasten my way out of the coffee house, vowing never to return.

Sean texted me later that evening. All the message said was: *You cock.*

I couldn't really argue with that.

Laura's Diary
Sunday, March 20th

Dear Mum,

I have the fashion sense of a demented chimpanzee. I am completely unable to put together a decent outfit that makes me look like anything other than a mad fishwife. My entire wardrobe is a sad collection of clothes from seasons past, none of which go together in an attractive ensemble. I hate to think how many hundreds of pounds I've wasted on this wardrobe – which looks like somebody has thrown a diarrhoea grenade into the middle of it.

I'm in this state because I have a date tonight with a guy called Graham, set up for me by my hairdresser Stephanie. Yes, that's how bad things are. I'm relying on the woman who hides my roots to sort out my love life.

I really must learn to keep my mouth shut when I'm in the salon. It's just so easy to blab about all your problems when there's soothing jazz being piped into your ears, as a chatty woman massages your head in a nearly orgasmic way. Steph should quit the hairdressing business and join the army as an interrogator. Five minutes with her magic fingers on his scalp and any terrorist will be giving up the location of his secret cache of explosives with an idiotic grin on his face.

I idly mentioned to her on my last appointment that I was feeling ready to get back into the dating game again, and that was all she needed to embark on Operation Find McIntyre A Penis. Graham is the luckless individual she's picked out for me from her roster of male friends.

'I reckon you two are a good match,' she tells me as she starts layering on the foils.

'I'm not sure, Steph. The last date I went on ended with a sticky hand and a twisted ankle.'

'Everyone has bad dates. You've got to kiss a lot of frogs before one of them turns into David Beckham covered in whipped cream.'

She's right, of course. I can't let one crappy date stop me.

'Okay, I'll do it,' I tell her. 'But he is *normal*, isn't he, Steph? I'm not going to end up with a guy dressed as Hitler who constantly sucks his fingers, am I?'

Steph snorts. 'Of course not! I wouldn't do that to you, babe.'

'Good. I'll give it a go then.'

'That's the spirit!'

Sadly my wardrobe does not share Steph's enthusiasm. *Sigh.* There's nothing for it, I'm just going to wear black. Black jeans, black cardigan, black high heels. I'll throw on a white T-shirt as well, so I don't look like a cross-dressing ninja. Wish me luck, Mum. I'm going to bloody need it. I'll report back on my return.

Three hours of Laura McIntyre's-life-that-she'll-never-get-back later . . .

Luck wasn't needed in the end. The outfit I wore wasn't

a problem. To tell the truth, I could have turned up dressed as a giant chicken and it wouldn't have mattered much.

I knew things weren't going to go well when my date for the evening arrived at Café Leon wearing cycle shorts. The really tight kind that show off a man's junk like prize plums in a greengrocer's window. They were shiny silver (the shorts, not his plums) mixed with what I can only describe as nuclear orange. So was the matching skin-tight T-shirt. And the helmet. And the shoes . . . and good God yes – the bike as well.

It's about four degrees outside and pitch black. This guy has turned up to a date wearing a thin Lycra body stocking that makes him look like a neon dildo.

Through the window I watch him ride up on the mountain bike. Sadly, Café Leon is not blessed with a back door so I have nowhere to run. I then watch with a sinking heart as he spends a good five minutes padlocking the bike to the railings outside. It takes him that long as he has *three* separate locks to clip round the frame and both tyres. He double checks each one before walking away from the bike . . . then goes back and triple checks.

It's plain that even if Graham turns out to be a wonderful guy who I fall head over heels in love with, I'll be spending most of my time warring for his affections with the bloody bicycle.

Having established that his beloved mode of transport is less likely to be stolen than the contents of Fort Knox, Graham makes his way into the coffee house . . . crotch first. I've never seen a man pull this off before (no pun intended) but he manages it with great aplomb. Some people lead with their heads, others lead with their feet. Graham leads with his penis.

The poor little bugger looks quite hamstrung and deeply uncomfortable in those shorts, but Graham doesn't appear to be bothered in the slightest.

Having entered the café, he scans the few people who are enjoying an evening coffee and sees me. I'm a little hard to miss as I'm the only single woman in the place. He smiles broadly at me and comes over to my table.

'Good evening! You must be Laura!' It's not just his clothes that are loud.

'Yes, that's me. Are you Graham?' I say this with a small catch in my voice. It's the last dying vestige of hope that there has been some kind of colossal mistake and Captain Crotchbulge is in fact here to meet some other poor unfortunate girl called Laura, who's just running a bit late.

'I am indeed!'

Bugger.

Graham sits down. His legs are as far apart as is humanly possible – putting his genitals on display for the world to see. I try not to look between his thighs, but it's rather like asking a man with a gun to his face not to look down the barrel.

I'm also wondering when he's going to take the bright orange cycle helmet off. He's shown no signs of doing so yet.

'Sorry I'm a bit late,' he barks. 'Been on a ten-mile ride and got lost in myself.'

What?

I've been lost in Hastings, Milton Keynes and Florida, but never *in myself.* Was this some kind of euphemism for masturbation I'd never heard of? If so, how did he manage to keep pedalling?

'Ah, okay. Well, don't worry. I only just got here as well,' I reply, a suspicious look creeping across my face. There is every chance I'm on a date with a lunatic. One who seemingly has a strange and painful medical condition that requires him to sit like there's a fucking horse between his legs.

'What can I get you to drink, Laura?'

'Flat white with an extra shot of espresso, please.' I've been up since five in the morning so this seems like an appropriate order.

'Gotcha!' he says . . . and does gun fingers. You know what gun fingers are, don't you? It's when people point their index finger at you and stick their thumb up. I say 'people' . . . I mean *twats*. It was a miracle he didn't make '*peow peow*' gun noises as he did it.

Graham's penis gets out of the chair and the rest of him follows it up to the counter.

I've never claimed to be a great judge of someone's character from a first impression, but I'm fairly sure I've got a handle on Graham. It's certainly obvious where his handle is, anyway. This is the type of guy who revels in strenuous outdoor activities. I'm sure he's no stranger to paragliding, rock climbing, spelunking and extreme mountain biking. He has a carefully controlled diet, no doubt – and probably checks his own faeces for fibre on a regular basis.

He's the type of guy who sees everything as a challenge, and stands in the mirror every morning telling himself how successful he's going to be that day in everything he does. *You're a warrior!* he says as he flexes his pectorals, before donning his Lycra body suit and going out into the world to thoroughly annoy everyone he comes across. I can't hear him place his order at the counter, but I'm willing to bet vital parts of my anatomy he's ordering something with soya in it.

I *hate* exercise. This is because I am a normal twenty-first-century woman. Exercise is only to be undertaken when a look in the mirror and a four-pound gain on the scales demand it. It is *not* something to be done in place of more entertaining pastimes, such as eating chocolate, watching soap operas or having sex. I'm pretty sure Graham would happily forego all of these things for a chance to cycle up the side of Ben Nevis in a force-nine gale, his penis merrily leading the way to the summit. He's probably watched every TV show Bear Grylls has ever made and thinks flushing toilets are for homosexuals.

My thoughts are interrupted by Graham's penis as he brings our drinks over. My flat white looks delicious. His latte looks anaemic.

'Here you go, Laura!' he booms. 'That's a lot of caffeine you've got there, you know. You want to watch how much you're drinking. It can cause a lot of gastrointestinal problems.'

Wow. He's got the charming small talk off to a T.

'Yeah . . . thanks for the advice,' I reply. I then take a gamble: 'How's your decaff soya latte?'

'It's great!'

Hah!

Graham slurps his coffee and I start to wish those gastrointestinal problems would strike me down right now.

'Stephanie tells me you've been single for ages!' Graham says, with no trace of tact whatsoever.

'Um. A few months, yes.'

'Yeah, me too! Been far too busy with work and the biking. Just haven't had the time to squeeze a woman in!'

'Has something changed, then?' I ask, wondering if he's finally given up on trying to have sex with his mountain bike and wants to return to basics.

'No, not really, but Stepho filled me in about you and showed me your picture – and you looked hot enough to have a go at!'

Oh good God.

'That's . . . *nice*. I certainly wish she'd told me more about you,' I say, biting the rim of my coffee cup.

'Yeah, I've got a really interesting lifestyle. You'd love it.'

'A lot of mountain biking involved, is there?'

'Absolutely! I'm about to enter the annual Lake District hundred-mile cross-country challenge.'

Really? I'm about to enter a state of abject despair.

'That sounds difficult.'

'It is! Going to be a real challenge, but I've been training for six months now. That's why I was out riding before coming here. Can't stop my regime just to meet up with a woman, you know!'

'No, no. It's perfectly understandable that you'd put

your training ahead of dressing to impress.' I try to inject as much sarcasm into that statement as I can. It falls on deaf ears.

'That's right! I'm glad you understand!' Graham takes another gulp of his pointlessly healthy coffee. 'You sound like the kind of girl who likes to be active, just like me!'

Do I?

'Do you bike, Laura?'

I'm pretty sure 'bike' isn't a verb, but I choose not to point it out. 'I've got one in the shed. It's pink.'

'Do much riding?'

'Not recently.'

Graham springs to his feet. 'Come on then!'

'What?'

'Come on, let's go outside. You can have a go on mine!'

I look with disbelief from Graham's earnest face to the dark, cold winter evening beyond the café window. 'Now?'

'Yeah! Why the hell not?'

Because I'm not a bloody mentalist, that's why, you stupid walking dildo.

'Um . . . it's a bit cold, isn't it?'

'Nah! Just brisk!'

Before I know it Graham has grabbed my hand and is pulling me to my feet. The sheer force of his idiocy overwhelms my reluctance and I'm powered towards the door with a stunned expression on my face. The other customers in the coffee shop watch me go. To them it must look like I'm being abducted by one of the Power Rangers. None of them jump on the phone to call the police, though – they're all leaving me to my hideous fate, the bastards.

Outside, the elements batter my cardigan-clad body. Graham appears completely impervious to the biting chill of the March wind.

The multiple locks come off the mountain bike and before I can protest further, Graham is waggling the handlebars in my direction. 'Hop on then! It's got active suspension, so it's the most comfortable ride you'll ever have!'

Shivering, I take the bike and try to mount it. It's a man's bike and my jeans are far too tight, so instead of throwing one leg over the bar I whack my knee on the frame.

'Oopsie daisy!' Graham says with a chuckle.

Oopsie fucking daisy?

I've probably just broken my patella and all he can offer in the way of commiseration is the kind of phrase my nan stopped using in the fifties?

'Never mind. These things can be a bit difficult to get the hang of, especially if you're a girl on a guy's bike.' His tone is so patronising I want to kick him in the penis. I never, *ever* intend to see Graham again for as long as I live. This 'date' will end with me handing over a fake phone number and showing him my heels as quickly as possible.

However, I'm not going to let the little bastard get one over on me like this. I don't like being patronised at the best of times, and I certainly am *not* going to let this walking sex toy with a handlebar fixation get away with it.

With a grunt of effort I stretch my leg over the crossbar, fighting against the tight jeans for all I'm worth. Having successfully negotiated my way onto the bike I sit back on the saddle with a look of hardcore female determination in my eyes. I must show this prick that women are capable of riding a stupid man's mountain bike!

'Good girl! Well done!' he cries with delight. I avoid looking down at his crotch just in case he's started to get an erection.

'You want to wear my helmet?' he offers, pointing at it, as if I don't know what one looks like. 'Safety first!'

'I'll be okay, thanks.' This evening is going badly enough without me ruining what's left of my hairstyle by putting on his ridiculous orange cycle helmet.

My heeled foot fumbles around on one pedal for a few moments, before finally getting a decent amount of purchase.

I breathe deeply, push away with the other leg . . . and I'm off.

I'm sure there are things in this world that are more difficult than riding a full-suspension mountain bike designed for a six-foot man, when you're in three-inch heels, spray-on jeans and a thin cardigan, but none immediately springs to mind.

The front wheel starts to wobble. My feet slide off the pedals. My bum cheeks grip the saddle as hard as possible. My hair whips into my face.

I'm concentrating so hard on not letting the bike fall over that I'm unaware I'm cycling straight towards the local branch of Burger King before it's too late to do anything about it. One of the spotty teenage staff is cleaning the windows and the door is propped open with a bucket.

I hadn't intended to visit Burger King that evening. Especially not on a bright orange mountain bike.

It's funny how your plans can change, isn't it?

'Oh fuck!' I wail as I cross the threshold. In my terror I forget I have brakes.

Two girls – the only customers at this time of night – watch in disbelief as a freezing cold skinny blonde in high heels rides right up to the counter, gets her wits together enough to brake before she flies into the chip fryer, and slowly topples sideways onto the freshly washed floor with a plaintive squawk.

Graham's penis enters in front of the rest of him.

'My bike!' he wails.

I disentangle myself from the flaming thing, knowing that I'm going to have a large, healthy bruise on my right hip come morning. Graham picks the bike up and starts checking it for damage. I see red.

'Oh thanks very much, you Lycra-wearing tosser! I could have been killed and all you care about is your bright orange girlfriend!'

'This thing cost me three grand,' he argues.

'Really? How much did the costume cost? How much is it exactly these days to make yourself look a complete *wank stick*?'

'Now, now. Calm down there, Laura.' He actually contrives to look hurt.

'No, I don't think so, *Graham*. All I wanted to do was have a cup of coffee with a guy and see where it might lead . . . and I end up nearly mounting a Burger King till!'

'Are either of you going to order?' says the teenager behind the counter.

'No!' I shout.

'Do you have any salads left?' Graham asks.

Throwing my hands in the air in disgust I storm out of Burger King, leaving the walking dildo to order his evening snack.

Stephanie rang the next day to ask me how the date had gone.

I started by telling her what Graham had been wearing.

'Oh, that's unfortunate,' she said. 'That's why everyone calls him Crotch Goblin.'

So there you go, Mum. Is it any wonder I'm single when people actively think it's a good idea to set me up with somebody called *Crotch Goblin*?

Love and miss you,

Your bruised daughter, Laura.

xx

Jamie's Blog
Thursday 21 April

I've always thought the phrase 'speed dating' was something of an oxymoron. When I do get lucky enough to score a night out with a woman, I spend an inordinate amount of time a) worrying about where to take her, b) deciding what to wear, c) trying to think of something witty and charming to say during the date itself, and d) worrying if she wants to see me again or not.

The concept of getting all of this over and done with in mere minutes sounds completely counterintuitive. Besides, finding the love of your life is surely something to take your time over, isn't it? This is a pretty serious life decision we're talking about here, not what take-away food to order on a Saturday night.

Come to think of it, I take ages deciding whether I fancy a Chinese, Indian or a kebab, so even that's not an appropriate analogy.

Nevertheless I'm desperate (as we know all too well) and will try anything once. Frankly, if this doesn't go well I'm just going to start walking up to random women in the street and begging them to fuck me until they either capitulate or call the police.

My sister Sarah saw an advert in the paper for

'One-to-One Speed Dating in Your Area!' and tore it out to show me. When your loved ones think you're so pathetic that they have to scan the back pages of the local rag to find you a partner, you know you're in trouble.

'Go on, give it a go,' she said.

'I don't want to. It's stupid.'

'Good grief, Jamie, stop being so stubborn. You never know . . . you might have fun!'

'I very much doubt it,' I predicted with a scowl.

'Please do this, Jamie,' Sarah said with a plaintive look on her face. 'Mum won't stop talking about how worried she is that you're still single. If it goes on much longer she'll start trying to fix you up with Wendy again.'

I groaned out loud. Wendy is insane. The daughter of one of Mum's upper-class gym cronies, Wendy is a robust and healthy maniac, with a penchant for driving Land Rovers and shooting anything with feathers. She's had a crush on me ever since I was forced into her gravitational field at one of Mum's cocktail parties. The speed dating idea is suddenly starting to look a lot more attractive as a proposition.

Besides, what do I have to lose, eh? Other than what's left of my self respect, anyway.

The event is held at The Cheetah Lounge – a nightclub in the heart of town known for its relaxed approach to licensing laws and casual violence. Apparently this is the most popular speed dating option in the area. I can only imagine this is because the bar is quite cheap and within easy reach after you've just spent the evening being reminded how single and pathetic you are.

I arrive at the front door to the club dressed in what I think approximates 'smart casual' and am ushered in by a large bald security guard, who can't quite suppress the smile on his face as he looks into the eyes of yet another loser who can't get laid. That's what his expression says to me anyway, but I admit I may be a bit paranoid at this point. It feels as if everyone I've looked at since I left the house knows exactly where I'm going and has had to resist the urge to laugh and point.

Following some barely legible handmade signs tacked up to various walls around the expansive interior, I wend my way to the rear of the nightclub, into a Latin-themed area called 'El Cheetos'. Maracas and sombreros clumsily painted on the walls tell me this is the kind of place where stereotypes come to die.

As I enter I'm greeted by an excitable stick-thin woman, who introduces herself as Natasha from One-to-One Dating. I'm amazed she isn't sporting a Zapata moustache and poncho.

'And what's your name?' she asks.

'Glen Artichoke.'

Now, you may be wondering why I'm giving a false name. If you're thinking it's because I'm embarrassed by this whole enterprise you're only half right. The other reason is I see far too many shows on the Crime & Investigation Network, which you'll find way up in the thousands on your Sky box if you can be bothered to look for it.

I've recently been watching a fascinating series called *Killer Broads*, about women who murder – and why. There are many reasons why these ladies choose to take a life, but all the victims have one thing in common: they're men. One particular lass from Alabama called Raylene Driscoll would stalk her victims via various dating services until she found one she liked the look of – and then she'd burn his house to the ground with him in it. The lunatic managed to cook six unfortunate blokes extra crispy before the law finally caught up with her.

Then there was the charming tale of good-time girl Mitzy Blake, who was dubbed 'The Scissor Lady' during her murder trial, due to her love of attacking her sleeping boyfriends with a pair of kitchen scissors. In the space of a week she gave a short back and sides with extra mutilation to three blokes she randomly seduced in bars across her local neighbourhood.

Given these heart-warming examples of what can happen to the unsuspecting single man, I'm not taking any fucking chances. If there is a murderous nutcase here tonight then she'll have a bloody hard time tracking down Glen Artichoke afterwards for some light murder before bed.

'Here you go, Glen,' Natasha says, handing me a badge with my fake name written on it in permanent marker, just below a large number thirteen. 'We'll be kicking things off shortly, but if you'd like to go in and order yourself a drink we'll let everyone know when we're starting.'

I pin the badge to my jacket, give Natasha a weak smile and walk into the bar area.

There are roughly two dozen men and women standing around, all looking as apprehensive as I feel. I order a drink and stand at the bar trying to look as inconspicuous as possible.

I spend more time checking out the competition than eyeing up the ladies, if I'm honest. There's probably something very wrong with this on a psychological level, but I just can't help myself. There's one guy in a white cotton suit who looks like he's no stranger to the gym, but he's the only stand-out in a group of unspectacular-looking individuals. This makes me feel terrible, as chances are I look as unspectacular as they do. I should have worn something that would make me stand out a bit more. I might not have got many dates if I'd come dressed as Batman, but by crikey, I'd have been memorable.

I'm also amazed to discover that none of the women look like they're on day release, or the backside of an angry cow, so my spirits rise somewhat. Maybe this wasn't such a bad idea after all.

Five minutes pass and I nervously sip my Diet Coke until Natasha bids us follow her into the large dance floor area that lies past a set of heavy blue curtains.

Inside is a selection of small tables and chairs, laid out in a ring around the edge of the dance floor. There are sixteen men and sixteen women altogether, so we'll get a chance to spend a whole *five minutes* with each member of the opposite sex before moving on to the next. The women stay seated while the men move one place to the left. There will be a break after the first eight dates, giving us a chance to wet our whistles and pop to the loo.

We're given forms that we're supposed to fill out

afterwards, indicating whether we'd like to see any of the dates again – and those that match are put together by the company in a subsequent 'proper' date.

It's a masterpiece of efficiency, and I can't help wondering if a German originally invented speed dating. Then I remember that the German word for nipple literally translates as 'breast wart' and decide that they're probably not much ones for romance, all things considered.

I go over to table thirteen and sit down opposite a wide-eyed redhead with an angular nose.

A buzzer sounds and the speed dating begins!

I won't recount every second of each date (mainly because I may kill myself halfway through) but here are the highlights:

Date one is Carol.

Carol is forty, a mother of four and loves to tango. I hate children, am not attracted to older women, and only dance when stupid drunk. Carol's husband left her for his masseuse, taking their dog Wuffly Frank with him. I'm fairly sure this is too much information for a five-minute date.

I tell Carol I'm a national yo-yo champion, can speak fluent Swahili and work part-time as an Elvis impersonator – figuring that I'm never going to see the woman again, so why not have a little fun? I'm telling her the Swahili for testicles when the buzzer sounds and I move on.

Date two is Angela.

Angela is thirty, has no children and permanently looks off to the left. It's highly disconcerting. The slightly worried look on her face doesn't help either. I keep thinking there's some mad axe-man or rabid Yeti standing behind me, about to attack at any moment.

I tell Angela I used to be a roadie for The Wurzels, have French-kissed Sinead O'Connor and can whistle through my eyeballs. Thankfully the buzzer goes before I am called upon to prove this.

Date three is Bryce.

Bryce is an American living in the UK, and working for Nintendo. Much like the games she sells, Bryce is colourful, irritating, hard to understand and loud. Unlike the games she sells she doesn't have an off switch.

'Oh my God, I love Ant and Dec!' she screeches at me.

I tell Bryce I'm employed as a chicken sexer, have never slept in a real bed and think Stephen Hawking is faking it.

She's asking me where a chicken's penis is when the buzzer goes.

Dates four and five are both so deathly dull I can barely bring myself to write about them. I can't even remember their names, but I know one of them thought tarmac was a beautiful word. One of them was wearing beige. I'm pretty sure the other one was actually made of it.

You know they say a minute can last a lifetime? They're wrong. It can last an entire geological epoch.

Date six is Magdalena.

The second foreigner of the evening is originally from Portugal, but now works as a medium up in London.

You'd think anyone with psychic powers would know that moving from the gloriously sunny Portuguese coast to somewhere where you have to spend an hour commuting to Brixton every day would be a bad idea, wouldn't you?

Before three minutes have elapsed she's grabbed my hand and is telling me that Glen Artichoke's future will contain overseas travel. I counter by telling her I suffer from a rare medical condition that means I can't move over bodies of water without the urge to masturbate.

Magdalena is learning all about hydromasturphilia when the buzzer goes and I move on.

Date seven is Maxine, the head of Human Resources at the newspaper I currently work for.

We sit awkwardly for five minutes discussing the changes to annual leave policy, before I rocket out of the chair when the buzzer goes. We both know that this evening will never, *ever* be spoken about by either of us.

Date eight is Barbara.

Barbara's surname is Toadingham, which almost makes me wish Glen Artichoke was real, as that would make one hell of a double-barrel.

By this time nearly an hour has gone by and I'm losing the will to live, so my conversation with Barbara is stilted and bland. I can't even be bothered to make anything up.

'You're not enjoying this, are you?' she says.

'Not particularly. You?'

'Am I fuck. I could be at home watching *Glee*. Instead I've had to hear all about Colin and his piano collection, David's wheat intolerance and Yuri's problems getting a permanent visa.'

I like Barbara. It's a crying shame I'm not attracted to her in the slightest.

'Oh thank Christ for that,' she says as the buzzer goes. 'I need a drink.'

She's up before I am, so for once I get to feel what it's like to have someone scuttle away as quickly as possible.

I slouch over to the bar and order another Diet Coke. Only eight dates to go . . . And by the looks of things Barbara might be the highlight of the night. I get a good look at the remaining women as they come to the bar.

There's at least three more made of beige, two who obviously got dressed in the dark, one who is old enough to be my mother – but thinks she can wear the same make-up as a teenage girl – and a scared-looking chubby girl I struggle not to feel sorry for. The sixteenth and final woman of the evening would be a looker if it weren't for the scowl permanently plastered across her face.

This might be due to the greasy-looking individual in the white suit that won't leave her alone at the bar, but I can't be sure. From the speed she's downing the bottle of Smirnoff Ice in her hand I can tell she's having about as much fun as I am.

Can't wait to chat with her.

I don't particularly want an alcoholic drink right now, but I could murder a cigarette. There's five minutes of the break left, so I slope off for one. I'm supposed to be quitting, but nothing raises my stress levels like trying to hold a polite conversation with eight complete strangers in a row.

It's raining outside. Not just raining, actually, but absolutely bucketing it down. I have the choice of getting soaking wet or not having a ciggie. Neither appeals.

A third option springs to mind when I realise that the nightclub is virtually empty tonight, other than us lonely singletons. Across the way is the corridor leading to the toilets. I'm not one for arbitrary rule breaking, but I need nicotine, *damn it,* so am more than willing to flout the law on this occasion.

As I walk down the corridor I have to dodge a very disgruntled-looking blonde as she hustles out of the ladies' loo. It's the same one from earlier, and getting a second look at the black expression on her face makes me even less keen to make her acquaintance.

She has a nice arse though.

I go into the men's loo and lock myself in a stall, lighting up with the combined feeling of guilt and relief I'm well used to. While I'm having a cigarette I might as well answer the call of nature, so I drop my trousers and assume the position. Ten seconds later I'm in creamy nicotine heaven, and the prospect of another eight speed dates doesn't feel quite as bad.

Maybe one of them will turn out to be a winner!

Not the one that's old enough to be my mother, though. That would be a step too far, regardless of how much make-up she's got plastered across her wrinkly face.

I never get the chance to find out if any of the other lovely ladies is a winner, though. You see, modern night-clubs are very well-equipped places. They have great lighting rigs, pin-sharp speakers and state of the art bar facilities. They also have *very* sensitive sprinkler systems.

A mere four puffs into my cigarette all hell breaks loose. A klaxon goes off that's so loud I'm glad I'm sat on the toilet. I scream in terror and drop the cigarette in my lap. This elicits an even bigger scream of pain as the red hot ember singes my pubic hair. I jump to my feet, brushing the cigarette away frantically just as the sprinklers get into action. There's one just above my head, so the toilet stall gets turned into an impromptu shower.

I scream for the third time in as many seconds as ice cold water gets dumped down the back of my neck, and I throw open the toilet door, stumbling out with my trousers and boxer shorts still round my ankles. This means the bald security guard from earlier gets a good look at my meat and two veg as he comes barrelling into the toilet to check that everyone has evacuated. With hands grasping at my belt in an effort to pull up my trousers and cover my embarrassment, I promptly slip on the wet tiles and fall over right in front of him, displaying my naked arse like I'm engaged in some kind of bizarre mating ritual.

It's one that I'm fortunate enough he doesn't want to respond to.

Instead, the guard helps me off the floor and back out into the nightclub once I've successfully dressed myself again.

I could have stuck around. I imagine the speed dating continued after a clean-up, but I was so embarrassed by this time that all I wanted to do was run home and hide for a couple of decades. I started the evening trying to get a date, but the only person I got close to that with was a burly, bald man who had arms hairier than the arse I'd presented him with on the toilet floor moments before.

I was already soaking wet, so the rain didn't bother me much as I traipsed back to the car, still smarting from the painful new burn in my crotch.

That was the beginning and end of Jamie Newman's foray into the wonderful world of speed dating. I failed to find the love of my life that night – but did come down with a nasty head cold, so didn't walk away entirely empty-handed after all.

Laura's Diary
Friday, April 22nd

Dear Mum,

I've finally scraped the bottom of the barrel and gone speed dating.

It was something I promised myself I'd never do, but the quest I'm on to find a decent man is turning out to be longer than the one Frodo and his mates went on trying to get rid of that stupid ring. At least they had some proper directions to follow. About the only ones I've got to help me are: 'Keep going straight and try to avoid the blokes that look like Peter Sutcliffe'.

I suppose I've been spoiled in the past. I never had much trouble getting a man in my late teens and early twenties thanks to the liberal application of tiny skirts, tight tops and red lipstick. Then Mike came along, rendering all that nonsense completely redundant. As far as I was concerned the chase was over. I'd been caught by what I perceived to be the perfect man, and was more than happy to forget all of my little seduction techniques in favour of a long-term, stable relationship.

This was all well and good right up to the point when I found myself single again and in a world where eligible bachelors are becoming scarcer by the minute. All those poor boys I wiggled my round little bottom at in the local nightclubs have grown up and paired off with other women, leaving Laura McIntyre with a much smaller pool of contenders – and a slightly less shapely bottom these days, if she's being entirely honest.

In light of this sorry situation, I am willing to give the speed dating a try.

Elise from the gym recommended I give it a go. She met her husband at a local event a couple of years ago and told me it was a really happy experience for her from start to finish.

Elise is one of those people completely untroubled by original thought. If it were possible to gaze into her head, it would probably look like a sun-dappled meadow, full of frolicking bunny rabbits and doe-eyed Bambis. The soundtrack to this bucolic scene would be a One Direction song. Probably one of the ballads. Her husband Malcolm is just as bad. He spends his whole day smiling at everyone, whether they want him to or not.

If these are the type of people speed dating works for, I'm not entirely sure I want to be a part of it. Nothing ventured, nothing gained though, eh?

Providing I don't have to give anyone a hand job or ride a mountain bike, I should be fine.

I traipse down to The Cheetah Lounge on Tuesday night with more than a little trepidation, praying to whatever gods of dating might be up there that I'll meet someone at least halfway decent.

I'm not in the best of moods when I turn up, if I'm honest, as I've developed piles.

Yes, *piles*. I'm twenty-eight for crying out loud. How can a non-pregnant woman in her late twenties develop a complaint usually reserved for those in their pensionable years? I can only put it down to the incredibly uncomfortable plastic chair I was forced to sit on for three solid hours at a wholesaler's presentation on Friday. Listening to a bunch of insincere salesmen trying to persuade you to buy their product via a series of incomprehensible PowerPoint slides is bad enough. Add squirming around on a chair that's slowly sending your backside to sleep and it makes the experience even worse.

With an itchy rear end and a cynical frame of mind I walk into The Cheetah Lounge to find that I've arrived a good half an hour early.

'We're not starting until eight,' says the anorexic girl standing at the threshold to the Mexican section of the nightclub. I'm quite familiar with the place, having downed one too many tequila shots here last Christmas.

'It said seven thirty on the website,' I reply, a scowl forming on my face. I hate arriving early for an event, especially one like this where I don't know anyone.

'Oh! Sorry. That should have been changed,' she says, giving me an apologetic, wet smile. 'The bar is open already, though, if you'd like to get a drink.'

'I suppose I'll have to, won't I?'

'What's your name?'

'Laura McIntyre.'

She looks down a piece of paper, ticks my name off and hands over a large plastic badge. I'm apparently blessed with being number five this evening.

'Thanks for coming tonight, Laura!' the girl says, plastering an enormous and completely fake smile across her face. 'My name's Natasha and I'll be your host. Please enjoy the bar area until the other attendees arrive.'

She says *attendees*, but I hear *losers*.

'Once everybody has settled in I'll issue further instructions.' Now it's starting to sound like we're about to embark on some kind of top secret mission into enemy territory.

'Okay, thanks,' I reply and walk over to ask the bored barman for a Smirnoff Ice.

'Hello there,' a male voice says from behind me. Without turning round I know this guy will be greasy. I can tell from his tone of voice. I take a swig of Smirnoff, re-arrange my face into an expression of pleasant neutrality and turn round.

Yep, greasy as hell. It looks like you could squeeze his hair and cook chips with what drips off.

'Hello,' I say, knowing I'm going to be stuck in a conversation with this bloke until somebody else shows up and saves me.

'I'm Angelo.'

Of course you are. With a white cotton suit and slicked-back hair, what other name could you possibly have?

'Laura.'

'That's a beautiful name, Laura. It means goddess, doesn't it?'

'I don't think so. I'm pretty sure it just means laurel shrub.'

In fact I know it does. When I was a kid I once sat with

some friends looking up what our names meant. They called me shrub-a-dub for weeks.

'Ah, I am sure it means goddess. Maybe it is Hebrew I am thinking of.'

This is obviously Angelo's go-to chat-up line.

I'm sure every woman on the planet has a name that means goddess in one ancient language or another as far as he's concerned. I'd love to see what he makes of someone called Helga.

'No idea. I was named after my grandmother,' I add.

'And a beautiful lady I'm sure she was as well.'

'Er, thanks.'

'And what do you do for a living, Laura?'

'I run a shop. A chocolate shop.'

'Really? That's wonderful!'

You wouldn't think that if you saw my bank balance, pal.

Angelo offers me the smarmiest smile this side of a politician in election year. 'If your chocolate tastes as delightful as you look, Laura, I'm sure you must sell a great deal.'

The rest of the Smirnoff Ice gets downed in one fast swallow. I do this mainly to head off the vomit that's rising from my throat.

'Would you like another drink?' he says.

'Double vodka and Coke, please,' I tell him, safe in the knowledge I'll be getting a taxi home due to my Ford Ka's engine exploding last week.

Angelo takes a thin black wallet out of his white trousers and calls the barman over.

I'm barely into the evening and I'm already being wooed

by a greasy Italian who couldn't be more stereotypical if he spoke like Super Mario and twirled a pizza in one hand.

I bet he wouldn't be quite so interested in me if he knew I was suffering from itchy piles. It's taking all my concentration at this point not to start scratching my backside. Mind you, if Angelo won't take the hint and go away soon, I might just start doing it anyway. It doesn't matter how much of a goddess he thinks I am, I can't see him staying around if I start working at my bottom like a dog with fleas. Thankfully I don't need to resort to such drastic measures, as at this moment three other women walk into the bar.

They've obviously come together safety in numbers and all that. With hindsight I should have done the same thing. I could have dragged Elise along if nothing else.

At least one of these women is a rather stunning dark-haired beauty, wearing an unfortunate ensemble of floral headscarf and gypsy skirt. Angelo's clocked her and I can see him trying to decide whether he should carry on chatting up the skinny blonde who keeps jiggling about on the spot, or go over and charm the Latin lovely with the deep brown eyes.

'It was nice to meet you, Laura. I look forward to our date,' he says and makes a move to leave. I am entirely unsurprised.

'And you, Angelo.'

He saunters off towards his next victim and I am left blissfully alone with my second alcoholic drink and itchy rear end.

More people start to trickle in. My nerves get worse as each one enters. I order another double vodka, hoping it will calm them – while also doing the job of making the men look more attractive into the bargain. I notice a guy walk in bearing the number 13 on his badge. He seems about as comfortable with proceedings as I do, but he's a handsome chap and the best of the bunch by far. I'm put off by his name though. I really can't see myself being called Laura Artichoke any time in the near future. He must have had a terrible time at school.

By the time the rabidly upbeat Natasha issues us with instructions to go through to the dating area, I've got a real buzz on from the vodka.

There's a card on one of the tables with a number 5 on it, so I sit down carefully, hoping the hard wooden chair isn't going to cause me too much grief over the course of the evening

Hah! Chance would be a fine thing.

I'm not two minutes into the first date – with a guy who won't shut up about how much he loves pianos – when my bum starts to itch worse than it has at any point thus far. An eye starts to twitch as my irritation mounts to suicide-inducing proportions.

What the hell do I do now?

I'm pretty drunk from the vodka, so my powers of reasoning have deserted me. I'm sure if I was sober and had some clarity of thought I could get myself out of this with the minimum of fuss, but the alcohol has well and truly invaded my cerebral cortex and is working its evil magic. I simply have *no idea* how to get myself out of this situation.

I'll just have to sit here for the next hour while a series of single men are trotted out in front of me, trying my hardest not to squirm back and forth in my seat like a newborn puppy.

'. . . and that's when it hit me. I should just buy one myself! What do you think of that?' says Colin the first date.

I have no idea what he's on about.

'Um . . .'

'I mean, it's not as expensive as I thought it would be. It's huge, but well worth the money! Maybe you'd like to see it if I do get one?'

Oh Christ. A new car? A new house? A penis extension?

I try to recall what little I picked up about Colin before my piles became all consuming. 'Good for you, Colin. I'm sure it's a lovely . . . *piano.*'

'Yes! Yes it is!'

Thank God for that.

I don't intend to ever see Colin again, but nobody likes to be rude, do they? I try a little harder to listen to him for the next two minutes, but when the buzzer sounds I really have no idea who he is beyond his predilection for ivory-keyed musical instruments.

Before my next speed date sits down – a tall, chiselled-looking individual called William – I shuffle my butt cheeks around a bit, which provides temporary relief. I'm tempted to lean sideways to see if that helps, but this will look like

I'm letting out a fart, which probably wouldn't be the kind of thing to impress a prospective husband.

William turns out to be the kind of guy Graham the mountain biker would get on with like a house on fire. This one's more into windsurfing than mountain biking, but displays the same idiotic propensity for casual sexism and random shouting. He also sits like his legs are spring-loaded.

I'm very relieved when the buzzer goes, because it gets rid of William before he can finish the story about how he won an Iron Man triathlon with a twisted testicle. It also means I can seat shuffle again for a few moments in an effort to relieve my haemorrhoidal discomfort.

Swiftly following William is Greg the Police Community Support Officer, who spends five minutes telling me all about Section 4 of the Protection from Harassment Act. As far as conversation topics at a speed dating event go, this must take the brass ring for the most inappropriate. He seems quite disappointed when the buzzer sounds and he's forced to move away. This is again a huge relief as I'm pretty sure he was about to tell me what the legal definition of rape is.

To me, the buzzer is becoming the countdown to my salvation. The sooner I hear the eighth and final buzz, the sooner I know this hell will be temporarily over and I can get to the ladies' loo.

Next in line is Tom.

Tom seems like a nice lad. He's quite good looking, and is charming and interesting when he talks about flying microlight aircraft – his great passion outside his work as a landscape gardener. Frankly though, he could have told me he was a millionaire underwear model who could breathe through his ears and loved giving sensual massages and it wouldn't have mattered.

Buzz!

Adam could have shown me a foot-long tongue with prehensile abilities, talked about his volunteer work saving the lives of abandoned puppies and African orphans, *and* told me he worked for Smirnoff and I couldn't have cared less.

Buzz!

Malik is another nice guy, who I would quite happily have chatted to in less trying circumstances. It turns out he's a graphic designer. I've been thinking about getting one in to improve the shop's image so he could've been a useful person to know. What better way to start a relationship than with someone you know because of work? It's a natural ice-breaker.

What prevents me from handing over my phone number and going out with him again (on a night when it doesn't feel like I've got a nest of ants in my underwear) is the fact he stills lives at home with his mother. I once made the mistake of dating a guy who lived with his parents.

Never again. The memory of seeing his mother's face from the doorway through my upturned legs still haunts me to this day.

Buzz!

Just one more . . . just *one* more . . .

'Hello beautiful Laura, whose name is a shrub.'

I feel like crying. Angelo sits himself down opposite me

with a flourish and proceeds to tell me all about his father's vineyard, his mother's singing voice and his own Maserati. It's just as well he loves the sound of his own voice because I'm not contributing much to the conversation. About the only thing I could discuss with any clarity right now would be the soothing effects of Anusol, and I don't think even Angelo would put up with that for too long.

Buzz!

'Let me buy you another drink!' Angelo cries, before the strident buzzer tone has died.

'No, no, that's okay,' I tell him, getting up from the horrible wooden chair for the first time in an hour with indescribable relief.

'Please, you are such a good listener and I think we have a real spark together. A drink is the least I can do for such a wonderful conversation partner.'

Seriously? He calls monosyllabic responses, a pinched face and a constant jiggle the hallmarks of a great conversationalist?

Before I can protest further, though, he's got an arm round me and is propelling me back to the bar. I really must stop men doing this to me.

Now, frankly I blame you for this, Mother. You always told me that when a charming man offers you a drink you should accept. I elect to avoid more vodka for reasons which should be obvious. I couldn't bring myself to ask for a soft drink though. Not on a night like this . . .

So despite the piles, the fact I'm already far drunker than I should be on a school night, and Angelo's towering narcissism, I stand there for another five minutes necking my second bottle of Smirnoff Ice while he waxes lyrical about how beautiful the rolling Italian hills are in the spring.

Angelo has ceased doing his bit for the Italian tourism board and has started telling me about the funk band he sings with when my resolve – and my reserve – breaks.

'I'm sorry, Angelo. Would you excuse me? I need to—'

To what? Whip down my jeans and have a good rummage?

'I need to . . . powder my nose.'

Angelo makes a face. This is understandable, as we all know what 'powder my nose' is code for. I may as well have said *I need to take a big shit.* I slam the half-empty Smirnoff Ice on the bar and hurry out in search of the toilet.

I won't detail what goes on over the course of the next few minutes. Suffice to say I am granted some small relief from the discomfort in my undercarriage by the application of cool water and warm air. Those multi-directional hand dryers are a godsend, I can tell you.

Having administered some ad-hoc first aid, there's no way I intend to spend another minute dodging Angelo and speed dating another eight single men tonight, so I head out of the toilet (nearly crashing into Mr Artichoke as I do) and make a beeline for the exit, hoping and praying Angelo doesn't spot me.

I let out an audible sigh of relief as I leave The Cheetah Lounge. I don't even mind that it's started to rain cats and dogs. When you've just been sitting on a hard wooden chair with the itchiest bottom in the known universe, getting soaking wet in a downpour is almost a pleasant experience.

I spent altogether far too much money on suitable ointments and creams the next day in Boots.

Love you and miss you, Mum,

Your now relatively comfortable daughter, Laura.

xx

Jamie's Blog
Sunday 1 May

Oh good grief, I went on a date with Wendy.

Wendy of the Land Rover, Wellington boots and homicidal approach to wild animals. A woman blissfully unaware of what the word 'mortgage' means – and one completely oblivious to the recession currently gripping the western world. Ask her where she thinks the best place to keep your savings would be and she'd probably reply 'Daddy'.

It's not her fault. No-one could blame her for being born into the upper-classes. I'm not from the same social rung of the ladder, though, no matter how much my mother would wish it otherwise.

'She's a lovely girl, Jamie!' Mum says to me a scant day after my humiliation at The Cheetah Lounge. 'I know she's always wanted to get to know you better.'

'Yes, Mum, I know. You tend to remind me every time I see you. Sometimes twice.'

'Her parents are wonderful people.'

What she really means is that her parents have a wonderful bank balance, but I let it slide. I guess if nothing else, Wendy can afford to pay for us both on any date we do go on. And her legs do look quite nice in a pair of jodhpurs.

'Oh alright. Give me her number and I'll give her a call. No promises though.'

Mum is so delighted she actually claps her hands together. The prospect of marrying her son off to one of the aristocracy is apparently enough to break her usually unruffled demeanour.

'Good grief, Newman! I never thought you'd develop the stones to ask me on a date!' is the first thing out of Wendy's mouth when I make the call. 'A girl could feel quite put out, you know!'

'Er . . . sorry?' Quite why I'm apologising for not asking somebody out on a date before is beyond me, but this is the effect Wendy has on you.

'I should jolly well think so! Are you free Sunday?'

'Um, yep.' I was going to ask her to the pub on Friday, but Wendy obviously has other plans.

'Excellent. Come to the house and pick me up at eleven o'clock.'

'Eleven o'clock? That's a bit early for the pub, isn't it?' I say, worried now that I've asked an alcoholic out on a date.

'Not for what we're going to do, handsome!'

Oh fuck, it's even worse than alcoholism – she's *religious*. 'What are we doing, Wendy?'

'It's a surprise! Just make sure you're on time and wear a pair of strong boots.'

Strong boots? Are we going to kick something to death? Possibly a bunch of atheists?

I put the phone down feeling less like I've just arranged a date, and more like I've just agreed to take out an expensive life insurance plan I don't need.

Still, as Sunday is usually reserved for buying my weekly stock of Asda Meals For One and lengthy periods of masturbation, I'm fairly happy to shake my plans up a bit – even if it does mean taking part in whatever hideous upper-class pursuit Wendy has in store.

The satnav takes me on what feels like a magical mystery tour of the local countryside before turning into the longest driveway I've ever been on. By the time the Mondeo has negotiated its way across the potholed gravel and up to the house, I'm starting to get worried I might not have enough petrol to back out again.

I say house . . . I mean *mansion*.

Bruce Wayne would take one look at the place and start contemplating where to put the Batcave. It's your classic British massive posh bastard with two wings, and looks several decades past needing a bloody good paint job.

I walk up the steps to the colossal double front door and ring the bell. I fully expect it to be answered by Alfred, telling me that Master Wayne is currently indisposed. It's Wendy who answers it, however, a look of glee on her face.

'Hi, Newman!' she exclaims. 'Glad you could make it.' She looks down at my footwear. 'Are they the best you've got?'

I also look down at the ancient Dr. Martens that have followed me around for the past decade and a half like a bad smell. 'I only wear trainers usually,' I say in my defence.

'Well, they'll have to do, I suppose.' Wendy turns her

head back towards the cavernous hallway behind her. 'I'm off out now, Mumsie!'

'Have fun, dear!' I hear a woman's voice drift from somewhere out the back. I bet she's feeding the horses.

Wendy takes about thirty minutes to shut the enormous front door, giving me time to check my emails.

'Come on then!' she tells me when it's finally closed, before waltzing off in completely the wrong direction.

'My car's down there,' I say, pointing to where the Mondeo is slowly rusting itself into the ground.

'Won't be needing that. We're not leaving the grounds. A brisk walk is all we need.'

The atheists must be chained up in the woods out the back somewhere. Wendy takes my hand in hers. It's quite calloused for a young woman. I try not to think about it.

'Off we go then!' she cries and starts dragging me in the direction of a patchwork of fields and forest to our left.

'What are we doing today?' I finally muster the courage to ask as I nearly slip onto my arse for the fifth time in as many minutes.

Before Wendy replies, I'm scared shitless by an apocalyptic explosion of noise coming from over a nearby hedgerow. 'That!' Wendy says and laughs.

We're shooting the atheists now? Isn't that a bit harsh?

We round the hedgerow and I'm greeted by the sight of a line of people all dressed like the cast of *Last of the Summer Wine* – only with more firepower. Each one is holding a shotgun, and they're all standing in and around a collection of wooden frames that are dotted around the edges of the small field we're standing in. Nearest to me is a couple of the frames lashed together, both facing out across another larger field in front of us. Two green Range Rovers, one old and covered in dirt, the other brand new and clean, sit off to the left. The participants of the shoot have obviously enjoyed a more comfortable and warmer trip out here than me and Wendy.

'PULL!' screams a man who vaguely resembles Boris Johnson from the double stand. A pink disc rockets from a fiendish-looking contraption far to his right and he follows it down the sight of his shotgun for a second before pulling the trigger. 'Bastard, fuck and buggeration!' he roars as the clay flies out of harm's way behind a tree.

I look at Wendy. 'We're going to shoot things?' I ask her.

'Yep! It's a huge laugh.' Wendy strides ahead and takes two large green jackets from a man whose face is predominantly beard.

I follow, a look of deep concern on my face. I'm not a fan of guns, especially enormous ones that sound like God sneezing every time you pull the trigger. I like my guns carried by Bruce Willis on a cinema screen, thank you very much.

'Is this legal, Wendy? Only I don't have a gun licence or anything.'

She waves one hand dismissively. 'Oh never mind all that rubbish. Peter over there is a chief superintendent and I'm sure he couldn't give a monkey's, so I certainly don't.' Wendy points at the Boris Johnson look-a-like, who has once again failed to hit his target and erupts into more sulphurous swearing. 'It really is a piece of cake, Newman. Just point and shoot, you know?'

I put on the sleeveless shooting jacket Wendy has given me. It weighs a ton. I then don a pair of ear defenders that she also hands over. They make me look like a West Country Cyberman.

'Over here then, let's see if you can do this.' Wendy once again grabs my hand and wrenches me in the direction of the empty wooden stand next to Boris. My heart is hammering as she picks up one of the shotguns leaning against the frame and gives it to me. It too weighs a ton. This is not my idea of a fun date.

'Right, hold it like this, press that lever there and pull down on that bit there.'

I do as I'm bid and the shotgun cracks open in the middle.

'Now put these cartridges in each chamber and snap the gun closed.' Wendy watches while I fumble like a fifteen-year-old boy with his first bra strap. 'A bit harder than that. Seriously, harder than that, Newman. Come on, boy, put a bit of welly into it! Ah, that was probably too hard. Is your thumb alright?'

I suck my recently pinched thumb and glower at her.

'Okay, hold the gun up like this,' Wendy instructs.

I try to bravely forget about my injury and follow her instructions.

'Now put the stock against your shoulder like this.'

I do so, and I actually feel myself relaxing a little. The shotgun feels a lot more natural to hold now it's taken up its rightful position.

'What you've got to do is shoot just ahead of the clay,' she explains. 'Otherwise you'll miss it. Once you're ready, shout "pull" and you'll be off. Just remember to look down the sights and breathe nomally.'

I nod once and turn to face the open field.

'PULL!' I squeal and point the gun down the range.

Fching! goes the trap, flinging a clay pigeon into the air.

Boom! goes the shotgun as I pull the trigger.

'*Ow! Bastard!*' I cry as the recoil nearly separates my arm from my shoulder.

Boom! goes the shotgun again as my finger twitches on the trigger involuntarily. Sadly the infernal contraption is now pointed at the earth in front of my feet, so a delightful spray of grass and mud flies up into my face as I shoot the ground from point blank range.

'Bloody hellfire!' Wendy cries and skips out of the way.

Everyone is looking at me now. The hot red flush of shame marches its way across my face. This is swiftly replaced by a deathly shade of white as I realise I've just come within inches of blowing of all the toes on my left foot.

'Are you alright?' Wendy asks, gingerly taking the gun from my hands.

'See what happens when you bring beginners along, Wends? Bloody waste of time!' exclaims Peter the chief superintendent.

'Leave him alone, Peter. We're not all good at this kind of thing you know. Newman's just a bit softer than us. Guns just aren't his thing, it seems – isn't that right, Newman?'

Great. Not only does Boris Johnson's dad think I'm a useless article, Wendy has also evidently decided I'm a sorry example of the male species. I could just nod my head and slope off with my tail between my legs. I could go home, cook myself a chicken korma with pilau rice and fire up *Cum Guzzlers 27*.

But then again, I do still have *some* pride swirling around in the ocean of neuroses I carry around with me.

'I want another go,' I say, not quite believing it.

'You do?' Wendy asks with a worried look.

'Yes. Can I have the gun back, please?'

'Okay . . . but please be careful and try not to blow your own face off.' She cracks the gun open and inserts two fresh cartridges into the barrels. Snapping it back, she hands it over . . . and takes a good three paces backwards.

Just breathe slowly, Newman, I tell myself. *Do your best and try to salvage some dignity, eh?*

I set myself. My shoulder throbs like hell and my pulse rate is higher than Mount Everest, but I'm determined to make a better show of it. I'm agonisingly aware that everyone else is watching me closely to see what happens. From the corner of one eye I can see the walking beard with the jackets pulling out a mobile phone, his thumb no doubt hovering over the number nine. I point the gun towards the sky.

'Pull!' I shout and the trap throws out another clay. I track it with the shotgun, remembering what Wendy said about aiming it slightly ahead – and squeeze the trigger.

The pink clay disintegrates into a fine powder. *I did it.* I FUCKING DID IT.

'Well done, Newman!' Wendy crows.

'Beginner's luck,' Boris Johnson's dad mumbles.

'Pull!' I cry again. The clay shoots into the air, and once more I pick it off before it can fly out of range.

Could it be? Could it possibly be? I'm actually *good* at this?

The next ten minutes are brilliant. Of the fifteen clays I try to hit, I pulverise eleven of them. Wendy reassures me this is exceptional for a beginner. She also grabs my arse and gives it a squeeze after I hit four in a row. I don't mind this at all, given the heightened state of macho stupidity I'm currently revelling in. I even feel my penis twitch as she does it. I'm starting to understand why shooting is so popular.

Peter the senior copper is becoming more and more annoyed, to my utter delight. He's only hitting half as many clays as me and I can tell that being outdone is driving him crazy.

I decide to get a bit cocky. 'Can I have two up at once, Wendy?'

'Of course you can,' she beams and turns to the homunculus squatting over the trap where it sits twenty feet away. 'Trevor? Be a dear and load a double for Newman.'

Trevor does this and I set myself once again for glory. Peter stares at me with jealousy. Wendy stares at me with lust.

The rest of the shooters are doing their own thing and couldn't give a fuck what the working-class idiot Wendy has brought along is doing. Trevor appears to be cleaning his ear hole with a lock knife. He is forced to pay attention though as I point my mighty weapon aloft, ready to rain thunder down upon two of the small pink clay pigeons at once.

'PULL!' I scream like Mars, the god of war himself.

The clays fly into the air, one slightly ahead of the other. With nary a pause I take the first and bring the shotgun around for the second.

Oh no, this one's going faster. It's going to get away from me!

I follow the clay, trying desperately to get in front of it to get the shot in. The rest of the world disappears. It's just me, the shotgun and the clay. Nothing else exists. I track the pink disc as it flies through the air. It's getting lower and lower. Faster and faster. It's nearly out of range!

I have to take the shot!

Boom! goes the shotgun. *Whizz!* goes the clay, having been missed completely. *Ktissshhhh!* goes the driver's window of the brand new Range Rover parked off to the left, as the glass broken by my wild shot peppers the entire side of the vehicle.

Now I'm familiar with the phrase *I wanted the ground to swallow me up* – as I'm sure you are. For this particular incident, though, I feel we have to go beyond the mere confines of 'the ground' and broaden our horizons somewhat.

Cold, hard silence temporarily descends over the field of shooters and every one of them regards me with a look of utter disbelief. As I lower the shotgun and survey the wrecked Range Rover, I wish that the entire *universe* would open up and swallow me.

In doing so it would transport me to another dimension. One where committing acts of toe-curling stupidity is seen as a sign of great breeding and stature. There, I would of course be crowned king of all I survey, for no other in that parallel universe would be able to come close to the kind of epic idiocy I can achieve when given enough time and a long run-up.

A tiny sliver of a scream escapes from my constricted throat as I drop the shotgun like it's a live snake.

'Bollocking fuckery!' Peter the senior police officer and Johnson look-a-like roars from beside me in the other stand. 'What have you done to my fucking Range Rover, you little tit?'

Of course it belongs to him. Why wouldn't it? His face has turned a volcanic shade of red. His hands tremble with fury, making the shotgun he's holding rattle loudly. *I'm going to die.* I've just shot the brand new car of a maniac with a badge and a shotgun licence. Any second now he's going to level that big black bastard at my head and do to me what he's singularly been unable to do to the majority of the pink clay pigeons he's shot at today.

Thankfully, Wendy steps in and saves my bacon. 'Oh, how awful for you, Peter! I'm sure Newman is very sorry . . . aren't you, Newman?'

'Mfnfnm.'

'There. He's very sorry.' Wendy grabs me by one shoulder and starts to lead me away.

'What about my fucking car, Wenders?' Peter roars.

'I'll get Daddy to take care of it. It'll all be fine.'

'Fine? FINE?!' He's now approaching Brian Blessed-like volume levels. 'I only bought the cocking thing three days ago!'

'It'll still be under warranty, then,' I say, instantly regretting it.

'You think so, you little tosser?! You think they'll cover damage due to a shotgun blast inflicted by a walking sack of chicken faeces?'

'Now, now, Peter. Everything will be absolutely fine.' I notice that Wendy's voice has gone up an octave and my arsehole starts to pucker. 'Why don't we go back to the house now?' she says to me and starts to hurry me away. I hear the unmistakeable sound of a shotgun being cracked open. 'Tell you what, why don't we have a little jog? It'll be good for our constitutions,' Wendy continues.

I don't need telling twice. Throwing dignity to the four winds I take off as fast as my muddy heels will carry me. Thankfully Peter has eaten one too many large meals to mount any kind of pursuit, and I start to worry less that I'm going to get shot in the back as I run further away, given that the mad old sod couldn't hit the side of a barn door from ten feet away with his gun.

By the time Wendy and I have got back to the mansion she calls home, I've decided I'm probably going to live to see another day. What I'm not going to do is continue this ballistic date for one more second.

'I think I'm going to go home now.'

'I think that would be best, Newman.' I'll give her some credit for what she says next. 'I don't think we should arrange another date, do you? I get the feeling we're just too different to be compatible.'

'Agreed. If we went out again there's every chance I might accidentally step things up from criminal damage to involuntary manslaughter.'

This actually makes her smile. 'All the best to you, Newman . . . *Jamie.*' She gives me a kiss on the cheek. 'Now get out of here before Peter sets the hounds on you.'

I don't know if she's joking or not, but I'm gunning the Mondeo's engine and rooster-tailing my way back along the driveway before I have the chance to find out.

As I wend my way down the country road that leads back to civilisation, I'm thinking long and hard about my recent brush with shotgun-related death. So preoccupied am I that I don't notice the microlight aircraft buzzing towards me until it's nearly scraping the car's roof.

'Bloody hell!' I wail and brake heavily.

With horror I watch through the windscreen as the microlight whizzes over the car, missing it by a matter of inches. Over the whirring engine I can faintly hear a woman screaming.

The tiny aircraft continues its erratic course for another twenty yards past the Mondeo, skimming the hedgerows, until the pilot finally regains a measure of control and the thing climbs back above the trees and out of sight.

That's it. If ever there was a sign from on high that I should go home as swiftly as possible and pull the duvet over my head, it's this one. It's barely midday and I've already narrowly avoided being shot to death and crashed into by an aircraft. Somebody is definitely trying to tell me something.

As I sit here writing several hours later, I have a large purple bruise forming on my shoulder where the shotgun kept recoiling into it. My arm hurts so much I can't even have a wank, and I had to eat my Asda meal with one hand this evening. Most of it ended up in my lap. If anyone asks me if I want to go clay pigeon shooting again I'll have to decline on grounds of sexual frustration and malnutrition.

Laura's Diary
Sunday, May 1st

Dear Mum,

Oh good God I've been stalked. I've heard about it happening to other women but it's a first for me. You remember Alison Krausner, don't you? The poor German girl I knew at college, who had to put up with three months of Ritchie Morris masturbating in her back garden before the police actually did something about it?

'I would open the curtains and see his wangler every morning, it seems,' she used to tell me.

My recent experience is vastly different from Alison's, in the respect that instead of calling the local constabulary, I agreed to go out on a date with *my* stalker. To clarify – and assure you that I'm not *that* big a loser – if I'm being honest I'm probably exaggerating the 'stalker' tag. My guy didn't waggle his penis at me or anyone else, as far as I'm aware. In fact, what he did was rather flattering – and guaranteed him at least one shot with this girl.

You may recall that I briefly mentioned a guy called Tom when I spoke about the horrible speed dating experience I had a couple of weeks ago. He only got a passing mention as I was so caught up in the discomfort of my piles that I forgot about him almost as soon as I'd mentioned him in these pages.

Turns out Tom certainly didn't forget me, though. It also turns out the speed dating company probably needs to speak to somebody about the Data Protection Act.

I get a phone call Thursday night: 'Hello,' I say.

'Um. Hello. Is this Laura?'

'Yes. Who's this?'

'Okay, please don't hang up the phone.'

'Are you about to start heavy breathing? Because it really does nothing for me and this phone will just make you sound like Darth Vader with sinusitis.'

'No, no. Nothing like that. My name's Tom. Do you remember me? We met at the speed dating at The Cheetah Lounge?'

'Tom? Are you the one who saves abandoned puppies or likes to fly around in mini-planes?'

'They're called microlights, actually. And that was me.'

'How did you get my number?'

'Well, I basically kept ringing the company over and over until they capitulated and gave it to me. It took a week, and I ended up having to go down to their offices. I wouldn't leave until they at least gave me your mobile. I was there four hours in the end.'

'Why did you do that?'

'Because I thought you were absolutely gorgeous. Easily the most beautiful woman there that night. I couldn't stop thinking about you and I had to get in touch.'

'You think I'm beautiful?'

'Of course! Can I take you out sometime?'

What do you say to that? On the one hand this guy has gone to a freakish amount of trouble to get my number, which implies some kind of mental imbalance. On the other, he thinks I'm beautiful. It's a poser.

'I don't know, Tom. This is all a bit sudden.'

'I know! I thought you might be hesitant, so I wanted to make sure I could offer you a date worth remembering. Would you like to come flying with me?'

'Flying?'

'Yeah. I have my microlight fuelled and standing by – if you're free on Sunday.'

My heart starts to race – not about going on yet another date, I'm frankly bored by them at the moment – but *flying*? That sounds *amazing*. I've loved it ever since Grandad took me up in that Cessna when I was twelve. Okay, a microlight isn't quite the same thing, but the idea of swooping around the sky in a miniature plane, the wind in my hair and the clouds whizzing by my head?

'You know what? Why not?'

'Brilliant! Thanks very much.'

'Pleasure. You tell me where to meet you and when, and I'll be there Sunday.'

Yes, I literally threw caution to the wind, but damn it all, if you don't leap at these opportunities, you'll only end up regretting it. Besides, what if Tom turns out to be Mr Right? I get to have fun in the sky *and* land myself a potential mate for life.

I woke up this morning with these thoughts buzzing around my head and made myself ready for a day's micro-lighting. Fantastically, this kind of hobby does away with the need to dress up. Tom had told me to wear something warm and old, which I was more than happy to do. It's quite the pleasure to know your date isn't expecting you to turn up looking a million dollars, so after less than five minutes standing in front of the wardrobe hating myself, I slung on a pair of old jeans, a thick jumper and that puffy blue ski jacket I've never worn before.

I apply the minimal amount of make-up I can get away with when venturing out into the world, and within an hour of waking up (possibly a new record) I'm away in what's left of my Ford Ka and headed towards the airfield in the middle of nowhere where I'm due to meet Tom. On arrival I see the man in question standing by his microlight, checking it over. He's wearing a set of black overalls, undone with the arms tied round his waist. The tight T-shirt he's got on underneath shows off some very attractive biceps.

Ker-ching.

The microlight is smaller than I expected it to be. It looks like someone has crashed a Sinclair C5 into a quad bike and welded it to a hang-glider. There are seven or eight of them in total scattered around the grassy field, being fussed over by a variety of people.

I park the car next to a corrugated-iron building right out of a Second World War movie, and walk over to join Tom. I have to admit to putting a bit of extra sway into my step. The kind calculated to target a man's libido. I may be wearing a big puffy jacket and jeans with at least two paint stains on them, but I can still rock the sexy bottom sway – just about, anyway.

'Hey, Tom,' I say as I reach him, just about managing to look at his face rather than the biceps.

'Hi, Laura,' he replies, brushing a lock of dark brown hair out of his eyes and leaving a manly smear of engine grease. 'How are you?'

Horny now, Tom, thanks for asking. Can I hang off your arm for a bit?

'I'm great. Really looking forward to this!'

'Great. I'm just going through a few last-minute checks to make sure everything's fine. Do you mind waiting?'

Nope. As long as you don't mind me staring at your arse when you bend over to tinker with the seatbelts, Tom.

'That's fine. Take your time with it.'

I would have gone home happy after five minutes of watching Tom fiddle with his microlight, but as it is, he eventually stands back from it, shrugs the overalls up and over his perfectly formed shoulders and comes over to me.

'All ready to go, then?'

'Oh my, yes.'

Oh my, yes?

Why the hell have I started talking like a character in a bloody Jane Austen novel? I might as well slap him coquettishly with a lacy fan and be done with it.

'Great, let's get you your helmet.'

Okay, Tom. But I think I'd rather see your helme—

I'm not even going to finish that sentence.

Tom fishes out a bright green safety helmet that will clash horribly with my blue jacket and hands it over. I pull it down over my head, and become painfully aware that I now look like a right numpty.

'It suits you,' Tom lies with a smile.

'Oh great. I'm going up in an aircraft with a man who is quite obviously blind.'

Tom laughs (thank God) and tells me to climb into the microlight. As he buckles me in with the six-point harness, his hand brushes the inside of my thigh – I therefore completely miss everything he's got to say about the flight we're about to take. I catch the odd word and phrase here and there. He mentions something about engine noise and the cold, but my mind can't get away from the sensation of his hand on my leg.

'So you happy with all that, Laura?' Tom says.

'Oh my, yes,' I say again, and mentally curse myself.

'Off we go then!'

Tom leaps into the tiny cockpit in front of me. I have to open my legs slightly to allow room for his broad back. This doesn't help my composure. Tom speaks into a headset, obviously checking with whoever's holed up in the corrugated building that it's okay for us to depart. He then fires up the engine and we begin to putter towards a large flat area of field with orange markers along it indicating the runway.

My heart starts to beat faster and faster. In all the objectification of Tom the pilot, I'd temporarily forgotten that I'm about to take flight, but the excitement of it returns with full force as we turn to look down the grassy runway.

'Ready?!' Tom shouts above the engine.

'Oh fuck, yes!' I holler as the microlight sends shuddering vibrations through my entire body.

These ramp up a notch as Tom accelerates the microlight to flying speed. We rocket down the airstrip and as my breath catches in my throat the tiny craft is suddenly borne aloft.

The microlight soars into the air. I start panting like an excited puppy. We clear the tree line and I can see the rolling countryside spread out before me. This is *fantastic*! This is *wonderful*! This is . . . bloody freezing cold, actually.

It may be the start of May, but it's the start of May in *Great Britain,* so the temperature on the ground is a lukewarm fourteen degrees. Up here in the cold grey morning sky, though, as we rocket along at seventy miles an hour, you can cheerfully shave twelve degrees off that.

I get a terrible runny nose when it's cold. I tend to go through boxes of Kleenex like they're going out of fashion in the winter. You can imagine how that looks when a freezing seventy-miles-an-hour wind is blowing in your face. I've never had a snot moustache before. I can't say I'd ever want one again.

As the ground whips by us below, I start to sniff like a cocaine addict while trying to wipe some of the snot away from my face with my hands. I wipe them on my jeans, leaving small glistening trails up my leg. So now I'm painting myself with my own bodily fluids. My face has gone the ruddy red of a Victorian butcher in a blizzard, my eyes have been blasted equally red by the biting wind and my teeth are chattering like a malfunctioning wind-up toy.

This is the moment Tom chooses to look back at me

to see how I'm doing. 'Are you having fun?!' he shouts. I mount what I hope is something approximating a smile onto my face and give him a snotty thumbs up. The smile is more of a frozen grimace, it has to be said. What with that, the bright red face and bulging eyes, I probably resemble the head of one of those dancing dragons you see at Chinese New Year. Tom smiles, whoops and punches one hand into the air. He's obviously having a good time, even if I'm not.

Unfortunately, my thumbs up may have been a little too enthusiastic, as Tom takes it as a signal to start performing a few acrobatic tricks. He pitches the microlight into a steep descent, before levelling us out briefly and steering the craft back towards the clouds above our heads.

This is the first time I'm made truly aware of what it is I'm doing today. Until now my mind has been preoccupied with the fantasy of flight, Tom's rippling biceps and my runny nose. I hadn't really thought about the practicalities of microlighting. It hits home now, as Tom pulls the juddering plane into a sharp left-hand banking manoeuvre that Douglas Bader would have been proud of.

I'm sitting hundreds of feet in the air on a plastic seat with an enormous engine behind me that could at any time decide to blow itself up. The only things keeping me, Tom and the heavy engine aloft are two wings made out of extremely thin-looking material. They don't look like they could take a direct hit from a splodge of pigeon shit without tearing themselves to bits. A whirring propeller the size of a coffee table is also only a few feet away from my head, and it's making the whole contraption shudder and vibrate so much I'm expecting to see the rivets and screws holding the microlight together start flying out at any minute, pinging off my bright green helmet before we plummet earthwards to a fiery death.

This isn't like going up in a Cessna with Grandad at all. That had proper wings, seats, windows and a heater. This is more like being strapped to the contents of the nearest scrapyard and catapulted into the air at a hundred miles an hour.

All this – married with my frozen face, snot-covered cheeks and Tom's carefree aerobatics – sparks off a panic attack of no small dimensions. I've only ever had one before, on the ferry coming back from France when a storm hit. That time I could at least sit with my head between my legs and order a vodka and tonic. All I can do today is grip the seat for dear life and hyperventilate.

As Tom takes us into another controlled dive, my breathing gets faster, my eyes bulge even bigger in their sockets, and my blood runs into my toes as the microlight hits the bottom of the flight curve. This is all a bit much for my addled brain. It decides it's had quite enough of this malarkey for one day and shuts up shop.

To put it another way: I black out.

I regain consciousness to find myself slumped forward, my face mashed into Tom's back. He is screaming and trying to push me back with his left elbow. I manage to sit upright to look over his shoulder – and immediately wish I hadn't.

Coming right towards us is a blue Ford Mondeo. This seems quite strange as a Ford Mondeo is a car which goes along the ground. We are in a microlight aircraft that flies in the sky. The two should never meet. Not at speed, anyway. It finally registers that we're now barely fifteen feet above the ground and headed for an imminent crash with a rusty motor car. This is an excellent time to start screaming at the top of my lungs.

Without my body weight impeding him, Tom is able to bring the microlight out of its fatal crash course. The wheels clip a couple of trees as we soar right over the Mondeo and back into the grey skies above.

'I want to get off. I want to get off. I want to get off. I want to get off!' I start to wail in a terrified chant.

'I'm heading back to the airfield now,' Tom replies, his voice cracking as he shouts over the engine.

The rest of the flight is spent in tears. These join the rivulets of snot still smeared across my dirty face. I look like someone's thrown a jar of Vicks VapoRub at me in a wind tunnel. Tom brings us in to land and we bump back to earth successfully, with no apparent harm done to either of us, or the microlight. The damage done to my chances of another date with Tom are insurmountable, however.

We putter along the ground and eventually stop back near my car. This gives me enough time to prise my fingers from both sides of the plastic seat.

Tom climbs out of the cockpit and looks down at me. 'Are you alright, Laura?'

'Haaaaaa.'

'Pardon?'

'Sorry. I'm not a hundred per cent right now, Tom, no.'

'What's going on with your face?'

'It's exploded. My face has exploded, Tom.' I hold up a plaintive hand. 'Could you see your way clear to getting me out of this thing, please?'

'That didn't go the way I wanted it to,' Tom says, once I'm back on my feet and have wobbled unsteadily over to the car.

'No. Nor me.'

We both stand in silence for a moment. Him in contemplative thought, me clearing snot from my face with the tissues I've discovered in the car door.

'Perhaps a trip to the pub would have been a better idea.'

'Maybe, Tom. Maybe. There would have been less chance of us dying, that's for certain.'

'Sorry I got a bit carried away up there.'

'No need for apologies. I'm just not cut out for micro-lighting, I guess.'

Silence falls again. It's excruciating. We both know this is going nowhere. Any chemistry there might have been between us is gone. Near death experiences will do that, if you're not careful. I feel weary to my bones and just want to go home.

'It was nice to meet you though,' Tom says. 'I'm glad I got your number.'

Yeah, you're really not, boyo. Not now you've seen my face covered in the glistening contents of my nose and have nearly been killed by my inability to stay conscious in a crisis.

'Nice to meet you too, Tom.' I turn to the car. 'I'm going to go home now. I need a shower.'

'Good idea,' he says, and realises it was the worst possible thing to say at that moment. 'I'm sorry, Laura, I—'

'Forget about it. Take care of yourself.'

'And you. Drive home safely.'

'I'll try to. Let's hope I don't crash into that poor bastard in the Mondeo, eh?'

This fails to raise a laugh.

The last few hundred words are testament to the value of the phrase *keep it simple* . . . when it comes to dating, anyway. It's the reason why first dates always follow the same old routine of pub, bar or restaurant. You can get into fun, heart-racing stuff further on down the line, but that first meet should really consist of an activity where you don't take your life into your hands. It's certainly better for your complexion, if nothing else. I still have a red face and my nose only stopped running about an hour ago.

I have now sworn off dating for the foreseeable future. Or at least until I can arrange some decent life insurance.

Love you and miss you, Mum.

Your snotty daughter, Laura.

xx

Jamie's Blog
Thursday 19 May

Somebody once said that a woman only comes your way when you're not looking for one. If you're spending all your time on the hunt for a partner, the smell of desperation is strong enough to put anyone off. It's only by relaxing, forgetting about the whole thing and getting on with your life that you inevitably meet Miss Right.

This is of course a load of horseshit, but it makes you feel better when staring at a future devoid of love, affection and blow jobs. Having said all that, after my experience today, I'd say a woman only comes your way when you're minding your own business doing a bit of shopping and she runs you down on a clapped-out moped. This sounds less poetic, but it's certainly more accurate – at least for me.

The woman in question is called Laura and despite her attempts to murder me with a Vespa I gave her my phone number. Yes indeed, it has come to the point where I'm willing to give a potential homicidal maniac a chance if it means I might get laid. In fear of you tutting with disgust and moving on to a blog written by somebody less pathetic, I will now attempt to justify my actions:

I woke up this morning with the overwhelming urge

to spend money on new pants. This is a rare occurrence for me, as clothes shopping is right up there with root canal surgery for pastimes I'm likely to enjoy. Nevertheless, on this particular morning I wearily pulled on a pair of faded black boxers and looked at myself in the mirror. So baggy and misshapen were the boxer shorts that they had started to resemble a loincloth worn by one of my mammoth-eating ancestors. This was not a good look, even for a single man with no-one to impress. Hence the desire to spend some of my pay package on new underwear that would adequately cover my personal package.

Sadly, I had an entire day of work to get through before being able to sally forth into the local Primark, so had to wait a full eight hours before getting my hands on ten new pairs of boxers to replace the sorry collection I currently owned.

With a hop, skip and a jump I left the office at five thirty and drove into town to take full advantage of Thursday's late-night shopping hours. While the purchasing of pants was my main aim, I was also after something to liven up my living room, which has been looking depressingly empty for some time now. A couch, TV and small bookcase do not make an aesthetically pleasing living space, unless you are a monk who enjoys *EastEnders* and John Grisham.

I'm reliably informed that plants are always a welcome and attractive addition to anyone's house, so I went in search of something suitable to spruce mine up a bit.

Whether or not the six-foot rubber plant I wound up purchasing could be considered 'suitable' is something you'll have to decide for yourself. It was certainly a bugger to shift, weighing what felt like several hundred pounds thanks to the large pot of earth it came in. Quite why I didn't just settle for a small orchid to stick on the window-sill is beyond me.

I always make terrible decisions like this when presented with too much choice. I stood in front of more decorative B&Q flora than you can shake a stick at, wondering which one would look best in my front room window. At least ten minutes went by before I lost hope of choosing some-thing based on how pretty it was, and decided to just go for the biggest bargain. As the rubber plant was half price I dragged it over to the till and slapped down forty quid.

I also made the schoolboy error of buying a large item before I'd done the rest of my shopping, so I had to negotiate Primark carrying my brand new green monstrosity, trying my hardest not to concuss with a huge, rubbery leaf the collection of reprobates that shop there.

It wasn't easy, I can tell you. The place was bloody packed. I've never been in to a branch of Primark when it wasn't full to the rafters of people who would otherwise be in the audience of *The Jeremy Kyle Show*.

I had one near miss with a walrus of a woman covered in tattoos. I'm fairly sure she could have broken me in half over one knee, so it was just as well I managed to divert the flailing plant away from her head as she stood deciding which pair of combat trousers to buy for three quid.

Primark is a paradox of a high street store. It sells everything at dirt cheap prices, yet you always manage to spend far too much money while you're in there. It's just so hard to resist a bargain, isn't it? They pile that shit high and sell it cheap.

I picked up my ten pairs of boxer shorts – along with four two-quid T-shirts, two pairs of jeans for a tenner, a pair of cargo shorts for seven, some cheap-looking gym trainers for nine, four short-sleeved work shirts for sixteen, and an absolutely disgusting Hawaiian shirt (perfect for a fancy dress party I've got coming up) for six.

So now I'm trying to negotiate a busy store carrying a gigantic rubber plant and enough clothes to fit out an entire African village. I get to the cash desk without committing any acts of rubbery assault and plonk down my purchases. The acne-ridden depressive behind the counter spends a few moments deciding whether to charge me for the rubber plant, before deciding that Primark probably hasn't expanded into the horticulture sector and starts scanning and bagging my other wares.

'That'll be seventy-six pounds please, sir,' it utters in the tones of one sick of living.

Seventy-six bloody quid? This is Primark, isn't it? How the hell can I have spent that much in sodding *Primark*? Not entirely sure I haven't been conned, I hand over my debit card and start to regret my tendency to impulse buy. I only came out for some pants. I've now spent well over a hundred quid on a massive plant and a wardrobe of clothing I'll probably never wear half of anyway.

Out I stumble into the mild evening air, rubber plant in one hand slapping me in the face with every step I take, bulging recyclable bag of horrendous garments in the other. I leave the pedestrian part of the shopping centre, my arms starting to ache under the weight as I stagger along.

Because the Green Cross Man terrified me as a child, I stop like a good boy at the kerb and look both ways before walking across the road in the direction of where I've parked the car down a side street. This is, of course, the perfect time for the recyclable paper Primark bag to break. Both handles give way under the weight of my new purchases and the bag drops to the tarmac, spilling its contents.

'Bollocks!' I tell the whole street, none of whom seem to care about my predicament.

It is at this precise moment, while I'm standing like an idiot in the middle of the road, contemplating how the hell I'm going to carry this lot now I have no bag, that Laura McIntyre enters my life . . . and nearly ends it in short order.

Laura's Diary
Thursday, May 19th

Dear Mum,

You may remember a conversation we had when I was thirteen, when I told you how I'd like to meet my future husband. I don't remember all the details, but I'm sure there was a desert island involved, along with a gleaming white stallion and a box of chocolates larger than my head.

Teenage girls are simple creatures, so I guess the rampant clichés were to be expected. Fast forward fifteen years and cold, hard reality has set in. I'm not really bothered if there's a desert island anymore, horses tend to smell bad anyway, and the box of chocolates would mean another month in the gym. Frankly I'd settle for meeting my future husband without suffering embarrassment, personal injury or great expense.

I *did* meet a guy today, Mum, and while I didn't spend much money, it was *bloody* embarrassing and I only just avoided serious personal injury by the skin of my teeth.

It started with panic. I'm not usually a forgetful person, but it's been a hard few weeks at the shop and my mind's been full of stock returns, balance sheets and advertising space, so I hope I could be forgiven for forgetting my goddaughter's birthday, surely? It was mortifying.

I walk in the door at six o'clock virtually dead on my feet, with plans to spend an exquisite evening doing absolutely bugger all, stretched out on the sofa watching soap operas. My flatmate Charlie is away for the week with her new boyfriend, so I have the luxury of an empty apartment. I think it's these little pleasures that keep you from going stark staring mad. The prospect of waltzing around your flat in just your knickers and a T-shirt, eating Ben & Jerry's straight out of the tub, is one that can keep you going all day at work if you let it.

With this delightful plan in my head I enter the kitchen and pass the fridge. I spot the picture of me, Melina and her beautiful little girl Hayley, taken at Thorpe Park last year – and my heart stops. *It's Hayley's fourth birthday tomorrow! I haven't bought her anything!*

I'm invited to the party that starts straight after I close the shop at six o'clock. With my current workload I'll have no chance to get out tomorrow and buy something.

I can't just pull something out of stock, as my chocolate is squarely aimed at the adult market. I can't see Hayley being all that impressed with a luxury praline gift box or truffle selection – at least not until she hits her twenties. There's nothing for it, I'll have to go back out now and get over to Toys R Us before it shuts.

This would be enough of a chore if the bloody Ford Ka was working, but it's knackered *again* thanks to the ongoing saga of the head gasket, so I've got no transport. I can't face another bus journey back into town and it'd take a month of Sundays anyway. *I'll have to get a taxi.*

Then my eyes fall on the bowl of keys by the micro-wave. One keyring belongs to Charlie. On it is the key to her 1982 Vespa moped. My flatmate has been nursing this monstrosity for the best part of a decade. Not quite vegetarian enough to ride a push bike everywhere, Charlie has nevertheless decided that riding round on a clapped-out scooter is better for the environment than owning an evil, polluting car.

I love the girl to pieces and the eight months we've shared this flat for have been largely trouble-free, but she does have some funny ideas about the world sometimes. I'm a little sick of the smell of joss sticks, to be honest. Still, she's reliable with her half of the rent and listens happily while I bitch and moan about my love life, so I can't really complain at all.

Standing looking at her keys, I'm reminded of a conversation we had a few weeks ago.

'You should have a go sometime, Laura. You're more than welcome,' Charlie said to me. 'What's mine is yours!'

'Yeah . . . maybe.'

This is fairly typical of Charlie. She shares everything and has a soul more trusting than a week-old puppy. I'm deathly afraid someone will take advantage of her good nature someday and bleed her dry of every penny in her bank account. I had absolutely no intention of taking her up on her kind offer to borrow the Vespa.

Until now.

I could (and should) just order a taxi, but things are tight at the moment money-wise, so I could do without the extra expense – especially because I'll probably end up spending a small fortune on Hayley's present. I spy Charlie's bright red crash helmet down by the recycling bin and my decision is made. It's a moped. How hard can it be?

Indeed, things go fine for the first few hundred yards: Twist throttle and off you go. I owned a little Honda Melody step-through as a student, so I'm familiar enough with mopeds to know how to ride one. Sadly, the Vespa is a *lot* more powerful than the Melody, a fact my neighbours are now acutely aware of, thanks to the ear-piercing screams that emanate from my mouth as I careen down the road, having opened the throttle a little too hard.

I narrowly avoid knocking the wing mirrors off every single car down my left-hand side as I grip the handlebars for dear life and try to steer the maniacal thing away from the parked vehicles. With my heart hammering in my chest, I apply the brakes, bringing the smelly silver beast to a halt, and resolve to take things a lot easier from now on.

Breathing deeply, I open the throttle with a level of caution usually reserved for bomb disposal and the moped moves off down the road at a sedate and less heart-attack-inducing pace.

The rest of the twenty-minute journey into town is relatively incident free, other than an expletive-filled exchange with a white-van driver and a hairy moment involving a Peugeot 106. I pull into Toys R Us with only a slight wobble and park in the motorcycle bay.

I'll be the first to admit that buying a four-foot doll's house when you're on a moped probably isn't the wisest move, but every little girl should have a doll's house, shouldn't they? I could just picture little Hayley's eyes lighting up as she opened the front of the house to see all those little rooms, with their miniature furniture and tiny glass-eyed dolls. I loved mine when I was a kid, so what better present for Auntie Laura to buy her?

I even got the gangly sales assistant to help me lash the thing to the back of the moped with some parcel tape and the collection of fraying bungee straps Charlie kept in the seat.

The look of terror in his eyes as I started the engine and moved (very, very slowly) away was entirely unjustified as far as I was concerned, as were the repeated car horns as I pootled my way along the road, wobbling all over the place as the doll's house unbalanced the Vespa with its colossal weight.

I was sure I could handle it though, and it was only a short journey home after all. Everything would have been hunky-dory if the crash helmet hadn't decided to fall back off the top of my head. I knew it was too big when I put it on back at the flat, but cinching the chin strap up as tight as I could seemed to stop it moving round too much, so I thought it'd be okay for the trip to the shops.

Nope. Not the case.

As I'm turning into the road that leads out of the shopping centre the bloody thing slips slowly backwards, nearly throttling me with the chin strap – and making my head tip upwards. I've barely been in control of the moped/doll's house combo anyway, so this latest development makes the situation ten times worse. Instead of looking at the road in front of me, I'm now getting blinded by the street lights above it as I whizz along completely out of control.

I lurch and weave across the road – now mercifully empty at gone eight o'clock in the evening – wailing like a banshee as I fight to avoid an enormous accident with something hard and unfriendly.

There are many effective ways to break the ice with a new man, Mum. A compliment about his clothes, for instance. A light touch on the forearm, accompanied by a warm laugh is always good. The wearing of a brassiere designed to lift and separate is even better.

Side-swiping him with a fifty-pound doll's house in the middle of the road *isn't* a good way to break the ice – though you'll certainly end up breaking something if you're not careful.

I've fought to bring my head forward again, straining against the weight of the helmet. Looking ahead, I barely have time to register the guy standing in the street holding a gigantic pot plant before I'm steaming right at him, applying the moped brakes for all I'm worth. Luckily, I get the speed down sufficiently to avoid serious injury to either of us – but I'm still thrown off the damn Vespa, earning a nasty scrape on my knee. My luckless victim is hit by the doll's house and is sent sprawling to the concrete, still hugging the pot plant like it's his firstborn.

'Oh you fucking bastard!' I scream in a combination of pain and fury as I clasp my new wound and hop about a bit. I try to wrench the helmet off my head, forgetting that it's still cinched tight around my neck. I now look like an escaped mental patient having a fight with a crash helmet. One I'm losing.

'You ran into *me*!' I hear my victim cry from beneath the pot plant, misinterpreting the source of my wrath.

'Not you! This stupid moped!' I reply, giving the evil little sod a hearty kick. 'Ow! Fuck it!' I exclaim rather inevitably, given that the Vespa's metal body is a lot harder than my pump-clad left foot.

Taking a deep breath, I remove the crash helmet and survey the accident scene properly for the first time. It looks like a branch of Primark has exploded. Cheap boxer shorts lie everywhere. The guy I've just nearly killed is now back on his feet and looking shell-shocked.

Apologising isn't something I'm keen on, but I also don't like the idea of being sued for every penny I'm worth, so I get up a good head of remorseful steam by the time I've dragged the moped to the side of the road and helped him carry his ridiculous rubber plant and broken bag of shopping over as well.

'It's okay. I'm fine!' he says, still clutching the oversized plant in front of him protectively, like I'm going to attack him at any moment. 'Are you alright?'

'Yeah. Just embarrassed is all. I really am very, very sorry.' I hand him a collection of damp, gritty boxer shorts and affect a smile that drips with an unspoken request for forgiveness.

He finally puts the pot plant down, having decided I'm not about to jump on him like a rabid spider monkey. As he stands up, there's a light of recognition in his eyes.

'Hey! Weren't you at that stupid speed dating thing down The Cheetah Lounge last month?'

Oh, terrific! Humiliation piled on humiliation. Not only does this bloke – who I'm starting to realise is really quite attractive, despite his obsession with potted green flora – think I'm a lunatic with a ballistic moped, he also knows that I'm a hideously *single* lunatic with a ballistic moped.

'Yes,' I admit. 'I remember you too. Glen Artichoke, isn't it?'

'Ah . . . that might have been a bit of a fib.' He extends a hand. 'My name's actually Jamie Newman.'

I offer a smile still laced with apology and take his hand. 'Laura McIntyre. I wondered if that was a made-up name at the time.'

'Yeah. Call it an insurance policy against any psychopathic women out there.'

That's a very nice smile you've got, Jamie Newman. Congratulations.

'We never got a chance to talk, did we?' I say, remembering how the awful evening had ended.

'No.' Jamie looks a bit guilty. 'That may have been my fault. I set the sprinklers off having a fag in the toilets.' Guilt changes to pride. 'That was my last cigarette, actually. It seemed appropriate to quit at that point.'

Jamie Newman and I spend a good ten minutes at the side of the road chatting before I have to stifle a yawn. Much as I'm enjoying speaking to what appears to be an intelligent, charming man, I am now virtually dead on my feet from near exhaustion. I can also feel blood trickling down my leg from the scrape and I need to get home to apply some TCP as soon as possible.

Not wanting to let this fish off the hook I decide to take a chance.

'Look, I have to get home before I fall asleep in the street, but maybe I could buy you a drink sometime?' I ask. 'You know, by way of an apology for nearly killing you with a doll's house?'

The smile he gives me makes my heart beat faster. 'That'd be lovely.'

I give him my number, which he puts into his mobile phone. He promises to give me a call in the next few days.

'Will you be okay riding home on that thing?' he asks, pointing at the moped, which now has a lovely fresh dent down one side to go along with all the others Charlie has inflicted on it over the years.

'Oh yes. I'll be fine!' I reply with more than a touch of bravado, and jump back onto the infernal contraption. I just hope I can ride away without crashing into the nearest lamppost.

Having again cinched the crash helmet up as tight as it'll go, I turn the key in the ignition and look back at Jamie, who is once more holding his rubber plant. It doesn't look like he's planning on throwing it at me this time though. I give him a wave, which he returns awkwardly – and I pray to all the gods in the universe that the moped behaves itself as I twist the throttle and ride away.

Happy thoughts manage to keep the Vespa upright all the way back to the flat.

I barely notice the car horns and screeching tyres that mark my uncertain progress.

I'm fortunate the local constabulary isn't out in force. Any copper would probably run out of the ink in his pen filling out all the penalty notices it would take to cover everything I'm doing wrong.

So there you go, Mum. I thought you had to dress like a high-class prostitute and go clubbing to find a man – when all it really takes is a day-old set of work clothes, a knackered moped and a hit and run.

Whether Jamie Newman calls me or not is another thing. Let's just hope he can see past the attempted murder and bright red crash helmet, in the same way I can definitely see past the silly rubber plant and cheap pants.

Love and miss you, Mum.

Your tired but happy daughter, Laura.

xx

Jamie's Blog
Tuesday 24 May

Today finds Jamie Newman in an astoundingly good mood, for I have had the best night out I've experienced in a long time.

First dates have always been something of a trial for me – even the ones that have resulted in a relationship – but the two hours spent in the company of the lovely Laura McIntyre last night at The Barley Corn pub were far more pleasurable than I expected them to be. If you had to compile a checklist of the details you'd want on the ideal first date, then last night would tick a majority of the boxes. Okay, Laura isn't a multi-millionaire and doesn't have a twin sister with whom she shares an extremely open relationship, but I'd pretty much given up on ticking those boxes years ago anyway.

The date started, as these things always do, with THE PHONE CALL. I'm using capital letters for extra added emphasis to indicate just how important THE PHONE CALL is. There are many times when you might phone a girl during the course of a relationship, but there is only ever one THE PHONE CALL – and it's always the first one you make. This phone call will determine the rest of your life.

Those few brief moments you spend speaking into a small electronic device can have ramifications on your future so profound it's hard to accurately put into words. People with beards can bleat on about chaos theory and the 'butterfly effect' all they like, but they pale into insignificance alongside the seismic shifts that happen in the universe based on what transpires during THE PHONE CALL. After all, if it goes well, the two of you may well end up having a child who could grow up to be the next Hitler – or worse, Justin Bieber.

The most important part of THE PHONE CALL initially is establishing whether the young lady in question is still interested in meeting up with you. This is never, *ever* a certainty when you dial her number. Just because she drunkenly scrawled it down in lipstick on a beer coaster, it doesn't mean she actually wants anything more to do with you three days later, when she's sober and watching *EastEnders*. Similarly, just because a woman feels guilty about nearly killing you in the high street with a moped and gives you her phone number, it does not automatically mean that she's got the hots for you.

Even if you do find out she *is* interested, you still have the thorny problem of engaging in a conversation with a complete stranger over the phone without saying anything stupid, offensive – or the worst sin of all, *boring*. It's not good enough to simply ask the young lady if she still wants to go out, and arrange a time and place before signing off – that's far too brief and to the point. Unlike conversations on the phone with other men, women want you to actually have something of *substance* to say, to prove that you're worth the time and effort. After all, as we all know, it takes them a month of Sundays to get ready for a date.

Most conversations with other men travel largely along the following lines:

Ring, ring.

'Alright, shitface.'

'Afternoon, you big homo.'

'Pub tonight?'

'Yeah, but only if I can get off your mum in time.'

Click. Brrrrrr.

Such brief exchanges are fine for anyone with a penis between their legs, but women are a different kettle of fish. Getting off the phone with one of them in less than ten minutes is practically impossible. This especially holds true when the woman in question is one you are attracted to, and therefore wish to impress.

You must have a topic of conversation prepared ahead of time for THE PHONE CALL. Nothing that'll take *hours* to get through (don't start telling her all about your hopes and dreams for the future, or your opinions on climate change) but something that will engage her interest for the aforementioned ten minutes, and will make you sound like a charming, upstanding individual. Avoid mentioning sex, football, cars, your personal hygiene, anal or your mother and you should be fine.

With Laura I elect to ask if her friend's child liked the doll's house she battered me with in the middle of the high street. This strategy proves that I listened properly to her explanation for why she nearly killed me with the bloody thing, and demonstrates an interest in something Laura clearly feels is important: her goddaughter.

In reality, I couldn't give a shit if the kid had taken one look at the doll's house and vomited into the chimney stack, but this is the type of bullshit you have to engage with if you're going to secure yourself a date.

Which I did, I'm happy to say!

THE PHONE CALL went well and we chatted amiably for a good ten minutes.

It transpired that the girl did like the doll's house, despite the dent in one side caused by my forehead. I made the appropriate sympathetic noises when Laura described the nasty graze she'd got on her knee because of the crash, and she was pleased when I told her I had no lasting effects from my fall onto the concrete. I assume this was out of a genuine concern for my health, rather than a desire not to get sued.

It was a blatant lie, in fact, because I'd actually woken up the next day with a nasty backache, but I sure as hell wasn't going to admit it. Backache is the kind of thing only suffered by men who have completely lost their grip on youth. This is not the impression I want to give Laura at the outset.

She even sounded pleased when I suggested the out-of-town Barley Corn pub as a location for our date. This is the riskiest part of THE PHONE CALL. The place you choose says a lot about your personality. The reaction you get says a lot about hers. A girl like sex monster Isobel would have been deeply disappointed with a quaint, quiet country pub like The Barley Corn, I have no doubt – as would Annika the Swedish goddess. They would probably have both found it far too prosaic and boring.

I took a chance with Laura, though. She struck me as being a down-to-earth, easygoing kind of girl, who'd appreciate the quiet atmosphere a place like The Barley Corn would provide – and I was proved right when she sounded genuinely pleased at my suggestion.

Having arranged to meet at seven thirty, I hung up with a huge sigh of relief and instantly began to worry about what the hell I was going to wear.

Laura's Diary
Tuesday, May 24th

Dear Mum,

Oh my. My luck just might be changing.

I'm not saying last night's date was necessarily the start of a love affair for the ages, but I can't remember the last time I walked away from one as happy as this.

Well, that's not entirely true. I seem to remember floating home on cloud nine after the first time Mike took me out, but I was a lot younger and more hormonal then, so I was probably more horny than anything.

Sad to say I'm a lot more jaded these days, and most of the time I come away from first dates either disappointed in them – or in myself. It was very different with Jamie, though. No disappointment in sight. In fact, I have to confess my heart was skipping a few beats as I drove home. I've heard people talk about 'clicking' with someone before. It always sounded like the worst kind of buzzword bullshit to me, but I have to say I've got an idea of what they're talking about now. Jamie and I just seemed to fit together well, and I couldn't be more pleased.

Blah. This is disgusting. I'm a twenty-eight-year-old independent woman with her own business and I sound like a giddy schoolgirl.

Three days after the crash Jamie phoned me. He'd obviously read all the right dating manuals as this is the accepted time any man should leave before getting in touch: long enough not to appear desperate, short enough to seem appropriately interested. To tell the truth, the call could have come at a better time as I was waxing my legs – something you want to concentrate on as much as possible with no outside interference. One false move with one of those strips and you can spend the rest of the evening swallowing Nurofen and looking for the nearest ice pack.

Besides, when a man calls, you want to feel at least a *little bit* attractive, even though he can't see you – for the psychological boost if nothing else. Being dressed in a fluffy blue dressing gown, enormous period knickers and sporting a set of legs hairier than Bigfoot is about as far away from attractive as it's possible to get. It's the kind of look you don't want a man to associate you with until at least four years into a relationship.

I could tell Jamie was quite nervous by the speed at which he talked. He was kind enough to ask whether Hayley liked her present or not, though he did call her Katy for some reason. I let it slide as the fact he even remembered who the present was for was surprising in itself. I suppose the one saving grace of the ridiculous manner in which we bumped into each other was that we had something to talk about in our second conversation.

Jamie asked about the graze on my leg. I neglected to

go into detail about the fifteen pitiable minutes I'd prodded at it with TCP-soaked cotton wool, tears brimming in my eyes. He did the typical guy thing of shrugging off being body-slammed to the road by a frantic blonde on a Vespa. I'm sure it must have hurt, but he dismissed it out of hand and moved on to talk about something else.

I nearly brought up how funny he'd looked hugging his rubber plant like it was about to leave him for another bush, but thought better of it. A man's ego is fragile enough at times like this and I didn't want to scare him off. Frankly, I was pleased he made light of the accident, just in case the date didn't work out and he decided to sue me.

The Barley Corn was a bit left field for a location, it has to be said. I'm so used to being invited to coffee houses and city pubs (where there are ample opportunities for the man to end the date early if he doesn't like the look of me) that the prospect of a quiet drink in one of the more picturesque pubs outside town seemed like a very nice alternative.

It also meant Jamie would be able to hide my body easily should he prove to be Ted Bundy's little brother, but I figured the risk was worth it.

My first impressions hadn't set off any alarm bells. Charlie would be instructed to ring me at half past ten anyway and inform the police if I didn't pick up. With the date arranged, Jamie said goodbye in a tone of voice that suggested he was glad the call was over. I took this as a sign of nerves, rather than buyer's remorse, and hung up with a faint smile on my face.

Now the only problem I had was deciding what clothes to wear that would effectively disguise the ugly two-inch gash on my right knee . . .

Jamie's Blog
Tuesday 24 May continued . . .

Somewhat ruining the ambience of our date location is the fact that somebody has left graffiti on the pub's sign so it now reads 'The Barley Porn' – which sounds like a skin flick set in the West Country. Not a good one, either. It would involve sheep. Still, it's a mild spring evening, I'm wearing my best bib and tucker and there's a young lady to be wooed, so I don't let it worry me unduly.

I've taken several strong painkillers to mask the agony I'm now in from the body slam into the road a week ago. The last thing I need is to be moving around like a crippled robot trying not to aggravate my back, so I'm pleased that the pills have taken the edge off, for the moment at least.

I figure a bit of Dutch courage is the order of the day, so I make sure to turn up half an hour early at seven to drain a swift pint before Laura arrives.

I could've taken my time and sipped the bloody thing, as I'd forgotten the first rule of dating: the woman always turns up late. If I hate one thing about the first stages of a relationship it's the little games we're forced to play in order to size up the 'opposition'. A woman arriving late tests *your* patience, and gives *her* a good idea of how keen you are – if you're prepared to wait around for her, that is. I'm keen enough on Laura to stand at the bar for nearly an *hour* before she walks in, dressed in a pair of blue jeans and a white vest top that's tight enough to show off her boobs to such a pleasing degree I temporarily forget my backache. She's obviously spent a great deal of time on her hair and make-up as she looks very pretty indeed.

Scratch that, she's *beautiful*.

The ensemble is only slightly marred by the fact she appears to be limping.

It's rather like looking at a Ferrari with a puncture. Mind you, I'm trying my best to hide the fact I can't move my head independently of my shoulders due to the sharp, stabbing pains I feel every time I try, so who the hell am I to be critical?

'Hi, Laura!' I say cheerfully as she walks over.

At this point my brain decides to ruin everything. It's been behaving itself all day, but now decides to throw in a suggestion which could potentially put a spanner in the works.

Why don't you give her a kiss on the cheek? it suggests, with no regard for my well-being whatsoever.

I can't do that! I argue. *It's way too forward for a first date.*

Don't be a pussy! it replies.

Now I'm stuck in an agony of indecision as Laura heads towards me. Do I chance a kiss on the cheek? Will she like it? Will it put her off? What's the dating etiquette here? Why the hell did I agree to do this? If the porno flick did have sheep in it, would they enjoy it?

I want to go home!

I eventually win the argument with my treacherous brain and just go for a brisk handshake.

'What can I get you to drink?' I ask.

Don't say a pint of mild. Don't say a pint of mild. Don't say a pint of mild.

'Small glass of white wine, please. Pinot Grigio if they've got it.'

Phew.

I order the drinks from a barman who is only just able to suppress a smirk as he notes the nervous first-date tone to my voice. He's seen this little act play out a thousand times, I'm sure.

Drinks ordered, it's small talk time. I hate this shit. The conversational topics you're forced into when speaking to someone you don't know all that well. I'd much rather launch into a conversation about how great I think zombie movies are, but I have no idea if Laura would agree, or think I'm a total dick. Therefore, I have to play it safe and pick a subject matter that won't offend.

The options on offer are: Weather, current events, sports, more about the weather, last night's television, and possibly more weather. All are boring, contrived and guaranteed to make me sound like a cretin with nothing valuable to say. I decide to throw caution to the wind and go meta.

'I think this is the point where we're supposed to engage in small talk, you know,' I say with a smile. It's a huge gamble – potential success or otherwise depending on Laura's sense of humour and level of intelligence. She's either going to find it funny, think I'm an idiot or not have a clue what I'm on about.

The gamble pays off! She gets the joke and laughs.

The smirking barman returns with our drinks and I hand over the cash. I pick up Laura's wine and twist round to give it to her, forgetting my back problems for a brief moment. A sharp bolt of pain rockets across my shoulder blades. It's like being burped by the Incredible Hulk.

Don't let her see! Man up!

I want to let out a contemptible gasp of pain and make a grab for my shoulder, but instead I internalise the agony. I think I get away with it without Laura noticing.

Picking up my pint with deliberate caution, I suggest we go over and sit in the corner at a quiet table, where the chairs have nice high backs for me to rest against.

As previously stated, the next two hours are fantastic . . . well, other than the fact I have to sit bolt upright all the way through it. Also, Laura has to pop off to the toilet several times, which is a bit strange as she only has one glass of wine and a Diet Coke.

I can tell when she needs the loo as her left leg starts to jiggle up and down a bit and her brow creases in apparent discomfort. I'm not going to let a minor thing like a weak bladder (or perhaps a cocaine habit) stop me from liking this girl, though.

It's gone eleven before I reluctantly say I'll have to wind the date up thanks to a six thirty start the next day.

This suits her as well. When you run your own shop, you have to be up at the crack of dawn every day apparently. Who knew flogging posh chocolate could be so stressful?

The dull ache that had settled across my shoulders roared into life as I stood up, and I couldn't stop a look of agony briefly crossing my face. Luckily Laura was putting her coat on, so she didn't notice. On the walk back to the car, my brain once again threw up the kissing suggestion, this time by way of a goodbye.

Go on. Do it. Just a quickie on the cheek, you bloody coward.

This time I didn't intend to argue. I liked this girl and thought it was worth a punt. We arrived at her bright red Nissan Micra. There was a nasty dent down one side on the driver's wing. 'That looks bad,' I commented, pointing at it.

'Yeah. Had to buy a car cheap. My old one was too far gone to bother fixing. This was the best I could find for the money.' She ran a hand over the dent. 'I call him El Denté.'

That clever witticism just made me fancy her even more. A tight body and a pretty face are one thing, but add a sharp sense of humour and I'm in heaven.

Time for THE QUESTION. This is much like THE PHONE CALL. Its importance can also never be underestimated in the grand scheme of things. One invariably leads to another. Plenty of men screw THE QUESTION up by getting ahead of themselves. *You wanna fuck?* for instance, is not the right question to ask at the conclusion of a first date. Neither is *Would you like to meet my mummy?* Both are equally awful, for very different reasons. Happily I'm not that much of a moron.

'I had fun tonight, Laura. Would you like to get together again some time?'

'Yeah, I had a good time as well. That'd be great.'

Woo hoo! Now go for the kiss, you idiot!

I do. And while this blog is full of embarrassing mistakes, social faux pas and idiotic moments in the life of Jamie Newman, this is not one of them. I don't accidentally head-butt Laura, or let out an unexpected belch into her face. I merely lean forward, plant a gentle kiss on her cheek and stand back. She offers me a heart-racing smile and her eyes twinkle.

'See you soon,' she says and jumps in her dented car. I see her off and walk back to my Mondeo at roughly three hundred feet above the ground.

That was yesterday, and I'm still buzzing. I had a hard time getting to sleep last night. Not because I was single, horny and needed a wank thanks to a three-hour date with a very attractive woman, but because I couldn't stop thinking about how Laura looked, smelled and about the stimulating conversation we'd just had. I was excited about our next date and couldn't wait to see her again. I had a wank anyway of course. She was *very* sexy after all.

All the bloody stupid game-playing that goes on during those first few dates could go to hell as far as I was concerned – and with no concern for my own welfare I called Laura *this morning* and asked her out again.

Thankfully she said yes. We're due a second date at the weekend!

I can't help but feel those seismic changes to the universe that start with THE PHONE CALL are beginning to shift into gear.

Laura's Diary
Tuesday, May 24th continued . . .

'Make sure you turn up late, darling,' Tim had advised me when he popped into the shop for a coffee that morning. 'The right man will happily wait for you.'

I'm never sure about these dating games, but Tim's had more relationships than I can shake a stick at, so I followed his advice this time and got to The Barley Corn at nearly eight. I would have been a bit late anyway, given the length of time it took me to deal with my stupid leg wound, which still hasn't healed. The gash needed a dressing over it, which usually wouldn't have been a problem, except that tonight I was determined to wear my best jeans, and the huge bloody plaster I'd put over the cut kept painfully ripping off every time I tried to pull them up. I had to resort to wrapping surgical tape tight round my leg to keep it in place, which meant I couldn't bend my knee properly. This caused a noticeable limp and Jamie would enjoy a lovely evening with someone doing their best impression of Long John Silver.

I hobble into the pub and see Jamie at the bar. I'm no expert at body language, but from the way he's standing so stiffly, it's obvious he isn't feeling any more relaxed than I am. First dates are not for the faint hearted.

'Hi, Laura!' he says, and I walk over, resisting the urge to cry *Aaar, Jim lad!* and offer him the black spot. As I hobble towards him, there's a very strange moment when Jamie appears to freeze in position, a blank expression plastered across his face. It's like somebody has switched off the power. His eyes flicker for a second before he blinks a couple of times and re-animates, sticking his hand out for me to shake.

'Hi, Jamie,' I say and take it. It's warm, smooth and feels very nice. He asks me what I'd like to drink. I've got my nerves just about in check enough to need only a small glass of white. I figure if he orders anything that's pink or has an umbrella in it for himself, I know I'm probably onto a loser.

'A small glass of Pinot Grigio and a pint of Foster's, please mate,' he says to the barman – who can obviously tell two people on a first date from a bloody mile away. Time to think of some small talk while the drinks are coming . . .

I hate doing this. What the hell do you say to a complete stranger you're trying to create a good impression with? Luckily Jamie saves me the trouble by coming out with something rather clever about how this is the point where we're supposed to engage in small talk. It's like he read my mind.

'Shall we not bother?' I reply. 'I don't care what the weather's doing, and I didn't watch any telly last night.'

He laughs, and the ice on this date is suitably broken with no injury or need to fill out complicated health and safety forms. Jamie hands me my glass of wine. For some

135

reason, as he does this, he lets out a little high-pitched squeak from the back of his throat and for the briefest of moments looks like he's just licked a battery. This is the second strange interlude I've seen so far tonight. I hope they're not a sign he has some kind of mental complaint. The advantages are outweighing the disadvantages, though, so I let it slide and we go over to a table close by the window.

Our conversation from then on is very enjoyable. Jamie is quite charming and can spin a good story. This is not massively surprising since it turns out he's a writer. I've never dated someone creative before – providing you don't count Mitchell The Snorter and the three chords he could play on that electric guitar he stole from a pawn shop. Mike was about as creative as concrete and the rest of my ex-boyfriends were of a similar nature. It's very interesting to be across the table from a guy who gets excited when he talks about something he evidently loves to do. It also makes a great topic of conversation for me as I love to put pen to paper as well . . . as this diary will attest.

I start to relax nicely into the date, but I get the impression Jamie is still nervous throughout, as he sits upright the entire time and only makes small, careful movements. I think it's quite endearing, really, and a good sign he's not a cocksure idiot.

The only bad thing that happens is when my leg starts to bleed. There I am, happily talking about how bad *Come Dine with Me* is and I feel the disconcerting sensation of blood trickling down my calf, towards the fifty-quid high heels I've only owned for a month. I have to beetle off to the loo on three separate occasions to sort the plaster out before the threat of a bloodstained shoe is completely averted.

Still, it isn't nearly as bad as the piles episode from a few weeks ago and I don't think Jamie notices I'm having a problem. As the evening wears on I become unpleasantly aware of the stock check I have to get up at six in the morning to do tomorrow, so part of me is quite glad when Jamie says he needs to leave since he has an early start as well. There's another part of me that hates the infernal drudge of the working week, though, as I'd be more than happy to stay here and keep talking with this handsome, funny guy for a lot longer – instead of having to rush off home early because I've got to pay the rent.

We leave together and I manage not to limp too much as we walk back to where I've got El Denté parked. After a slightly embarrassing exchange about how the little red terror came into my life, Jamie asks if I'd like to see him again, and for what seems like the first time in a long while, I don't have to hesitate before saying yes.

My heart skips a beat as he leans forward to plant a soft kiss on my cheek. I feel a little electric shock run down my back as he does. Having said our goodbyes, I drive away from The Barley Corn with the dumbest smile in history plastered across my face.

So there you go, Mum, that's how I officially met Jamie Newman. We've already planned a second date. He's promised to cook for me!

I'm expecting to be struck down with some hideous, disfiguring disease any moment now.

Or he'll turn out to be a serial killer. Or worse – *married*.

Love and miss you, Mum.

Your surprised daughter, Laura.

xx

Jamie's Blog
Saturday 4 June

I should have known. I should have bloody *well known*.

Whenever things look like they're going well, along comes Captain Cock-Up to ruin everything.

It's my fault really. What else did I expect from being so optimistic about a new woman?

It simply isn't in the great, galactic plan of existence for me to be anything other than a hideously lonely single bloke. Jamie Newman is simply *meant* to be a champion masturbator and video games expert. All that successful relationship stuff is for other men, who haven't gravely offended the gods at some point in their lives. I don't know what I did, but it must have been a transgression of enormous magnitude to deal me such a harsh blow – and remove yet another chance of a happy relationship from my miserable little life.

Everything started out well. On paper it looked like a good idea as far as second dates go. Instead of the usual trip to the cinema or repeat pub performance, I thought I'd invite Laura round to my house for some grub. Now, I'm fully aware that this kind of thing is usually third-, or even fourth-date territory – but sue me, I liked this girl a lot and wanted to make a good impression. It's so easy to just keep coming out with the hoary old dating chestnuts if you're not careful, so I thought mixing things up a bit would be the best way to keep Laura interested.

And what better way to prove that I'm the right man for her than knocking up some tasty fajitas, along with a bottle of expensive red? I didn't plan on this being some kind of seedy night of seduction, just something a little bit different, with more effort on my part than buying a round. I fully intended to sit at one end of the couch with her at the other – a suitable amount of second-date distance between us.

From asking around, I'm led to believe that fajitas are a popular meal for couples in the very early stages of courtship. I have no idea why this is. I'm sure somebody with a beard and too much time on their hands would say it has something to do with sex – but they'll say that about anything if it'll make girls more attracted to their beards and improve their chances of a bunk-up.

Regardless, Laura seems to approve of the fajita idea. 'Not too spicy though, please,' she asks, and I'm more than happy to oblige. While I'm not going to attempt any horizontal shenanigans, it would be nice to get a proper kiss at the end of the evening, and having breath like our old friend Isobel probably wouldn't be a particularly good idea.

Ever since I burped into a girl's mouth when I was a teenager I've been terrified of food-related disasters while dating. I promise Laura to keep the spice to a minimum.

A speedy shop in Tesco provided all the ingredients I needed. Such was my desire to create a good impression

I didn't even plump for the own-brand cheap stuff. I went straight for the top of the range. I was particularly pleased to have acquired some of that very expensive free-range, corn-fed chicken, which had been put in the reduced section at fifty per cent off because it was on its sell-by date. Remember this fact, for it is important in the hideous pantomime about to play out.

Laden with various ingredients including peppers, salsa, the chicken and an onion (chuck in the spice mix and that's pretty much the recipe for fajitas if you've never attempted it), I wend my merry way home to begin my cooking extravaganza.

As usual when I'm doing something outside my comfort zone, I overcompensate. Instead of just going for a few fajitas, I also decide to cook nachos, cheesy jacket potatoes and a mixed salad – with an enormous chocolate torte for afters. You know that African village I could have clothed with my Primark purchases? Well tonight I was going to cook enough to feed the buggers for a week as well.

I was a bit worried that cooking all this food would be time consuming and complicated, but it turns out that all you have to do is chuck the fajita stuff into a frying pan, sling the potatoes in the oven and nuke the nachos in the microwave. Easy peasy, lemon squeezy.

By seven thirty everything is cooked to my satisfaction and I leave it to stand while I go upstairs to get dressed. I braved the crowds in town this afternoon to pick up some new clothes for the occasion, which proves that I'm keen to make a good impression, if nothing else. I didn't even go into Primark. I thought Laura at least deserved a swift look round Burton and Topman.

The doorbell rings at eight o'clock (Laura is on time for this date – officially a good sign) and I answer it smelling and looking my best in a black Burton shirt and dark blue Topman jeans. She's wearing a very pretty cream dress, which looks fabulous, but probably isn't the best thing to wear when you're about to eat messy Mexican food. I don't point this out, of course . . . I'm not a *complete* idiot.

She makes appropriate noises over how good the food smells, and as I pour her a glass of red, I'm very pleased to hear her compliment me on the way I've laid the table.

This delights me more than it usually would because I had to borrow the table (and the matching cutlery) from my sister. The table had been a right bugger to lug back to the house in the car. Single men don't have much call for dinner tables (it's much easier to eat your pizza straight out of the box while sitting on the sofa) and I sure as hell wasn't going to buy one just for this evening. I like Laura a lot, but let's keep things in proportion, eh?

I nearly picked up some candles from Wilkinsons to top the whole thing off, but thought better of it, as it'd be laying it on a bit thick for a second date.

Unfortunately the table is quite small, so can't handle the ridiculous banquet I've cooked. I have to resort to dragging over the coffee table, which wouldn't be too bad were it not for the fact my mate Ryan drew a penis on it in permanent marker last month while he was arseholed on cheap gin.

I cover the offending phallus with the bowl of potatoes before Laura sees it and we sit down to try and wade our way through the piles of Mexican cheesy goodness I've rustled up. The meal itself goes off without a hitch. The non-spicy fajitas come out well, Laura likes the cheesy jacket potatoes and the chocolate torte is demolished with no concern for calorie intake.

Admittedly, there's still a mountain of food left at the end, but that's what Tupperware and freezers are for, after all. We stay sitting at the table chatting for well over an hour with no problems whatsoever. Laura isn't even bothered when she lifts the bowl of potatoes and sees Ryan's handiwork.

By nine thirty I'm confident that the evening is going well and that the meal has been a roaring success. I'm already daydreaming about the kiss I shall receive as a reward for my cooking prowess before Laura leaves.

Oh Lord have mercy, how wrong I was.

Laura's Diary
Sunday, June 5th

Dear Mum,

I knew it was too good to be true. I don't think I'll be seeing Jamie Newman again.

Things happened on Friday night that I am only now able to put into words.

I've spent the weekend in mortified shock and while I'm usually happy to tell people about my dating mis-adventures, this one will stay between me, you, Jamie and whatever heavenly deities may have been watching (and laughing their celestial bottoms off, no doubt).

The evening began with the customary hatred of my wardrobe. It's almost got to the point now where I wouldn't feel comfortable going out without first spending ten minutes berating my pathetic fashion sense. There was literally only *one* item I could wear that was suitable: the lovely cream dress I'd picked up for Melina's wedding to Travis last year that I never got round to wearing because of the 'incident'. You know . . . the one I told you about? Where she found all those pictures of her cousin naked on Travis's phone? The fallout has only just settled from that one.

Anyway, that was the dress I wanted to wear. One

problem though: I was going to be eating fajitas. Sloppy Mexican food and cream dresses do not a happy combination make.

But what choice did I have? It was either that or the purple maxi that sagged at the boobs, the cocktail dress with the permanent absinthe stain, or the Elvis jumpsuit I'd bought for a Halloween party two years ago. I almost went for the Elvis just to see the look on my date's face. Maybe if we were a couple of months into things it would have been good for a laugh, but turning up at his door singing 'All Shook Up' in a sequinned onesie on a second date would have definitely been a bad idea. Nope, the cream dress was my only real option. I'd just have to eat very, *very* carefully, that's all.

It's apparent when he opens his front door that Jamie has decided to wear an entire can of Lynx deodorant this evening. I let him off (and hold my breath) as at least he's made *too much* effort instead of *none* . . . which is always better in my book. The shirt and jeans are nice though. He's obviously only just bought the former, as the Burton tag is still swinging around outside his collar on his back. I nearly say something, but don't want to embarrass the poor guy. If I'd have known then what was going to transpire that evening I wouldn't have had such concerns for his discomfort.

The rather lovely smell of cooking fajitas that wafts from the kitchen is even stronger than the Lynx Jamie is wearing and I feel my stomach rumble in anticipation. I've virtually starved myself all day to make sure I'm hungry. Even if Jamie is a terrible cook, I'll eat whatever is put in front of me. This is another one of Tim's valuable dating tips – one which actually makes some sense in a twisted, masochistic way.

I needn't have worried. Jamie is in fact a very good cook – even if he has made enough to feed an entire football team. Seriously, do I look like I eat that much? I couldn't have consumed the mountain of food he put in front of me if you'd put a gun to my head like they did to that poor fat bloke in *Seven*.

Jamie's house is quite tidy for a boy. The *Raiders of the Lost Ark* poster hung on one wall is a bit much, but at least it's in a frame.

'Signed by George Lucas himself!' he says with pride, as if this is supposed to mean something to me. Other than that – and the vast collection of DVDs that seemed to exclusively feature things exploding – Jamie's bachelor pad is more than acceptable.

I firmly believe the way a man keeps his house says a lot about him. There was one guy I dated years ago called Nathan, who thought that purple suede-effect wallpaper all over the house was a good idea – along with a black sofa, black curtains and a matching black coffee table. It was like living inside a bruise. His penis, along with his conversation skills, was very small.

Then there was Terry, who thought nothing of inviting a girl to his house, even though he had no less than *thirty* posters of Page Three girls stuck up with Blu-Tack in various places. There was even one on the toilet door, to be gazed at whenever he was taking care of business. Terry could talk the hind legs off a donkey, but was also severely under-endowed – and threw up when he laughed too much.

Finally, there was Zach. Zach was hung like a horse and a very witty guy. Unfortunately, he also had the hygiene habits of a pig with chronic sinusitis. There were *things* growing in his kitchen that still give me the willies every time I think about them. Zach therefore never managed to give me *his* willy – no matter how many times he invited me over to his cesspit of a flat.

Once Jamie's meal is finished (including a bloody huge Gü pudding that's going to take weeks on the infernal cross-trainer to get rid of) we sit at the table with contented full bellies, chatting about anything and everything for a couple of hours. The night goes swimmingly and the conversation is sparkling. We talk about work, our friends, holidays, religion, sport, politics . . . the whole nine yards, really. I've never been able to communicate with a man as easily as I do with Jamie Newman.

The first indication that something is horribly wrong is when I have the uncontrollable urge to fart. I asked Jamie not to put much spice into the fajitas for just this reason. Spicy food plays havoc with my internal work-ings. They were mild fajitas – but not mild enough, it seems.

So while he's telling me all about the time he went kayaking in Colorado, I'm squeezing my bum cheeks together and trying to ignore the urgent rumblings in my nether regions. I hold on to the fart successfully until Jamie goes out to make coffee. With relief I negotiate it out of my body without noise. But oh my, it's a *stinker*.

You cannot imagine how embarrassed I feel. Here I am on a second date with a man I already like a lot and I've just turned his front room into a gigantic Dutch oven. All I can do as he returns is hope his sense of smell is terrible.

Jamie puts down the coffee and takes a sniff.

'Oh no,' he says, as I turn crimson. 'Sorry, Laura, the bin smells a bit. I'll just and go and empty it.'

So there it is . . . my backside officially smells like a rubbish bin. As Jamie bashes and crashes around in the kitchen I feel a *very* unpleasant rolling motion coming from my stomach. Then a blinding wave of nausea passes through me.

'There we are, all better,' Jamie says as he comes back into the room.

'Where . . . where is your toilet, please?' I ask weakly.

'Upstairs. Second on the left. Are you okay?'

'Yes, yes I'm fine.'

No, no I am not fucking fine!

Out of the chair like a shot, I'm over to the stairs faster than you can say salmonella. I experience the onrush of another enormous pocket of air in my bowels and hurry up to the first floor.

Sadly, the motion of rushing up the stairs is too much for my delicate innards and as I get three quarters of the way up I fart again. A long, sonorous wet number that carries all the hallmarks of somebody in imminent danger of soiling themselves. It was so loud Jamie *must* have heard it.

I wish I had time to be suitably mortified, but my

bowels are sending me such strenuous emergency signals
that all other thought is banished from my mind. In the
bathroom I get my dress pulled up and my knickers down
at the speed of light and park myself on Jamie's toilet (I
still have bruises on the backs of my thighs from where
I sat down so heavily on the seat).

Blessèd – and noisy – relief then follows.

This is such a terrible turn of events I should be feeling
that the bottom has fallen out of my world – were it not
for the fact the world is now falling out of my bottom.

It's only a small house, so Jamie must be able to hear
what's going on. I'm pretty sure the people in the neigh-
bouring houses can too. It's a wonder they don't call out
the fire brigade.

'Are you okay?' I hear Jamie cry from downstairs. 'Only
you looked a bit green when you—'

He stops mid-sentence. I then hear the sound of heavy,
fast footsteps and the clatter of pots and pans coming
from the kitchen. A cry of horror, a couple of gasps, a
plaintive squeal, and then hideous, *hideous* silence . . .

I remain locked in my death struggle for a good ten
minutes. Finally – mercifully – the tide abates and I can
prise myself slowly off the bowl. My legs are shakier than
earthquake jelly and pins and needles start to run up and
down my thighs as the blood flow gets going again. I still
feel pretty nauseous as I lean against the sink, and fear
that there will be an encore performance in the near future
– but for now the worst is over.

I flush and wash, breathing deeply to restore some
measure of composure. The walk back downstairs is . . .

cautious. Jamie is nowhere to be seen so I walk across his lounge, along the hallway and into the kitch—

Oh sweet mother of God!

Jamie is squatting over the pedal bin, his trousers round his ankles. He looks up at me in horror.

'I'm sorry!' I wail and back away as fast as I can.

In a state of skin-crawling disbelief, I stand in the lounge waiting for Jamie to (oh God) *finish up* and compose himself. He eventually reappears, holding his stomach and shuffling slowly into the room. He looks like a zombie with trapped wind. The look on his face is one of such abject misery I feel a pang of sympathy. I'm sure the expression on my face isn't that much different.

On the surface it's because of the rampant food poisoning we're obviously both suffering from, but on another level I'm sure we also realise that there's no hope of a relationship blossoming between us now. Not after he's heard me fart like a sumo wrestler with irritable bowel syndrome.

Explosive diarrhoea is not something you can simply overlook after two dates.

. . . nor is watching someone shit into a stainless steel pedal bin.

There are no words. The mutual embarrassment is so cringeworthy there's simply nothing that can be said. I scuttle past Jamie into the hall and grab my coat. My stomach rolls again as I catch a whiff of the kitchen.

'You don't have . . . have to go,' Jamie says.

'I really think I should,' I counter. 'This might not be over yet. I want to get home.'

His little face crumples. 'Aah. Okay.'

He opens the front door and I walk out into the blissfully cool night air. I know I should turn and say goodbye, but the mortification is too much to bear. All I can do now is keep my head down, run back to El Denté and drive back to the flat (with its lovely clean girls' toilet) as quickly as possible.

As I reverse the car out, I look back at Jamie still standing in his doorway, watching me go with a face like a kicked puppy. I see him clutch his stomach again and grimace – and know he'll be running upstairs any moment to finish the evening with a bang.

I feel another wave of nausea pass through me and hope I get home before the rotten fajitas assault my lower intestines again. El Denté's dashboard may be wipe-clean, but that is of scant comfort. Besides, the seat sure as hell isn't.

In the space of two hours this has gone from the very best date I've ever had to the very, *very* worst. I'm frankly surprised the whole debacle hasn't given me severe emotional whiplash.

I did make it home, Mum. *Just.* Things finally settled down about two in the morning and I dropped into an exhausted sleep.

It's been two days now and I managed to eat some dry toast for tea this evening. I think I might be ready to try something more exotic like a tin of baked beans tomorrow. What I won't be trying again for an *extremely* long time is dating. When it results in a near-death experience and the most embarrassing moment of your life, it's probably time to give it a rest for a while, don't you think?

Love you and miss you, Mum . . . as always.

Your poorly daughter, Laura.

xx

Jamie's Blog
Monday 4 July

Today marks the one-month anniversary of the worst night of my adult life.

It eclipses the day I was fired from a lucrative freelance contract with a popular restaurant chain due to a spell-checker changing the word 'taste buds' to 'testicles' in a promotional pamphlet I was responsible for. Thousands of people got a chance to read all about how the cuisine on offer would 'tickle their testicles with flavour'.

It was also worse than the time I broke my ankle while pretending to be Spider-Man at a fancy dress disco, and had to spend eight hours in casualty dressed as the web-slinger, because there was nobody sober enough around to bring me a change of clothes.

It even overshadows the night I was arrested for cow tipping, and spent two hours covered in manure and stinking up the meat wagon before the copper who'd nicked us thought better of it and let us go.

Yep, straight to the top of the pile of shame is the night I gave a pretty girl food poisoning, causing her to take the shit from hell upstairs in the bathroom, while I defecated painfully into the pedal bin downstairs.

Look, I had no other choice, alright? By the time I

reached the kitchen, my bowels were screaming at me to do something constructive. It was either the bin or the sink, and when you lift the bin lid it looks a *bit* like a toilet seat. I wouldn't recommend it as an alternative to the more conventional set-up. Let's just say there's a real danger of *splash back* and leave it at that.

It wasn't until last week that I was able to tell somebody about what happened during my second (and last) date with Laura McIntyre.

Ryan tried his hardest to stop laughing after about an hour, but eventually had to go and splash water on his face to calm down a bit. I sometimes think that he only stays friends with me for the dating anecdotes. Since I first met him at college the number of times I've left him a snorting wreck after recounting another tale of romantic woe must be in the double figures by now. I'm convinced he's writing them all down somewhere and intends to write a book once I'm dead.

I keep him around as once he's got over the side-splitting laughter he tends to be a good shoulder to cry on. 'When you fuck up, Newman, you really go to town, don't you?' he says, mouth twitching with mirth. 'Or should I start calling you Pedalo?'

Needless to say I didn't attempt to contact poor Laura again. I mean, what the hell do you say? The text would go something like: *Hi! Sorry I gave you the galloping shits. Fancy a movie? I'm sure the popcorn won't be full of salmonella!*

There was a tiny part of me that hoped I might hear from her though . . . but that hope has thus far come to nothing. It's been over four weeks now and I'm fairly sure Laura (and her intestinal tract) have got over the night of the uncontrollable squits. I'm sure she just wants to put the whole thing behind her and move on with her life. Which leaves poor old Jamie Newman mired back in the world of the single man again.

To compound my misery I was invited to a dinner party at the weekend. Now, I know this makes me sound initially ungrateful. After all, an invite to a party is not to be sniffed at, and at least goes some way to proving that I'm not a complete social pariah. However, you have to bear in mind that the people inviting me to the party are a couple.

Couples invariably invite other couples to parties. This is the way of things. Similarly, single people tend to mainly ask other single people to their shindigs. I'm thinking of ringing up the Natural History Museum and telling them Darwin got it wrong. Not all human beings are the same species, after all. There are in fact two distinct types, who only like to mix with their own kind whenever possible: *Homo couplus* and *Homo singlus*.

Sure, there is interaction between species when necessary, but it is often stilted and awkward. It always comes as something of a relief when the other one eventually buggers off to do something else. As very much a member of the *Homo singlus* crowd I had to weigh up the pros and cons of being invited to a party that would no doubt consist predominantly of the enemy camp.

Was it worth the discomfort and possible social inadequacy to avoid another Saturday evening on my own, watching whatever crap Ant and Dec were hosting at the moment on ITV? I concluded that it probably was.

It would have been bad enough if there had been a sprinkling of my fellow *singlus* species at the party, scattered amongst the happy couples, but it turns out I'm the *only* single person invited. Yep, it was three happy partnerships and one miserable Jamie Newman sitting round the dinner table eating Chinese food. I was the legendary spare prick at the wedding.

Hosts for the party are my mate Dave and his wife Katherine. They've been married for seven years, so have reached the stage where the shine has well and truly rubbed off the apple. I've watched that shine fade from the sidelines. Dave fell for Katherine while we were both shop staff at HMV. She came in once and asked us to find the latest Iron Maiden album for her little brother. Dave found a copy before I did, so he got first dibs.

Still, it seems they still love each other and have the most stable relationship I know of – despite the familiarity of seven years' marriage. This suits me fine, as if I'm going to engage with members of the *Homo couplus* crowd, I'd prefer them not to be enthusiastic about the whole thing. There's nothing worse than a new relationship being flaunted in front of you when you're all on your own. As for couples two and three, they are the epitome of horrifying middle-class self obsession, and have both ostensibly been invited along for the entertainment value. One couple are Dave's friends, the other Katherine's.

'You've got to come along, mate, it's going to be hilarious,' Dave told me over the phone. 'You know how bloody awful they both are – especially when they get together.'

That's what really swayed it for me. I very much doubted Ant and Dec could come up with anything as potentially amusing as two middle-class couples trying to outdo each other in the materialism stakes. Angela and Mitchell know Dave and me through work, while Katherine introduced Sophia and Iain to our social circle about six months ago. Ever since then, whenever they're in the same room together, you can almost feel the tension crackling back and forth between them.

I begged Dave to let me be the one to get the ball rolling this evening. I hadn't been given the chance yet and was thoroughly looking forward to it. So, about an hour into the dinner party, with most of the kung po chicken eaten and a relaxed, convivial atmosphere in the room, I drop the following bombshell:

'So then, everyone, are any of you going on your summer holidays in the next few weeks?'

It'd taken me mere seconds to decide on this particular opening gambit. I knew damn well that both couples hadn't been on holiday yet and were planning to go away, so this was the perfect catalyst for tonight's entertainment to begin.

Dave stifles a laugh and Katherine has to get up to pour another glass of wine before she gives the game away.

'Oh yes!' Angela says happily. 'Mitchell and I are off to the Maldives for a fortnight at the end of the month!' Mitchell nods smugly as she says this.

'We're not that keen on the Maldives these days,' says

Sophia. 'Getting far too commercialised for our liking. We're heading for the Seychelles.'

'Really?' Mitchell pipes up, barely able to disguise the sneer on his face. 'I never feel it's exclusive enough there.'

'Oh, it is indeed,' Iain retorts, sitting up in his chair. 'We get the same vibe from going there as we do when we ski in Val d'Isère every year.'

'Aspen's the place for us when we want a bit of après-ski,' Angela says, attempting to smile. It looks more like she's chewing a dog turd.

'Pfft!' Sophia exclaims, sounding like a tyre going down. 'The place is full of Americans. It's all so heavily commercialised.'

'Maybe the parts you've been going to, hon.'

Zing! That's round one to A&M.

'We're going to Devon in a caravan next week!' Dave says happily, draining his glass. I have to get a piece of this.

'Really? I'm going camping in the New Forest! Even going somewhere this year with toilet facilities, so I won't have to shit in a bucket!'

Katherine spits her wine out. Angela, Mitchell, Sophia and Iain all look at Dave with barely concealed contempt. They don't even bother trying to conceal it when they look at me.

Dave ratchets things up a notch by moving on to an even more electric topic: 'See you're driving the new Mercedes SLK, Iain.' He turns and regards Mitchell. 'Tell me, Mitchell, has that got a better spec than your BMW or not?'

Ooh. That's a good one . . .

Mitchell and Iain spend the next ten minutes arguing about who has the better traction control system, heated rear seats and on-board computer. They probably should have just whipped down their trousers and measured – up it would have saved a lot of time. I have a feeling neither would win any awards if they did.

Iain wins the car round by correctly identifying that his over-priced German executive cruiser costs about a grand more than his opponent's. I thought Mitchell did very well to not bite into his wine glass.

'My Punto went through its MOT last week!' Katherine tells us all.

'Good for you,' I congratulate her. 'My Mondeo's suspension makes a noise like a cat throwing up whenever it goes over a speed bump!'

Dave nearly chokes on a prawn ball. It's Katherine's turn to stoke the fires now and she really hits a home run with: 'I see you've got a new handbag, Sophia. Chanel, is it?'

Perfect. If cars get the lads going, handbags are sure to set the women off.

'Yes! Wonderful, isn't it?' Sophia holds up a ghastly brown snakeskin monstrosity that features two golden buckles slightly larger than my head.

'I had that one last year,' Angela comments in an off-hand manner that in reality is anything but.

'Really? What have you got now?' You could have cut diamonds with Sophia's tone.

Angela pulls out a slim, silky grey number that is

certainly more aesthetically pleasing than the bulky Chanel job and waggles it in Sophia's face. 'Prada.'

Game, set and match Angela and Mitchell!

Silence descends. You can almost hear Sophia chewing on her own liver. Iain has gone a somewhat disturbing shade of puce. I'm trying very hard not to giggle every time I take a sip of wine.

Then Angela ruins it. 'Have you found yourself a girlfriend yet, Jamie? Maybe you can take one camping in the New Forest with you?'

Bitch.

'Not yet,' I tell her and knock back the rest of my Merlot.

'Oh, that's a shame. You should try speed dating.'

I bite back a suitable retort and resist the urge to jump across the table and throttle middle-class Angela, with her shameless materialism and oh so *helpful* nuggets of advice.

'Or the internet?' Sophia adds. 'My assistant Karen found somebody on a dating site, bless her. She'd been single for *years* by the time she gave it a go. It's not something I'd ever consider, but it looks like it's worked for her, the poor girl.'

Is it possible to throttle two people at once? Or should I just go and buy a shotgun?

Then I come out with the well-rehearsed and practised lie that every singleton knows off by heart: 'I'm not really looking at the moment, actually. Happy being free and single, to be honest.' *You pathetic, lying bastard, Newman . . .*

Katherine sees the look on my face and quickly pours

more Merlot into my empty glass. I can see veiled sympathy in her eyes, which is almost worse than the barbed comments from the other two women at the table.

'How are things at the company, Iain?' Dave asks, trying to steer the conversation away from my barren love life. Iain and Mitchell proceed to try and beat each other in the 'who gets the better job perks' argument, but frankly my heart's not in the contest anymore. For the first time I'm acutely aware that I'm the only single person at the table. The half bottle of red wine I've now consumed is not helping my mood, so by the time the clock hits ten thirty, I make my excuses to leave and get up from the table.

I manage to suppress the urge to strangle both Angela and Sophia as they air kiss me goodbye. Dave claps me on the back as I walk to the front door, blackening my mood further. I don't need people feeling sorry for me anymore than I need to be told I should try internet dating like that 'poor girl' Karen.

My house is about a thirty-minute walk from Dave's place so I amble home in no particular rush, attempting to lift my mood by breathing in the fresh summer night air and thinking happy thoughts. Needless to say, even though it's nearly eleven at night, there are still reminders of my terrible singledom everywhere.

This always happens. There's nothing more guaranteed to bring hordes of happy, loving couples out onto the streets than when you're trying to forget how single and lonely you are. I decide to count how many examples of *Homo couplus* I come across in the two-mile walk back to my house.

Eleven. *Eleven* bloody love partnerships between me and my front door. Can you believe that? The bastards were coming out of houses, passing in cars, walking hand in hand down the street. There was even one pair walking a dog. One of those poxy little Chihuahua things. That's just not fair. Who the hell walks a dog at eleven at night? Is the sodding thing nocturnal?

I stumble back into my house, lock the door and sit down in the lounge to watch a bit of Saturday night television. The first programme that pops onto the screen when I turn on the Sky box is *Dating in the Dark*. Luckily I'm still quite drunk, so my aim is off and the remote control thankfully misses the telly.

I regret my outburst – and the broken remote control – ten minutes later when *Four Weddings* . . . comes on and I have no way to turn the bastard thing off. It's a good job I went to bed before *Snog Marry Avoid?* started, otherwise the next day's paper would have carried the story of my late-night homicidal rampage through the streets, killing anyone who looked remotely like they were in a relationship . . . or walking a fucking Chihuahua.

Laura's Diary

Sunday, August 14th

Dear Mum,

The sunburn has finally faded and stopped hurting as much. I now look like a human being again, instead of a boiled lobster. It was a fantastic holiday, but boy have I paid for not taking the Italian sun seriously. Still, two weeks soaking up the Tuscan heat was just what I needed after the year I've had so far.

The shop is just about making a turn back into the black thanks to the new deal I've struck with the wholesalers, and getting Tilly in as an assistant has been a godsend. I was sad that Tim had to leave the shop. It's been a pleasure having one of my best friends working with me all this time. When the job came up over at the Gap, though, I couldn't really ask him to stay on at the paltry pay I was able to offer; so I sent him on his way into the world of V-neck sweaters and skinny-fit jeans with my blessing.

Thank God Tilly came along. I won't lie when I say that paying her a lower wage than Tim has really helped balance the books – and kept me sane. God bless teenagers and their willingness to work for peanuts.

My series of dating disasters put me on the back foot

as well – particularly the fajita episode with Jamie Newman. There were a couple of times I almost texted him to say hello, but as my finger hovered over the send button, I had flashbacks to thunderous stair farts and pedal bins – and hit delete instead.

The anniversary is always hard, Mum. No matter how many years pass, I still dread 17 July. It never gets easier without you here.

When Charlie suggested the trip with her to Italy I was ecstatic. She's a lovely girl and has become a real friend – as well as a housemate who pays the bills on time. I knew closing up the shop for a week wasn't the best idea in the world, but it's been a real slog these past few months, so the time off was much needed – and the rewards outweighed the risk. No bugger buys much fancy chocolate in the middle of summer, anyway.

So off I went with Charlie to Europe for seven days in the villa her cousin April owns with her yachtsman husband Gerard. Charlie may be a hemp-smoking throwback to the Woodstock festival, but her extended family appear to be social climbers of the highest order.

The villa was gorgeous, right out of a romantic novel. I drank my own body weight in Pinot over the course of the week and managed to catch the eyes of a couple of local Tuscan men when Charlie and I ventured out to sample the nightlife. During our last night in the villa, I could have easily pulled a particularly handsome chap called Ezio, who had been following me around like a puppy ever since I bumped into him in the trattoria nearest to the villa. Unfortunately two images kept swirling into my head every time I considered accepting his advances: Angelo the greasy lothario from the speed dating debacle, and Jamie Newman squatting over a pedal bin.

I didn't want to ruin the delightful time I was having by complicating it with a penis, even if it was attached to someone who wouldn't look out of place on the cover of *GQ*. Ezio's attentions were very flattering though. It reminded me that searching for Mr Right can have its benefits. Despite the crispy lobster complexion I walked around with for the fortnight after coming home from the trip, I can safely say it was one of the most relaxing weeks of my life.

So content was I (and horny, thanks to Ezio, if I'm being honest) when I returned I even agreed to go out with Martin – the blond, attractive salesman from the wholesalers I'm now working with. It was completely out of the blue. We were doing a stock check at the warehouse and discussing a potential increase in the amount of truffles on my monthly order, when he straight up asked me if I'd like to go for a drink.

I never even knew he was single. I said yes (much to my surprise) and we had a very enjoyable lunch date at one of the local bistros in the shopping centre a few days later. He paid for everything, managed to maintain my interest conversation-wise, and I noticed that he sported a very nice bottom under his trousers when he went up to the counter to get the bill.

The second date was just as pleasant, this time in the pub just down the road from me. He paid for all the drinks, still wasn't boring me after two hours, and the bottom looked even better in tight blue jeans. It was only when we hit the third date that things unravelled spectacularly . . . resulting in a *very* unexpected development, it has to be said. I'm not the kind of girl who believes in things like fate, but after Friday night I may have to re-evaluate.

In a change of pace Martin suggests we hit the town together and visit some of the clubs dotted around the city centre. I'm pretty keen on this idea as I don't think my mortal soul can stand yet another quiet country pub or coffee house. Instead, we meet at The Frog and Figment – one of the popular bars in the part of the city frequented by the hip, happening young people. I freely admit to being someone who happened about eight years ago, but I'm willing to revisit the hectic Friday nights of my youth just this once.

We both turn up in taxis, so we can drink without fear of subsequent criminal proceedings. Martin certainly seems in the mood to let his hair down and has sunk two Jack Daniel's before I've even got halfway through my first vodka.

'It's good to be out on a Friday night, isn't it?' he shouts at me over the Lady Gaga spilling from the enormous speakers mounted close to the ceiling.

'Yeah, sure is!' I reply enthusiastically, trying to get into the spirit of things.

'Rock 'n' roll, baby!' Martin shouts, knocks back the tequila shot he's just bought, and loudly claps his hands together.

It appears Martin becomes a somewhat different proposition once he's got a couple of drinks inside him. He was quite a straight-laced, quiet guy on our previous two dates, so I'm rather surprised to find myself in the company of a guy who says things like *rock 'n' roll, baby* with no trace of irony when approaching the legal limit.

Still, it's been ages since I let my hair down and Martin is a good-looking guy, so I decide to forgive him some alcohol-induced exuberance and try my best to catch up in the inebriation stakes. This proves impossible, given the pace at which Martin is downing shots. You'd think alcohol was about to be made illegal.

'Lesss go to the Sheeter Lounge,' he says about an hour later, draping an arm around me. 'I wanna do some dancin'!'

The Cheetah Lounge isn't my favourite place, for obvious reasons, but I'm willing to give it a try. 'Okay!' I holler over the Kings of Leon.

'Great! C'mon then!' He downs the dregs of his pint (this is one boy not afraid to mix), grabs my hand and drags me towards the exit before I have time to finish my vodka.

It's gone ten o'clock by now, so the queue to the club is starting to grow.

Martin and I stand with a selection of people younger, better dressed and more excitable than we are. Actually, scratch that last one as far as Martin is concerned. One of his legs is jiggling up and down and you can tell he's dying to get on that dance floor and bust some shapes. He pays for us both to get in (which my over-draft thanks him for) and we push our way into the already full club.

'How about El Cheetos?' he suggests. 'They're doing cheap tequila all night!'

'Can we just go to the Jungle Bar instead?' I respond. I don't really fancy the Mexican section, after the itchy couple of hours I spent in there. Also, Martin appears to have quite the taste for tequila. I don't think being near a bar selling it for next to nothing would be a good idea.

'Yeah! Alright! Rock 'n' roll, baby!' he virtually screams and does the hand clap thing again. To use a phrase like that once can be considered unfortunate, but twice in one evening suggests we might be skirting close to the edges of a catchphrase here, which is a distinct no-no in my book, especially when it's punctuated with that annoying hand clap.

Still, I've downed four vodkas, so I once again put the issue out of my mind as we head to the Jungle Bar and the dance floor Martin is no doubt desperate to shake his booty on.

And boy, does he shake it. I've never seen somebody have an epileptic fit while simultaneously being electrocuted with a cattle prod, but they would still have more co-ordination than poor old drunk Martin. There's a strange jerking of the hips going on, accompanied by wild arm flailing that makes him look likes he's directing air traffic during a hurricane. I'm sure he's breaking at least two of the fundamental laws of physics here, but I can't quite decide which.

As the Pendulum track gets into its stride, my date's wild undulations achieve dangerous proportions. The other people on the dance floor are now starting to give him a wide berth. There's every chance he's about to head-butt his own knee.

'I'm just getting a drink!' I shout. 'Do you want one?' This should get me away from the blast zone for a while.

Martin takes time out from his erratic thrashing to tell me he wants a Jägermeister.

'Make it a double!' he adds.

'Okay!'

'Rock 'n' roll, baby!' Hand clap.

Oh shit. So this date's gone south then. A third use of the catchphrase, accompanied by a style of dancing that would make Morris Men weep, means I've had enough. I start formulating excuses to leave as I'm waiting for the drinks. I've elected to go with a Diet Coke, as I'm going to need all my wits about me. Mind you, I'm not sure Martin would even notice if I just sloped off without telling him, as caught up as he is in his body-popping extravaganza. Nevertheless, I decide to go with an *I feel sick and need to leave* excuse as I carry our drinks back over.

If he pushes it I'll just tell him it's period related. That should shut him up. I hand Martin the drink, and he mercifully stops his one-man assault on the art form of dance to take a swig.

'Phew! I'm really hot!' he hollers.

Hmmm ... with your hair sticking up, face as red as a baboon's arse and sweat patches under your arms? I'm not so sure, buddy.

'Shall we go outside, Laura?'

This is actually a pretty good idea. I'm pretty damn

sweaty myself and could do with some air. It might also be easier to give Martin my excuses to leave if I don't have to shout at him over more Lady Gaga.

'Okay!' I shriek and lead the way out onto a broad veranda at the back of the club.

The terrace is packed with smokers and clubbers looking for a breath of fresh (hah!) air, but we find a corner to stand in, having squeezed past them. The cool air is glorious and Martin is starting to resemble a normal human being again now he's not in sight of a dance floor.

'You having a good time?' he asks.

He's got such a happy smile on his face that my resolve crumbles. I can't bring myself to throw out a spurious excuse for leaving. Damn my manners!

'Yes I am,' I lie.

'Yeah, me too. Wouldn't mind leaving soon though.'

Brilliant! It sounds like I won't need to use an excuse after all.

'Getting a bit hot and bothered here and wouldn't mind going somewhere quieter.'

Martin leans closer to me. *Oh dear.*

'Um . . . that's nice,' I say and try to back away. Sadly I'm right up against the railing that runs around the veranda and have nowhere to go.

'Maybe we could blow this joint and have a little fun on our own,' he says and waggles his eyebrows.

He then does something so incredible I still have trouble believing it happened. He leans against the railing and starts to gently massage his right nipple through his shirt with one finger. My eyes widen in shock. *He must be mucking about.*

'How would you like to come back to my place?' he says, leering at me while continuing to play with his nipple in a slow, 'seductive' circular motion that makes me feel quite ill. I look around for the cameras. This must have been set up by one of my friends. Yes, that's it. Tim has hired a jobbing actor called Martin to play the part of the Nipple Man and is recording it for posterity. Any moment now he's going to jump out with a look of glee on his face and we're all going to have a jolly good laugh about it.

I stand and wait. Nothing happens. Martin continues to revolve one damp finger around his sweaty areola. *Oh good God, this is actually serious.* Martin has gone from potential relationship material to potential restraining order material in the space of two hours. I have to suppress a horrified laugh as he starts to caress both nipples. He's also pouting at me. Like a washed-up porn star with an addiction to Botox, the idiot is shoving his lips out and rolling his eyes at me in what he probably thinks is a suggestive manner. It certainly is suggestive . . . suggestive of the fact he's fast losing his grip on his sanity.

Time. To. Escape.

'Sorry! Feel ill! On my period! Have to leave!' I blurt out and shove past him.

'Wait! Laura!' he calls after me as I speed back into the club, heading towards the main exit as fast as I can through the tightly packed throng of people. I can hear Martin calling my name even over the bombastic music, so I know he's close behind me. *If I can just get to a taxi as quickly as possible, I'll be okay.*

Bursting from The Cheetah Lounge I hurry along the pavement to the taxi rank. There aren't any. *Unbelievable.* Martin is now right behind me again.

'Oi! Where the hell are you going, baby? The night's still young.' He grabs me by the arm and spins me round. 'You can't just fuck off and leave me like that.' He drunkenly stabs a finger at my face. There's an edge to his voice that makes my heart pound.

Okay, this has now gone from plain weird to downright scary. I look over his shoulder to see the bouncers busy with a herd of scantily clad girls. No-one is looking at me – or the maniac who looks like he could swing for me at any moment.

'I reckon you should just relax and give me a kiss,' Martin says, leaning in. His breath is horrendous.

'Let me go, Martin,' I tell him firmly and try to shake off his grip. He outweighs me by a good four stone though and his arms are very strong, so I can't get free. 'You're hurting me.'

'Nah . . . I'm not hurting you. You're fine. You just need to loosen up a bit.' He tries to kiss me and I turn my head away in disgust. 'Don't be a fucking bitch, Laura,' he hisses. I try to pull away again. Now I'm scared to death.

'Let her go, mate,' a calm voice says to my left.

I look up and Jamie Newman is standing there.

'Piss off, dickhead,' Martin replies.

What happens next is scary, but quite wonderful at the

same time. Jamie walks forward, grabs Martin round the throat, puts his face right up to Martin's and stares at him with a look of absolute hate.

'I said let her go, or I'm going to beat the living crap out of you right here and now . . . *dickhead.*'

Martin is a good three inches taller and two stone heavier than Jamie, but the venom with which the threat is issued causes the bigger man to instantly release me. Martin pushes Jamie away and steps back. You can see his intoxicated brain trying to size up the situation. Jamie looks to be stone cold sober, so it could be something of a one-sided fight. Mind you, if Martin starts busting out some of his head-butting dance moves it might end up being a close-run thing. Once those arms get whirling there's no telling how much damage he could cause.

Given the look of fury on Jamie's face and his sobriety, Martin wisely decides this is a fight his inebriated body is very likely to lose and puts up his hands. 'Chill out, mate. Jus' mucking about.'

'Go muck about somewhere else.' Jamie couldn't be my hero any more right now if he had his pants on over his trousers and wore a cape.

Martin looks back at me. 'You're a fucking slut,' he says and points a finger.

Charming. The drunken idiot then turns and marches back towards the club.

I lose sight of him in the crowd of girls and turn to Jamie. 'Thank you so much,' I say with relief.

'Not a problem. I was walking along and saw you over

here. Wasn't going to bother you, but I saw him getting handy.'

'Yeah. That was scary as hell. Don't know what I'd have done if you hadn't come along. Very brave of you. Thanks.'

'Brave? You're kidding, aren't you? I think I've just shat myself.' The fury is gone and Jamie now looks as white as a sheet. 'I'm glad he didn't kick off. He probably would have beaten me senseless. The last time I won a fight it was because my best mate broke my favourite He-Man.'

'I thought he was a nice guy,' I say in a small voice.

'He-Man? He was. Skeletor was the villain.'

'No . . . Martin. That guy you just saved me from.'

'Ah. Apparently not, no.' Jamie fishes out a packet of cigarettes, pulls one out and lights it. He looks at me and misinterprets my expression. 'Sorry, I keep meaning to quit but don't seem to get round to it.'

'No, no. That's fine. You mind if I have one?'

I haven't had a cigarette for seven years, but as I've nearly been sexually assaulted by one man – and certainly saved from it by another – I figure a smoke can't hurt at this point.

It turned out Jamie was only in town to pick up his friend Ryan and Ryan's new girlfriend, Isobel. He offered to give me a lift home and I gratefully accepted.

As I climbed from his car outside the flat, I paused and looked at Jamie. This was the man who had been the cause of the single most embarrassing moment of my life. But he was also now my knight in shining armour. I was still drunk at this point, remember, so probably wasn't thinking straight, but I decided that the second thing cancelled out the first.

'Would you like to go out with me again sometime, Jamie?' I asked him, eliciting a wide-eyed look of surprise.

There's that smile again. I've missed it.

'Yeah, I'd love to.' He looked worried for a second. 'I promise I won't cook.'

So we're going out on a second first date together. Or should that be a third date? I can't quite decide.

I can't say how I really feel about the whole thing now I'm sober and writing it down on the page, but I *think* I've made the right choice to go out with him again. Jamie is the only man I've felt a connection with for many years, and despite the horrors of Fajita Night I'm well aware of the fact that finding a man you feel that way about is rarer than rocking-horse poo in this day and age.

Love and miss you, Mum.

Your karmic daughter, Laura.

xx

Jamie's Blog

Sunday 21 August

This being the twenty-first century, I was under the impression that to pull a member of the opposite sex you had to be in touch with your feminine side, openly express your emotions and have 'empathy' with other people (whatever the hell that is).

However, it turns out all I had to do to get another date with the lovely Laura McIntyre was threaten to beat up another man.

Who says chivalry is dead, eh?

After the fajita debacle I'd tried to convince myself that Laura really wasn't worth the trouble anyway – and that it didn't matter that I'd never see her again. A load of old hogwash, of course. I was really hung up on Laura McIntyre, whether I liked it or not. I admitted this to myself for the first time the other night when I was in town meeting Ryan and saw Laura being roughed up by some prick in a cheap suit.

I am not by nature a violent (or particularly brave) man, so it was testament to how much I still fancied her that I threw caution to the wind and stepped up. Thank God he wasn't some ju-jitsu expert who could lift half a ton and crack walnuts with his arse cheeks.

It was the look of fear in her eyes that spurred me into action. The second I saw it I was consumed by some kind of unholy, indignant rage that propelled me through the confrontation to its successful conclusion – and out the other side into the cool, calm lagoon of reflective dread known as the *What the fuck have I just done?* feeling. You know, when you've narrowly escaped serious physical harm and can't help dwelling on what might have been.

When my heartbeat had returned to normal and my bottom had stopped twitching, Laura and I held quite a sensible conversation. Explosive bowel movements and pedal bins weren't brought up once. I further secured my position as her knight in shining armour by offering her a lift home. This was only slightly marred by Ryan and Isobel making some unsubtle comments about Laura and me, which probably sounded like the height of comedy genius to them in their drunken state, but was embarrassing as hell.

I really shouldn't have introduced those two to one another. I had to do something to stop Isobel texting me though, and Ryan was always one for the 'earthy' kind of girl, so it seemed like a good idea at the time. I just wish I didn't have to hear about their sex life. It puts me right off my food.

Once I'd chucked Isobel and Ryan out of the car at her mum's house – to parting cries of '*Wahaay! Get in there, Newman!*' and '*Watch out! He spunked on Jesus!*' – it was a far more pleasant drive through the quiet early-morning streets. Laura was wearing perfume that targeted my libido nicely, and I found it quite hard to stay on the right side of the road.

You can imagine how surprised I was when she asked me out on another date. I think she was pretty surprised herself, judging from the look on her face after she'd suggested it. I wasn't going to give her a chance to back out though, and immediately said yes.

It seems, gentle people of the blogosphere, that the cure for giving someone chronic food poisoning is to save them from a drunk sex maniac. I don't know that you'll ever be called on to use this piece of advice constructively, but you can't say I didn't tell you.

Right then: third-date time! Usually, these are pretty easy to arrange. By this point you've generally established a mutual interest in one another and the third meet-up is really just an excuse to get the two of you together in an environment conducive to snogging. Unfortunately, my situation with Laura was somewhat unusual.

This was indeed the third date, but given the disaster of the second I felt a bit more effort was required on my part to make sure that she fully forgave The Fajita Debacle. This meant spending a decent sum of money on an interesting and exciting activity that would bring us closer together – but one that wouldn't scare her off by being too overtly romantic. Perhaps you're imagining that a nice bike ride in the country, followed by drinks and a meal in a pub sounds like a good idea? How about a show in London? A musical, possibly? Or how about something more unusual, but potentially rewarding, like a pottery class? After all, it worked for Patrick Swayze in *Ghost*, didn't it?

You may be considering all these things and more, but please don't forget for one second that I am a *colossal* idiot. In my infinite wisdom I decide we should spend the evening go-karting. Yes, you read that correctly: *go-karting*.

I panicked, you see. The weather wasn't nice enough for riding a bike; I wouldn't know a good musical if it bit me on the arse and then sang about it; and if I attempted pottery I would inevitably end up producing a giant ceramic phallus.

About a week beforehand I'd been chatting to somebody at work. They'd mentioned how much fun last year's works outing to the local go-kart track had been. It sounded like a brilliant idea to me, so I rang and booked two places on an open session. I watch Formula One when I get the chance, and this was the nearest I was ever likely to get to being like Jenson Button.

You'll be *completely* unsurprised to learn that Laura was less keen about the whole thing.

'Go-karting?' she says over the phone when I tell her of my plans. I can tell by her tone of voice that it isn't her cup of tea. I grimly plough on, because once I've got an idea in my head, it's very hard to dislodge it, no matter how hard you smack it. 'Yeah! It should be great fun.'

'Er . . . okay,' she says, trying to sound positive. 'It's different, I guess.'

The doubt in her voice makes me wince. I give her the

details of where to meet and I hang up to begin some hardcore hand-wringing. This is another one of Jamie Newman's legendary dating gambles. As the last one ended up with me having to buy a new bin for the kitchen, I'm not altogether confident it's going to pay off.

We meet outside 'Go-Karting For Fun' on Friday night. I only managed to get us booked in at nine thirty, so this will be a pretty short date, whether it goes well or not. Laura looks nervous. As do I. I'm guessing it's for very different reasons.

'I've never done anything like this before,' she tells me.

'Neither have I. Still, nothing ventured, nothing gained, eh?'

'Hmmm.'

She follows me into the building and we walk over to the cash desk, the drone of kart engines filling the enormous metal warehouse.

'Hi,' I say to the race director standing behind the counter. He's about the same age as me and is wearing the expression of a man who knows that things went horribly wrong at some point, but can't quite remember when.

'Can I help?' he says, hoping I'll say no.

'Yeah. I booked an hour for two people. Name of Newman?'

The guy picks up a pen and asks us to sign in. We write our names down on a sheet of paper that contains several paragraphs of small print – no doubt designed to absolve the company of any blame should either one of us get decapitated while out on track. He then points out the changing room just along the way and we head off to get into our racing overalls.

Unlike the type Formula One drivers wear, these look like oversized babygrows. I've never worn a onesie before so this is a new experience for me. Laura gives me a nondescript look as she stands up and folds her arms over the expansive material.

'I don't feel much like Lewis Hamilton,' she remarks. 'Well . . . maybe when he was two years old.' She sticks her thumb in her mouth and crosses her eyes.

'These things aren't flattering, are they?' I say, doing a couple of quick squats.

Laura joins in the impromptu exercise routine, and before long we're both laughing our heads off doing squats and lunges in our enormous overalls.

We then add helmets to the ensemble, which makes us both look like those bobble-head toys people stick on their dashboards. I start wobbling my head around like a maniac while continuing to do expansive lunges, making Laura actually snort a couple of times with laughter.

'Ready to go, are you?' the race director says, poking his head through the doorway and looking at us both like we're lunatics. Laura and I sober up fast.

'Oh yes,' I say. 'Roger that!'

Quite why I've started talking like a fighter pilot is beyond me. It seems appropriate though, what with the helmet and everything. The director favours me with a withering look and turns to leave. Laura and I trail in his wake like naughty children. She starts wailing like a toddler (thankfully muffled by her helmet) and waddling as we make our way onto the track. I follow suit, much to the disgust of the surly-looking marshals who are standing around waiting for us to bloody well get on with it.

There follows a mind-numbing ten-minute safety lecture, delivered in a monotonous tone of voice by our bored host. I've almost lost the will to live by the time he's pointing out where the toilets are. Then finally the talk is over and the fun can begin.

In the next hour (for which I had to pay an obscene amount of money, I should add) I learn a lot more about Laura McIntyre than I would have had we done something more prosaic like bike riding or pottery. I can thoroughly recommend a bit of competition laced with mild danger to show you a person's real character.

We're barely out of the pits before Laura is bumping into me from behind, telling me to get a move on. All traces of the nerves she displayed when we arrived have well and truly disappeared. Laura apparently suffers from some kind of multiple personality disorder, brought on by the sound of a two-stroke engine firing up. One minute she's a bright, beautiful blonde with a cheeky smile, the next she's Mad Max with anger management issues.

'Come on, slow coach!' she shouts and moves out to overtake me as I sedately take the hairpin. Our karts bump into one another, sending me into a tank slapper that I only just manage to recover from as Laura goes whizzing past. Given that I was still trying to make up for giving her food poisoning, I should probably have let Laura run rings around me. I am a heterosexual male, however, and am therefore incapable of letting a woman get the better of me while sitting in a mechanically propelled device. To do so would let down my entire gender. With red mist descending, I take off after my date – sorry, my *opponent* – with the pride of the male species at stake.

The next forty-five minutes of my life are humiliating to the point of absurdity.

Laura laps me. *Twelve* times. It appears I've tapped some hitherto unknown talent for motor racing in Laura McIntyre that puts my hack-sawing at the wheel to utter shame. She's frankly brilliant. While I spin the kart almost every time I try to take a corner with any speed, she's on and off the gas with expert timing, hitting all the apexes perfectly. It's evident that when presented with some competition, Laura becomes an altogether different person . . . one I wouldn't like to meet in a dark alley. Every time she comes haring past to put me another lap down, I'm treated to an insult or abusive gesture, each one more obscene than the last:

Lap one: A mocking wave.
Lap two: 'Speed up, Jamie!'
Lap three: 'Put your bloody foot down!'
Lap four: Pokes her tongue out.
Lap five: 'My granny's faster than you!'
Lap six: 'You suck!'
Lap seven: Middle finger.
Lap eight: 'Twat!'
Lap nine: 'You're my bitch!'
Lap ten: Wanker sign.
Lap eleven: Double wanker sign.

Lap twelve: Double wanker sign. Tongue poked out. 'You're fucking crap!'

By the time the buzzer goes to signal the end of our session I'm feeling so emasculated I might as well be wearing a dress and pigtails. As I trundle into the pits, she jumps out of her kart and starts to do a bizarre victory dance. This alternates between wiggling her arse at me and jumping round like Zebedee, singing about how much of a loser I am. I stand there and watch her do this with a rueful smile on her face.

I should be feeling terrible. I should be feeling embarrassed. But I'm pretty sure what I'm actually doing is falling in love.

Here's this beautiful girl – who was prepared to give me a second chance after I nearly killed her – so completely at ease that she can make herself look a complete *pillock* in front of a man she's met three times and a bunch of bored race marshals.

Hell, I even enjoyed the trash talk while we were on the track. I've never met anyone quite like her. She's amazing!

Oh fuck me, I'm in trouble.

Laura continues to berate me about my driving skills as we get rid of the overalls and helmets. We head out of the building over to our cars and Laura starts questioning other aspects of my manhood, including my general sporting prowess, my physical strength and even my skills in the bedroom. I have the feeling she's getting her own back for the embarrassment of the fajita incident and I'm (more or less) happy to let her rant. Besides, she's very funny and I can't help but laugh.

'Now, would you like some tips before you drive home, Jamie?' she says as I open my car door. 'We wouldn't want you crashing the second you pull out of this car park, would we?'

'Ha ha. You're not doing much for my self esteem here, woman.'

Laura affects a quite hideous expression of misery. 'Ooooh. Is wittle Jamie feeling bad about himself?' she says in the silliest baby voice I've ever heard.

'Give it a rest, McIntyre.'

'Oh yeah?' Laura pulls herself up to her full five foot six inches and steps forward. 'And what are you going to do about it if I don't, Newman?' She puts her hands on her hips and thrusts her chest out in an age-old gesture of defiance.

I've never wanted to kiss anyone more in my life.

'Guess I'll have to prove to you that my go-karting skills have no bearing on my manliness.'

'Oh right . . . and exactly how are you going to do—'

I've thrown caution to the wind and gone in for the kiss. Luckily for me (and future instalments of this blog) she kisses right back.

It's not the most romantic place for a first snog – in a dark car park on an industrial estate, up against a P-reg Nissan Micra with a dent in the wing – but it's still ten of the best minutes of my life.

'Okay,' she eventually says in a breathy whisper and pulls her head back. 'That's enough of that for one night, pal.'

I let out a little whimper of disappointment. 'Alright.'

Actually, this is to be expected. Women are much like the monster in a good horror movie. They don't like to give away too much too quickly. It's all about the slow build-up and teasing glimpses that keep you on the edge of your seat, all of which lead to the exciting climax when you finally get to see the shark properly and Robert Shaw gets bitten in half. A horrible analogy, obviously, but I'm hoping you get the point.

'Thrashing the pants off you has knackered me out,' Laura continues, separating herself from me and the gargantuan erection I'm now sporting.

'Well you can thrash the—'

'Don't even think about finishing that sentence,' she tells me.

Yep, I'm in love. *Bugger.*

'I'm off home to take a nice bath before bed. I stink of oil.'

'You smell pretty good to me. When can I see you again?'

'Not sure yet. I'm swamped with work. I'll give you a ring though.'

Laura jumps into her car and starts the engine. 'Despite the fact you drive slower than old people have sex, I really enjoyed this evening, Jamie.'

'Me too.'

'You certainly kiss better than you take a corner. See you soon.' She pokes her tongue out and goes momentarily cross-eyed. 'Loser!'

And she's gone. Out of the car park at speed in her

little dented Nissan, driving like she's still in the go-kart. I stand there for another few moments, a dumb smile on my face. I probably would have been there longer, were it not for the fact that the race director came outside for a smoke and started giving me the stink eye.

A woman ran rings around me tonight – in more ways than one. Some guys would probably hate that. I couldn't be happier.

Laura's Diary

Sunday, August 28th

Dear Mum,

It was up to me to arrange the fourth date.

I couldn't keep expecting Jamie to do it. God knows what he'd come up with next. I didn't really fancy a day rock climbing or shark fishing.

That's being a bit unfair. I really enjoyed the go-karting in the end, despite initial reservations. After Tom and his microlight back in the spring I wasn't sure any activity where I would have to wear a helmet was advisable, but I'm glad I agreed to it in the end as I had a blast. Even if it did bring out a side of me I've never seen before – and don't particularly want to see again. I've spent the past few days being very careful not to earn myself a speeding ticket. Whenever I see a corner now, I want to take it with my foot buried in the throttle. I also find myself swearing at other motorists and making V-signs. I may require counselling at some point in the near future.

Anyway, I said I'd come up with the idea for our next date. It's the twenty-first century after all, so the woman should be allowed to set the tone of the evening as often as the man. Sadly, I couldn't think of a bloody thing for us to do. The shadow of Fajita Night still hung over us, so a meal was out. I can't stand ten-pin bowling – and since he was a typical bloke, I doubted Jamie would like a long, romantic walk in the country.

Hmmm. Cinema it is then! Yes, I know it's dull, but all I really wanted was another go on those lovely soft lips of his, so I couldn't give a damn what the actual content of the date was beforehand. The choice of movie wasn't important either, so I took a cursory glance at the local listings and saw something called *Bound Together*. It looked like a thriller, which was perfect. Not a girly romantic comedy he'd have hated, and not a stupid action movie I would have been stone cold bored with after five minutes.

I went for the small cinema on the waterfront that shows independent movies. I can't stand the multiplexes – partly because the smell of rancid popcorn turns my stomach, and partly because at this time of year they're packed to the rafters with people going to see the latest CGI-infested blockbusters. The Harbour Cinema is a much more enticing proposition.

We meet in the car park outside and I have to resist the temptation to kiss Jamie there and then, as no-one likes to be easy, so I just let him give me a quick peck on the cheek and we go in. The woman behind the counter gives me a funny look when I ask for two tickets to *Bound Together*. I should have realised something was amiss right then. Her expression doesn't register, though, as I'm quite preoccupied with how nice Jamie smells. He's standing right behind me, and whatever he's wearing is making me a bit weak at the knees.

'Did it sound good in the write-up?' he asks as we walk away from the counter.

'Mmmm. Yeah. Yeah it did,' I reply. I don't have a clue whether it sounded good in the write-up or not. I don't care either. As long as I can sit nice and close to Jamie in a darkened room then I'm happy.

We settle in to our seats. There are only a few other people in the cinema with us. All of them men – another vital clue I completely missed thanks to Jamie's aftershave.

There are no trailers, so we move straight into the movie. The first few minutes seem innocuous. A pretty girl is walking through an indeterminate Eastern European city. A suitably airy piece of incidental music plays over the scene as she meanders through a flower market. Then a large black van pulls up and whisks her from the street. Exciting stuff . . . but not nearly as exciting as the fact Jamie's leg just brushed up against mine.

The screen fades to black. Then we see the girl again, this time tied to a chair. She's naked. Two men enter the room. The music isn't light and airy anymore. The men move closer to the girl and *things* start to happen. The next few minutes are eye-opening to say the least.

While not quite hardcore pornography, there's certainly enough flesh, grunting and bodily fluids on display for it to be borderline. There's also a nasty misogynistic element that makes me squirm in my seat even more than the piles did at The Cheetah Lounge. God knows what Jamie is thinking.

I barely paid attention to which movie I chose, figuring

it wouldn't matter. He must think I've actively decided that the best movie for us to see on our fourth date is a seedy European S and M movie. I daren't look at his face. *Mine* must be bright red. I can feel the embarrassment radiating from my cheeks like a convector heater. I've got nowhere else to look but at the screen, where it appears one of the gentlemen concerned is now slapping the poor young girl on the forehead with his penis, while the other one is inexplicably putting her feet into a bucket. I have no idea why. Perhaps the Eastern Europeans find galvanised steel sexy.

The penis slapping goes on for another few seconds. I can't quite decide whether the girl is enjoying it or not. The other guy starts washing her feet in the bucket with icy water. He also appears to be masturbating feverishly. The music in the background now sounds like something you'd hear at a fairground. I'm now so shamefaced by all this I've sunk down into my seat far enough for my knees to be hitting the back of the one in front.

Look at Jamie. See what expression he's got on his face. No! I can't do that. *You have to, you idiot! If he's looking disgusted it's bad . . . if he's looking horny it's worse.* I sneak a glance at my date, terrified I'm going to see him cross-eyed and dribbling with pleasure – much like the guy sitting about eight seats further down the row.

Jamie is in fact crying . . . with laughter, that is. It's one of those silent laughing fits that are almost painful to experience. He's holding his sides, and it looks like someone's shoved a broom up his backside. The tears flow down his cheeks and he keeps making high-pitched squeaking noises in an effort not to burst out laughing and disturb all the mouth breathers – who are no doubt loving every second of the penis slapping.

Laughter is infectious as we all know. My cheeks rapidly turn bright red through suppressed hilarity now, rather than embarrassment. We both manage to hold it together for another couple of minutes, but then the penis slapper calls the girl a 'cock-a-holic' in a thick Polish accent.

I've never laughed so much in my life. It doesn't help that the other guy is now sucking the girl's toes like his life depended on it, while simultaneously slapping his own meaty posterior with a tennis racket. Jamie and I jump out of our seats to a chorus of angry *shushing* noises from the mouth breathers. There's nothing like two idiots laughing like hyenas to put you off your stroke, I suppose.

We burst out of the theatre in a gale of laughter. Jamie has to lean bent double against a wall for a few moments while the giggles do their terrible work and I have to sit down in a nearby chair to get my breath back.

'Why . . . why did you think we should see that?' he asks between gasps. 'I thought you said it looked good?'

'I lied! I didn't . . . didn't look at the reviews properly.'

'Really? You don't say?' Jamie wipes his eyes. 'I'd love to have seen them though,' he continues, making writing gestures with his hand as he intones: '*If you only see one movie this year with a man slapping his penis on a girl's head, make it this one! Five stars!*'

This sends me off into another wave of laughter and we only sober up enough to leave the cinema when the woman from behind the counter comes storming round the corner, telling us to be quiet.

With our movie-going experience cut short, we elected to visit the nearest pub, where Jamie proceeded to tease me mercilessly about taking him to see a porno flick. After I rubbed his nose in his total lack of racing ability the other day, I guess it was nice for him to get his own back.

'Now, Laura,' he said, leaning forward and taking my hand. 'If that was your way of saying you like having your feet sucked, you could have just told me, you know.'

'Sod off.'

'And indeed, if it makes you feel sexy, I can go and buy a sausage and smack you over the head with it. It's not quite the same thing, but this is only our fourth date.'

He spends another fifteen minutes coming out with similar witticisms before I get bored and shut him up by moving my chair right next to his – favouring him with a lingering kiss that definitely wakes *his* sausage up. Frankly, I wanted sex there and then, but if there's one weapon a woman has in her arsenal when it comes to assessing a man's worth, it's seeing how he reacts when you hold off getting naked and sweaty for just *a little bit longer*.

We parted company in the car park after virtually dry humping against his Mondeo for ten minutes. We were like two rampant teenagers with nowhere private to go. Any of the audience for *Bound Together* would have probably enjoyed watching what we were doing. Provided we both put buckets on our heads, I suppose.

As I drove home, I knew that the next time I saw Jamie would be when I'd finally go all the way with him. I just had to decide the best way for that to happen, on my terms.

As ever, love and miss you, Mum.

Your very distracted daughter, Laura.

xx

Jamie's Blog
Tuesday 6 September

Good grief, it's hotter than a mustard vindaloo out there. This is not the weather you'd expect for September in the UK, but then if you want a predictable climate, this isn't the country to live in. People are wilting in the streets. Dogs have their tongues permanently out. The local chavs have rolled up their tracksuit bottoms and are only shop-lifting from the frozen food section in Asda at the moment.

The unseasonable warmth was an appropriate backdrop to the consummation of my relationship with Laura McIntyre on Sunday night. While the country was sweating thanks to the clammy Indian summer, we were sweating for far more enjoyable reasons. Don't fret, I'm not dumb enough to write about it here without having run it by Laura first. I'm smart enough to know that telling the world about your first sexual encounter with a new woman without getting her permission isn't likely to win you many brownie points.

She's given her blessing . . . and actually said she's looking forward to reading it. No pressure there, then.

Turns out she writes a diary herself, though she's very cagey about it. My mind's aflame with curiosity. I've never dated a woman who likes to write as much as me. It's quite disconcerting. There's every chance she might be better at it than I am, and I don't think my already fragile writer's ego can take it. Part of me would really like to get a look at her diary, but part of me would rather avoid it, if it means reading something funnier than I can put together.

I got the idea that Laura might be ready to go a little further than the public display of affection stage when she suggested I come over to hers for the evening. When a woman invites you into her home it tends to suggest things are proceeding in the right direction. While I didn't count my chickens before they'd hatched, I did make sure a fresh condom was secured in my wallet, just in case. I won't lie and say that my heart wasn't beating faster than usual as I rang her doorbell. I was really looking forward to having the opportunity to, well . . . ring her bell.

'Evening, handsome,' Laura says with a cheeky smile as she opens the door.

'Christ, you look incredible,' I reply.

This is no word of a lie. Laura is wearing the classic 'little black dress'. If someone has invented a sexier outfit than this, then I certainly haven't seen it, especially when the woman wearing it has a figure to die for. To trot out a hackneyed expression: *there she stood with all those curves and me with no brakes.*

I quickly stop speculating about what she might be wearing underneath the dress, otherwise I'm likely to spend the next five minutes on the doorstep staring at her and dribbling. I hand over the bunch of flowers I just picked up in Tesco and give her a kiss.

Stop making that face. Tesco flowers are *perfectly* accept-able in my book – provided it's a last-minute thing. It only occurred to me that I should buy her some as I walked out of my front door. Admittedly, I should have thought it a lot sooner and visited one of the local over-priced flower emporiums, but at least I didn't pull into the nearest Shell forecourt and pick up a bunch that stank of petrol.

Originally our plan was to get take-out, but Laura surprises me by stating that she's cooked us a spaghetti Bolognese.

'Don't worry,' she says when she sees the look on my face. 'I made sure the mince was fresh and cooked prop-erly. We've got two toilets though, just in case.'

'Very funny.'

'Got us a movie to watch afterwards as well. My flat-mate's out, so we can watch it in the lounge.'

Movie? Lounge? These are not the things a horny gentleman wishes to hear on a night he's designated for first-time rumpy-pumpy. Watching a movie (along with eating a meal) will fill up the majority of the evening, leaving little time for hanky-panky. Maybe this is Laura's plan though. Perhaps she wants to take things slow, and not jump right to the winky-wonky.

Yes, I did make that last one up.

This turn of events does not meet with approval from my penis. He's not happy in the slightest, and if he had a face it would have a very sulky expression on it right about now. My stomach is quite content, however, with the smells emanating from Laura's kitchen. I would have been more than happy with a bowl of chow mein from the local Chinese, but home-cooked food is always a better alternative – so long as you're not drunk out of your mind at two in the morning, when only something covered in MSG will suffice.

I walk into the lounge and sit at the table while Laura dishes up the meal. We chat about our respective days through the serving hatch as she wrestles with the pasta. Before you accuse me of being a lazy misogynist, I did offer to help, but she told me to stay put. This is probably wise as the last time I was let loose in a kitchen I nearly killed the both of us.

To head off any thoughts you might be having of a repeat performance of Fajita Night, the Bolognese is fabulous and there are no unpleasant after-effects (other than my need to break wind expansively later that evening – garlic has that effect on me).

We continue to chat about nothing in particular over the meal, though I have to admit to being somewhat distracted by the soft whispering sound her stockings make every time she crosses her legs. The words 'Agent' and 'Provocateur' swim into my head and I find it very hard to dislodge them. If my penis had a voice, he'd be chanting them over and over again at increasing volume.

'What movie is it?' I ask.

Please be a short one. Please be a short one.

'*Slumdog Millionaire*. I've never seen it. Have you?'

'No, but I've heard good things about it.'

Mainly that the bugger is a good two hours long, *damn it.*

'Great!'

'Completely devoid of slapping penis, I'm led to believe.'

We clear away the plates and settle down to watch the flick.

To be fair to Danny Boyle's tale of life in the Mumbai slums, we did manage to get through a whole thirty-seven minutes before turning our attention to more exciting activities. While the acting, storyline and cinematography are all very nice, they really can't compete with a beautiful woman in a tight black dress, who's had three glasses of wine and is feeling frisky.

By the time Slumdog (I never catch his real name) starts getting close to winning the twenty-million-rupee jackpot, I'm getting pretty damn close to scoring a jackpot of my own. Upon discovering what Laura has underneath her little black dress, my penis goes on a metaphorical victory lap and high fives my testicles: black stockings, black frilly knickers and suspenders with red bows – it's every red-blooded man's dream. If for some horrible reason I never see Laura McIntyre again after this night, her ensemble will be stored forevermore in my mental wank bank, to be brought out at regular intervals.

I'm not sure she's so enamoured with my Primark boxer shorts, but at least they are clean on today, which hopefully counts for something. She has no trouble snaking one hand under the elastic band, that's for sure. Ten more highly enjoyable minutes go by before Laura says something that sends my penis off around the track again for another lap.

'Let's go upstairs,' she whispers into my ear. There have

been some very good ideas throughout human history – starting with *Why don't we climb down out of these trees?* all the way up to *Why don't we just cover it in chocolate and charge twice as much?* I'd venture to argue, though, that Laura McIntyre suggesting we go upstairs is by far and away the best idea ever put to one human being by another.

As this isn't a bad romantic comedy from the eighties, I don't attempt to pick Laura up and carry her to the bedroom. I let her climb the stairs under her own steam – which is fine by me, as I'm right behind her and get a good eyeful of her bottom. She hasn't pulled the dress back down properly, so the tops of her stockings are visible. My penis is now pulling champagne corks and jumping up and down on the podium with the national anthem playing in the background.

It's baking hot in her bedroom so Laura throws open the windows, letting in a pleasant breeze, which is only slightly blocked by the curtains she pulls to prevent the neighbours getting a free show. It's still fairly early in the evening so I can hear voices coming from the gardens of nearby houses.

Within a minute of hitting the bed I'm naked apart from the budget Primark pants. Laura allows me to divest her of most of the lingerie, to her apparent relief.

'This stuff looks good, but it's a pain in the backside when it's hot like this,' she says as she rolls one stocking down her long, tanned leg.

'Mmmm,' is about all I can manage in response. My brain has pretty much frozen solid watching the stocking as it makes its way down her thigh. I couldn't take my eyes off it if a three-ton bull came bursting into the room holding a live hand grenade between its teeth.

There's a moment when you're in bed with someone for the first time that you realise you're completely naked in front of them. This usually leads to a strange combination of sexual excitement and neurotic anxiety. It's one thing to see someone else's sweaty naked body, but the prospect of them also seeing *yours* – with all its blemishes and imperfections – is somewhat disconcerting. Luckily, sexual excitement generally wins the battle nine times out of ten, and worries about self image are lost in the ensuing tangle of body parts.

The foreplay is brief. We both want it that way. There will (hopefully) be plenty of time for long, languid sex sessions in the future, but right now we are both in such a state of excitement that delayed gratification really isn't on the cards. My penis has worked himself up into such a frenzy that the prospect of this going on for more than a few minutes is about as likely as Megan Fox winning the best actress Oscar.

I climb on top, look into Laura's deep blue eyes, plant a gentle kiss on her lips and slide slowly into her, making us both gasp. My eyes stay locked with hers as I run a hand down that long, tanned leg, marvelling at how soft and sensual—

'MITTENS!'

What the bloody hell is that?

'WHERE ARE YOU, MITTENS?!'

From what seems like right outside the window, the

sound of a highly upset little girl's voice breaks the mood like a sledgehammer thrown through a sheet of glass.

'What the hell's going on?' I exclaim.

'Oh Christ . . . it's the girl in the block across the way,' Laura says. 'She's got a cat. The bloody thing's always going missing.'

For a few moments we stop, listening out for more from beyond the curtains.

When there isn't, I look back into Laura's eyes and start to move my hips forward again, watching her reaction as I—

'MITTENS!'

Bollocks.

'COME HOME, MITTENS!'

Now I'm really getting put off my stroke.

I stop again . . . and we both wait once more for another outburst.

This time a good couple of minutes go by.

'You think she's given up?' I ask.

'Yeah. She doesn't normally do it for long.'

'Okay.'

I kiss Laura and again start to move my hips back and forth.

At first I expect to be interrupted, but by the time I've worked up a bit of a rhythm, I've forgotten about Mittens and have my mind firmly back on the job. It's not long before Laura starts to moan loudly. She's starting to build to a climax and I increase my speed, her moans becoming gasps with each thrust.

We're moving together now, faster and faster . . . the

orgasm getting closer as our bodies work in harmony and our—

'MITTENS!'

Laura starts laughing – partly at the timing, partly at the look of angry frustration on my red, sweaty face.

'Astrid?' a man's voice says. 'Will you stop calling that stupid cat? It'll come home when it wants to.'

Judging from how annoying 'Astrid' is, I'd wager Mittens has done a runner in an attempt to avoid going deaf, and won't be back any time soon.

'But Daddy! He might have been run over!'

'I doubt it. Inside with you, I'm sure it'll be back soon.'

I would have genuinely liked this bloke for dragging his noisy daughter inside, were it not for the fact the idiot had called her Astrid.

The moment somewhat lost, I climb off Laura and lie next to her while her giggles gradually dissipate.

'Sorry about that,' she says, draping one leg over my body. 'The flats are close together round here. You get to hear a lot.'

'No worries. Let's just hope nobody heard *us*.'

'I was being as quiet as possible. It wasn't easy though . . . you know what you're doing, Newman.'

Excellent.

'In fact, I feel like I should step up my own game.'

For once, I'm glad that Laura is a competitive little soul, as she now slides down my body and starts to give me the single best blow job I've had in years. She can't get my balls in her mouth like Isobel, but she also isn't making a noise like a dozen pigs with head colds, so we'll call it a win.

I'm in absolute heaven. Before long I can feel my climax building again. I'm caught in a wave of total pleasure as Laura licks me. This is simply the best feeling I've had in months and I never want it to—

'MITTENS!'

We ended up watching the rest of *Slumdog Millionaire* on Laura's portable TV, figuring that Astrid would eventually go to bed and we'd be left in peace. The credits rolled on the movie at about eleven, and Laura and I finally got to have some uninterrupted fun. I just about managed to put Astrid and Mittens out of my head, but I have to confess I didn't relax entirely until the deed was properly done and Laura was wrapped in post-coital bliss in my arms.

I ended up staying the night and was late for work the next day. There's nothing quite like waking up with a warm, soft female body next to you to put a smile on your face on a Monday morning.

In the end it was a fantastic night, but I don't think I'm ever going to be able to look at a pair of children's gloves in the same way again.

Laura's Diary
Monday, September 19th

Dear Mum,

It's at times like this I really miss your advice. Something's happened that has set my head spinning faster than a washing machine on 'heavily soiled'. I'll try to explain. Maybe writing it down will clear my head and help me come to some kind of decision.

Last time I spoke to you, I was telling you about my first time with Jamie. Despite the next door neighbour's insistent attempts at ruining the moment, Jamie and I had sex for the first time – and it was quite exceptional. There's nothing like a hot, sweaty summer's evening to kick-start your libido, even if it does mean being part of one small girl's hunt for her missing cat.

Having got past the semi-awkward first time together, Jamie and I embarked on what could only be described as a rampant sex-a-thon. Over the course of the next week we rocked the kasbah every night. Sometimes twice. By the end of seven days I was so knackered from trying to combine a newly discovered sex life with work I could barely keep my eyes open.

I always tend to get emotional when I've not had much sleep, so I'm afraid I let the side down a bit last Wednesday when I burst into tears in front of Jamie as we lay together in his bed.

'Are you alright?' he said in a panicked voice. 'I didn't do anything wrong, did I? I know I didn't go for the wrong hole, so—'

'No,' I assured him as I wiped tears from my face. 'It's nothing to do with you. Today is my mum's birthday.'

'Aaah.' He didn't really have anything else to say, bless him.

Jamie already knew that I'd lost you, Mum, but we'd never gone into much detail. Things were different now though, so I spent a few minutes explaining what had happened.

'A friend of mine died of cancer about three years ago,' he said when I told him what had taken you away. 'I know it's nothing like what you've had to go through, but it was horrible.'

He planted a soft, gentle kiss on my forehead. This made me cry again – for somewhat different reasons.

'What was she like?' he asked, wrapping his arms around me. I'd never felt so safe. I told him all about you. The big things and the little things: How you brought me up on your own after Dad left us, working yourself into the ground so I could go to college and university. How you loved chocolate, eating and cooking with it, and the hours we'd spend in the kitchen when I was a little girl, rustling up all sorts of sugary treats . . . which led to three fillings in my twenties, I should add. I even told him about my twenty-first birthday, when you surprised me with the trip to Rome.

'Why Rome?' Jamie asked.

'I'd always wanted to go there, ever since I saw *Roman Holiday*. Audrey Hepburn was my idol when I was a girl. It's a truly beautiful place. Mum started to get sick just after the trip, so it was the last time I got to spend quality time with her. It was the happiest weekend of my life.'

'That's lovely,' Jamie said. 'Nice that you have a memory of her like that.'

I'm going to stop writing about this. It's getting difficult because I'm having trouble seeing through the tears.

Moving on, then. Suffice it to say, things were going very well with Jamie at this point. The first few hiccups of our burgeoning relationship had been successfully brushed under the carpet (or thrown out with the pedal bin, if you prefer) and we were entering what I like to think of as the second phase in proceedings, which generally involves a lot of inventive sex, fun nights out and a giddy sense of well-being that propels you through even the most stressful days with an idiotic smile on your face. I was very happy, which is a feeling that I've missed a great deal in recent years.

Then my bloody ex-boyfriend Mike came along and threw a gigantic spanner in the works. I hadn't seen him for over a year and a half, and was at the point where the break-up was a distant memory, rather than the all consuming agony I'd carried around with me for the first few months after he dumped me. It was last Friday when Mike Adams walked back into my life and turned it upside down. *Again*.

It was lunchtime and I was standing behind the counter

enjoying a lull in foot traffic. I'll never complain about having lots of people in the shop parting with their hard-earned, but it's nice to have a break now and again when you've been on your feet for five solid hours.

Sipping a cup of coffee and munching on a prawn mayo sandwich from Marks & Spencer, I was neatly ensconced in a pleasant daydream about what filthy things I intended to do to Jamie that evening. It involved the French maid's outfit that had been hidden at the back of the wardrobe for four years, and the tube of play lube stuck in the front pocket.

The speculative smile dropped off my face when I looked over to the entrance to see Mike standing there looking tanned and annoyingly healthy. A jolt went through my whole body.

'Hi, sugarbear,' he said and walked towards me.

My stomach rolled. The last time I'd heard him call me that was the night he'd finished with me. The night he sat on my bed, the sheets crumpled from the desperate sex I'd just had with him, and told me all about Le-Anne, the girl who worked with him at the gym.

'We've done nothing together yet,' he'd assured me, as if that would make it any better. 'But we really like each other. I don't know what it is about her. We just seem to get on so well.'

. . . well enough to send a five-year relationship with me down the drain, anyway.

Enough! I spilled this all out last year in these pages. We don't need a repeat performance. Needless to say all the tears and misery come flooding back as Mike strolls up to the counter – that *oh-so* charming lop-sided smile plastered across his face.

'What are you doing here, Mike?' I ask, from roughly ten thousand miles away.

'I would have come in sooner. It just took this long to work up the courage.'

'What do you mean?' I drop the half-eaten sandwich. My appetite has deserted me.

'I've been walking past for a few weeks now. Every time I think about coming in, you look busy with customers so I don't. How's the shop doing?'

'It's . . . it's doing fine, thanks. *Why* have you been walking past?'

'To see you, baby.' He looks genuinely sad. 'I miss you so much.'

'You miss me?'

'Yeah. Of course I do.'

'What about *Le-Anne*?'

He contrives to look guilty. 'Well, we didn't work out in the end.' Those big green Irish eyes look deep into mine. 'She just wasn't you, hon.'

It's impossible to describe the mixture of emotions that cascade through me.

I open and close my mouth a couple of times like a hungry guppy, before pulling my wits together enough to respond.

'I'm seeing somebody,' I say, altogether too quickly. Jamie's kind, open face pops into my head. 'It's too late for me and you.'

Mike actually looks like he's about to cry. 'I was afraid

you'd say that. Should have known you'd get snapped up by somebody else. I'm so sorry I left you. I was an idiot.'

'Yes. Yes you were.'

'But I realise that now. I love you, Laura. Always have. Is there *any* chance for us? Do you like this guy that much?'

God help me, *I don't know*. I should be showing him the door. I should be telling him this boat has sailed. I should be kicking him to the kerb. But damn me, I'm *not*.

Jamie's face is replaced by the five years I spent with Mike: The holiday to Koh Samui. The way he used to nibble my toes. The long weekend in Paris. The way he'd kiss my neck just behind the ear. The Christmas at his parents' house in Donegal. The feel of his hands moving across my breasts. The smile. The green eyes . . .

Oh bloody hellfire.

'You dumped me for another woman, Mike.' I'm trying to keep some steel in my voice. It's not working.

'I know. I'm an idiot. I threw the best thing I ever had away.' He moves around the counter, removing the barrier between us. 'Please, Laura. Just come out with me. We can talk. Then if you want, I'll just leave you alone.'

Somehow, he's taken my hand in his. I didn't notice it happen.

'I don't know.'

'For old times' sake, if nothing else?'

'Maybe, Mike, maybe. Just let me think about it on my own for a bit.' He looks a wee bit crestfallen. 'It does sound like a nice idea though,' I add, making him smile again.

Jamie's face reappears in my head. I feel terrible.

'Great. I'll call you,' Mike says. 'Same number, yeah?'

I nod, dumbfounded by this turn of events.

'Great.' He turns and notices an old couple walking into the shop. 'I'll leave you to it.'

I don't even flinch when he leans forward and kisses my cheek. What the hell is wrong with me? This man put me through the emotional wringer and here I am contemplating letting him back in my life again. I'm like a junkie who's spent years in rehab and has just got their life back together again when someone wafts a joint under their nose.

I watch Mike leave, my jaw slack. The timing is incredible. I finally meet a new man I really, really like and the old one comes barging back in, turning everything upside down. I'm consumed by guilt at the idea of even considering a meet with Mike. There's a part of me that loathes the ease with which he's more or less talked me into it. Jamie doesn't deserve this.

But how the hell else am I supposed to feel? Mike was my *entire life* for five years. I've known Jamie a few weeks. I don't have the history with him . . . or the memories. And let's not forget that he was the guy who gave me food poisoning.

So what's worse, McIntyre? Breaking your heart or giving you the galloping shits? Good point . . . *Damn it.*

I'm nervous, excited, sickened, ashamed and angry – all in equal measure. Mike has a lot of explaining to do if I do agree to meet up with him, but God help me, I think I want to hear what he's got to say, even after all this time. I'm supposed to be seeing Jamie tomorrow as well, though I might try to get out of it. I owe it to the poor guy to get my head straight before anything else happens with him.

What's a girl to do, Mum?

Your confused daughter, Laura.

xx

Jamie's Blog

Wednesday 21 September

I knew something was wrong with Laura the second she answered the phone.

There was reluctance in her voice that she couldn't disguise. It sounded like she couldn't wait to hang up.

Until yesterday she'd always sounded happy to speak to me, but when I rang her at work mid-afternoon there was a definite change. I've been on the receiving end of this tone before and it always signals that bad news is coming. Carla spent a whole month talking like that until she finally worked up the guts to end the relationship with me. In many ways that month was worse than the ones that followed. Laura might have been different though, so I swallowed the tight feeling of panic and tried to affect a breezy tone.

'So what do you fancy doing this evening?' I asked.

'Um. Not sure. Might just have the evening in, actually. Quite tired.'

Hmmm. She'd sounded keen about getting together the last time we'd spoken on Sunday. Something was definitely up.

'Okay. How about I just come over and hang out for a while?'

'I don't know, Jamie.'

The cold clammy feeling that had been settling in across the back of my neck got worse. I tried to ignore it.

'I won't stay long if you're tired. I'd really like to see you though.'

'Yeah . . . okay. Come over at seven thirty.' Her voice was dull.

Maybe she *was* just tired. *Or maybe she's decided she's had enough of you.* I said goodbye and hung up with a sinking feeling in my stomach. I didn't have a clue what I'd done wrong. I certainly hadn't poisoned her again. The sex had been pretty fantastic from my point of view . . . hers too, judging from the noises she'd been making. I hadn't made any social faux pas (much to my surprise) and had been on my most charming behaviour every time I'd seen her. I literally had *no* idea what the problem could be. It was therefore with some trepidation that I rocked up to her flat that evening.

'Hiya,' she says, the smile on her face a bit forced.

'Hi,' I reply. I'm too worried to smile.

'Come in, Jamie.'

The rather formal use of my name doesn't bode well. Neither does the way she ever so slightly backs away when I lean in to give her a kiss.

'Is something the matter, Laura?' Two can play at the formal game. I don't get a reply immediately, but I know the dreaded phrase 'we need to talk' is fast homing into view like a runaway oil tanker.

Say anything else, woman. Tell me you've come down with herpes. Tell me you have to leave the country because the KGB has caught up with you. Tell me you've been in contact with your home world and are being called back to the Orion Nebula.

'We need to talk.'

Bollocks, fuck and shit.

'Alright,' I sigh deeply and make my way through to the lounge like a man heading to the gallows. She sits in the chair across the room from me, a sure sign she's about to say something unpleasant.

'You're not about to tell me you've won the lottery, are you?' I say, trying to make light of the situation.

She smiles in a half-hearted way. 'No.'

'Go on then. Put me out of my misery.' I point a finger at her. 'But if you don't want to see me anymore because of the bloody fajita thing, I won't be happy.'

'I don't want to stop seeing you.'

Well, that's unexpected. A small bloom of hope makes the stupid mistake of forming in my chest.

'Then why have you got a face like a bulldog chewing a piss-covered thistle?' I can't help it. I get crude when I'm nervous.

'It's just that . . . I have to . . . I don't want . . . Oh for fuck's sake.' She puts her head in her hands.

'Make like your head and come to a point, woman.' I know this isn't really the time for banter, but I can't help myself.

'My ex, Mike, came into the shop the other day. He wants to see me again. Says he misses me and wants me back.' This comes out very fast in one breath, like she wants it out there as quickly as possible.

Nick Spalding

In these situations, a man more in control of his emotions (and one more experienced with the vagaries of the female mind) would have handled things *much* better. I'd only been seeing Laura for a few weeks, and this guy – whom she'd told me about only a week beforehand in one of those 'whose ex is worse' conversations you always have early in a relationship – had been a part of her life for half a decade.

Of course she'd still be conflicted about it. *Of course* she couldn't just brush his reappearance off without a thought. *Of course* I should let her explain. After all, the best way to show that I was the man for her – and not the guy who'd dumped her unceremoniously a year ago – was to act in an understanding, mature manner.

'You fucking *what*?' I say in a semi growl.

'It's very confusing, Jamie. He wants to see me and I've agreed, just so I can get my head straight about him, you . . . everything. Please don't be angry.'

'Don't be *angry*? Your cock of an ex walks back into your life and you don't kick him straight back out again?'

'I said it's complicated.' There's an edge to Laura's voice now.

'Looks pretty simple from where I'm sitting. You'd rather give the prick that dumped you another go than carry on seeing me.'

'That's not what I said! I don't want to stop seeing you. I just need to hear what he's got to say. I was with him for years.'

Shamefaced humiliation is fuelling my anger. I'm far too het up now to back down.

'Oh, well that's *fine* then! Perfectly reasonable to expect me to sit back and wait for you to make your fucking mind up about whether you want me or your ex.'

I'm off the couch and heading towards the front door in a flash. Laura follows.

'That's not fair, Jamie!'

'You know what's not fair? Actually thinking a girl's into you and finding out you're just a bloody seat-warmer until the real love of her life prances back on the scene. I hope you and marvellous Mike will be very happy together.'

'It's not like that!'

'Bullshit! You're a bitch!'

I throw the front door open and stalk out.

I know I've completely over-reacted. I'm already starting to regret it even as I walk into the street and storm towards my car. I should go back, apologise and try and salvage this mess. I know this girl is worth the effort. Sadly, I'm hurt, humiliated and angry. Logic has flown right out of the window. I gun the car angrily and drive past the flat. Laura is standing in the doorway with tears in her eyes. There are tears in mine too.

So here I sit, two hours later and still in a right old mess. Laura hasn't called me and I sure as hell don't intend to ring her. Every time I think I should phone and apologise, I remember that she's agreed to see her ex, even though she's supposed to be seeing *me*. It's just so *unbelievable* that she'd let him back in her life like that! How am I supposed to compete with a guy who can screw Laura around, dump her for another woman and *still* get his way, even though he's been gone over a year? She obviously wants to check whether he's changed – and come right back to me if he hasn't.

Well, bugger that for a game of soldiers, I'm *nobody's* second choice!

From a quick Google search it appears there are many ways I can become a monk. The idea of living halfway up a mountain, somewhere hundreds of miles from the nearest woman, sounds incredibly appealing. Maybe I can learn martial arts, come back in ten years and snap Mike's neck.

I hate my life.

Laura's Diary
Friday, September 23rd

Dear Mum,

I am a colossal idiot. A gold-plated moron. A five-star pillock. An all-singing, all-dancing twat of the highest order.

Seeing Jamie went about as well as I'd feared. He went totally overboard, of course.

Can I really blame him? The last thing a man wants to hear is that the woman he's been dating intends to meet up with her ex for a chat. I didn't expect him to go *quite* as mental as he did, though. The storming melodramatic exit from the flat was well executed, I'll give him that.

It left me feeling pretty damn shitty about myself, if I'm honest. As I watched his car roar away down the street, I knew I'd potentially ruined a good thing just to get some kind of closure on my relationship with Mike. But was that what I wanted? *Closure?* Or was there a part of me that still loved Mike and really was willing to take him back? I knew I'd done the right thing in agreeing to see him. It was a real pity I had to hurt Jamie in the process.

The last thought I had as I shut the front door was that Mike Adams had better have changed his bloody tune and be worth all this trouble.

Naturally Mike said we should meet at Langtree Lakes. We'd spent a lot of time in this gorgeous nature reserve when we were together. It's still one of the most beautiful places I've ever been to and I have very fond memories of the long walks we used to take, before heading into The Langtree Arms for a refreshing drink. I hadn't been back since the break-up, though.

The big problem with getting dumped is that so many of the places you love suddenly become completely off-limits. I've often thought it would be better to just visit a load of shit-holes with the love of your life. Then, even if the relationship does grenade itself, you're not going to mourn every beauty spot in the area, as well as your ex.

It looks exactly the same as I turn the Micra into the small gravel car park. The last vestiges of the Indian summer still hold the country in its embrace, so it's a gloriously sunny evening. And there he is . . .

Mike Adams. Sitting on the very same bench he always used to while he waited for me to arrive. We've kissed on that bench. There was even one occasion – on a hot summer's evening much like this one, with the car park deserted – that we did a little more. It's like going back in time.

A cynical part of me suggests this is all a very deliberate ploy on Mike's part to keep me thinking about the good times we shared, rather than the raging arguments that peppered the latter stages of our five years together. I try to ignore it though. Dredging up the past won't get us anywhere, and I want to go into this meeting with an open mind. He gets up and walks over to the car.

'Hello, beautiful,' he says in his charming Irish lilt, opening the car door for me like a perfect gentleman.

'Hi, Mike.'

I'm struck with nervous anxiety. I've gambled a hell of a lot on the idea Mike has changed. I've put all my chickens in his basket. He certainly hasn't altered physically one bit. That shock of dark brown hair is as unruly as ever. He still favours his chequered shirts and black jeans. The gym instructor's body still moves with the same consummate grace and poise.

Calm down, woman. Getting horny isn't going to put you in the right frame of mind to deal with this, is it?

'It's great to be back here with you,' he says, closing the car door behind me. 'Shall we walk the old route?'

'I guess so.'

We stroll past the first of the four lakes Langtree gets its name from. There's still enough sun at quarter to seven to bathe the calm waters with lazy heat. I decide to get straight to the point.

'So, why the hell should I consider taking you back, Mike?'

'Because I love you.'

'Not good enough. You broke my heart last year.'

'I know I did . . . and I'm sorry.'

I stop and look at him. 'Why, Mike? Why did you run off with that twelve-year-old?'

'She was twenty-one,' he protests.

'I know. I was exaggerating for effect.' This is an

annoying habit Mike always had. He can't resist correcting an error you've made, even if he knows damn well it's a deliberate one.

'I was stupid. She was just there all the time . . . and you were working such long hours.'

'I was trying to get my business off the ground!'

'I know. But I didn't see you for what seemed like days on end, and Le-Anne was there for me.'

'Not anymore though, eh? She's had enough of you, so now you're back, I suppose?'

I walk off in a huff. He catches up and takes my arm. For some reason, I'm horribly reminded of the confrontation with Martin the salesman outside The Cheetah Lounge. No Jamie Newman here this time, though.

'That's not true, baby. I finished with her, like I said.'

'Why?'

'There was nothing to her, you know? Once you got past the physical attraction. I only realised how unique you were when I had somebody else to compare you to.'

This is probably the smoothest line delivered in history. If you examined it with an electron microscope you wouldn't find a single flaw in its surface.

'It's not like I was the *only* busy one,' I remind him. 'You were off out with your friends so much back then. I remember the arguments when you'd stumble back in at two in the morning.'

'Yeah. I was selfish. I just got too . . . *relaxed*, you know? Took you for granted.'

'Yes. You did.'

'But I'll never do that again. It's been awful without

you. Not a day goes by when I don't wish things had happened differently.'

'Like not sticking your cock in a gym assistant?'

'I told you I never cheated and I meant it!'

And there it is. The old Adams anger. It's only ever boiled over once into physical violence, when he pushed me against a wall and banged my head. The apologies were as heartfelt as the ones I'm listening to right now.

'Alright, Mike. I believed you then and I still do,' I say.

He takes my hand and leads me down onto the small wooden jetty that sticks out over the second and largest lake on the reserve. This is another highly romantic place from our past. Memories come flooding back, *Good ones.* And as those deep-seated memories return, the more recent ones of poor old Jamie Newman fade away, I'm very sorry to say.

'All I want,' he says as he turns to face me, 'is another chance. Put the past behind us. Not try to get the old relationship back, but to start a *new* one.'

God almighty, he's still a beautiful man.

'I don't know, Mike. We'd have to take it slow.'

'I know! That's fine with me. We'll do it your way.'

I take far less time to make a decision than I would have liked.

'Alright. A second chance,' I tell him. I'm not sure whether this is the right decision, but the green of his eyes, the gold of the sun and the blue of the lake are doing a good job of convincing me it is.

Mike leans in and I let him kiss me. I'm not sure

whether it's better than the way Jamie Newman does it or not.

'So the shop's going okay, is it?' he asks as he pulls away. This is something of a sharp change in subject, but I don't immediately think too much of it.

'Not too bad. Sales have picked up recently, but it's still a bit shaky.'

'You're in the black then?'

'Yes. At last.'

'That's great to hear. I'll be happy to get involved again.'

What?

'What?'

'You know, with the shop? That's one thing I've really been looking forward to about getting back together.'

'How do you mean?' This is confusing. Mike's only contribution to the shop was the five grand he gave me when I was starting out. He never showed a moment's interest in it after that. There was even one time when he said he thought that Thorntons sold better-quality chocolate. He slept on the couch that night.

'You know? With the shop? Things have been tight for me recently. The gym shut its doors so I've been out of work for a few months.'

My eyes narrow. 'So what are you expecting from me?'

Mike can't look me in the face. 'Well, I did put a lot of money into the place when you opened it. In a way it's kinda partly mine.'

'Really?' The lazy evening sun can't melt the ice in my voice.

'Yeah. Don't you think it's fair I get something back?'

This is when I realise what a complete and utter fool I've been. I feel faint.

I've been well and truly suckered. Mike doesn't want me back. He wants a *job*. He wants a cut of my profits. The scum-sucking piece of shit has lost his job (and probably the girlfriend at the same time) and wants to lean on me for support. All the talk of the past, the meeting at the lakes, the apologies, the charming smile, the deep green eyes – all of it is *bullshit*.

And I've fallen for it hook, line and sinker. Just like all those times he came home late saying he'd been out with the boys. I believed him at the time, but now? When he's finally shown his true colours? *He was with her, you stupid twit.*

I feel on the verge of tears. A hopeless sense of frustration, self-pity and betrayal washes over me. It's like he's dumping me all over again. I'm probably going to stand here in this beautiful place and cry my eyes out in front of the man that's made my life a misery. The man I've once again trusted, like a total idiot.

Jamie Newman's earnest, honest face pops back into my head . . . notably the look of hurt in his eyes as I told him about seeing Mike. If I had a mirror handy I bet I'd see that same expression reflected back at me now.

Grief and self-loathing turn instantly to anger. I've let Mike ruin the best thing in my life. I've traded a good man (with horrific cooking skills, admittedly) for a pathetic coward.

'Are you okay, baby?' the coward says. 'Everything I

said makes sense, yeah?' he continues, unaware of the turmoil going on in my head. 'Shall we give it a try? I can start at the shop on Monday. It'll be great!'

Do you know that I've never punched someone in the face before, Mum? It's quite a satisfying experience. Even if it does mean you take an age writing an entry in your diary because your hand is throbbing so much.

I cock one arm back and try to remember what I've seen them do in all those action movies. Making a fist, I bring my arm back round with a scream of rage and connect soundly with Mike's left cheek. It isn't the hardest punch ever thrown. Any other time it would be one Mike could shrug off without much trouble, but today I catch him completely by surprise. He lets out a squawk and topples backwards . . . straight off the side of the jetty and into the lake.

I lean over and watch him flounder.

'Fuck you, you little shit!' I yell at the top of my voice. 'I can't believe I gave you another chance!'

The birds in the trees fly off in terror.

'You're the most pathetic, loathsome little cock I've ever met!'

'You're insane!' Mike howls, clutching his jaw with one hand, scrabbling for purchase on the jetty with the other.

'Yeah. I must be to believe a word you say! I ruined a really good thing with Jamie for you!'

'Who the hell is Jamie?'

If I could have punched him again I would have. If I could have pulled his penis off and rammed it up his backside I would have. In lieu of either option I show him two of the angriest middle fingers I can produce and stomp away. Ignoring his pleas for me to come back and help him out of the water (I later remember he can't swim – what a crying shame) I walk away and head back in the direction of the car park.

By the time I've climbed into El Denté my anger has burned off and I can't help bawling my eyes out as I drive away. So much so that I have to stop in a lay-by a bit further along to get it out of my system. I feel used, gullible and stupid . . . but that's not what is making me cry. It's Jamie Newman's smile, and the fact I'll probably never see it again thanks to Mike *fucking* Adams.

It's taken me a good three hours to spill this onto the page, Mum. I feel exhausted. My hand is killing me as well. The painkillers have worn off. I'm going to bed now, and will try to put this entire week behind me. I'm seeing Tim tomorrow and a bit of retail therapy in town will make me feel better, with any luck. I only hope I don't see any rubber plants. I just might kill myself if I do.

Miss you more right now than I have in a long time, Mum.

Your distraught and drained daughter, Laura.

xx

Jamie's Blog

Sunday 30 October

Crying in front of a woman who's holding your manhood isn't an ideal way to celebrate Halloween, but that's exactly how I ended up doing it Friday night. I also had a very important epiphany about the future of my life . . . but we'll get to that in due course. First, let me explain the crying.

It started with a party. Specifically, a party *at work*. These gatherings are usually attended by a gaggle of disparate human beings who would never normally hang out together. They are thrust into a social event organised by the management, in order to build team spirit and foster good working relationships.

This never works of course, and as such, events of this type are *always* abject failures. However, if the management deliberately organised these get-togethers to bring long-simmering disputes to a drunken climax, damage valuable office machinery and create circumstances leading to excruciating levels of embarrassment the following Monday morning, they would be classed as an unqualified success.

This particular office party is the brainchild of Alex, the editor of the news desk. Alex is the kind of guy you'd feel uncomfortable stuck in a lift with. Morale at the paper has been at rock bottom for months, so this is his attempt at making us all feel like valued members of the team. The festivities have a fancy dress theme . . . inevitably. Here's what I consider to be an undisputed fact: nobody actually *likes* going to fancy dress parties. If the government declared tomorrow that fancy dress parties were banned, nobody would mind. Why? Because you spend the weeks before the bloody thing worrying about what to wear and how much it's going to cost you. Then you either trawl around the charity shops every afternoon until you find a leather jacket that looks slightly like the one Indiana Jones wears, or you throw in the towel and buy one of those mass produced nasty costumes that come in a bag and fall apart before you've even arrived at the party. Then you realise that everybody's costume is a hundred times better than yours, and you look like the special kid who always stands at the back of the school concert waving at the fire exit.

Next time you go to a fancy dress party, count how many people are still in full costume by half past nine. If it's more than half then congratulations, you work in the entertainment industry. I considered turning up to this particular fancy dress party in a straightjacket covered with blood, with a sign hung round my neck saying '*Alex after the breakdown*' but I thought better of it in the end.

Lacking inspiration (and taking the freezing cold weather into account) I go along as Neo from *The Matrix* – which requires the wearing of a lovely thick long black coat, black jeans, black T-shirt and a pair of cheap sunglasses I picked up in Asda. I look like an utter tit. But I'm a *warm* utter tit, which is the important thing.

The most depressing thing about office parties is that they are held *in the office*. At work. The last place you tend to associate with the word 'fun'. It doesn't matter how many pretty decorations they hang to cover the whiteboards and filing cabinets, or how loud they blast the dance music across the cubicles, you're still stuck in the same bloody place where you've already spent eight hours of that day. I have to resist the urge to check my emails once I arrive at the party, to see if the marketing suggestions I've made recently have been approved or not.

Others have made more of an effort with their costumes. There are two pirates, one ninja and a Doctor Who. The insufferably annoying trio from Personnel have come as Harry, Ron and Hermione. Pete, the skinny part-time assistant from reprographics is dressed as Wolverine from *X-Men*, which consists of spiking his unruly ginger hair up and gaffer-taping a few unbent coat hangers to his hands. Clare, the chunky lass who writes the lifestyle section, obviously can't let go of the nineties and has come as Lara Croft. Alex, whose grip on sanity is tenuous at best these days, is dressed as the Joker from *The Dark Knight*, which everyone agrees is *very* fitting. All in all it's a motley collection of half-arsed, thrown-together outfits. The local charity shops must have had a field day.

In light of the fact I'm dressed like Keanu Reeves's older, chubbier brother, and am in the office at eight thirty on a Friday night surrounded by people I can barely tolerate in the harsh light of day, I decide to get as insanely drunk as possible.

With stupendous success, it has to be said. By ten o'clock I've polished off three quarters of a bottle of Jack Daniel's and am starting to think I look really cool in my sunglasses and trench coat. I send an email to the chief editor demanding that my genius marketing ideas are approved immediately, or I'll punch his wife in the face.

I giggle as I hit 'send' on the keyboard. I doubt I'll be giggling when I get into work on Monday morning. Nevertheless, my spirits are high right now and I'm enjoying myself . . . as long as standing on a desk, sweating my arse off in a thick leather trench coat, singing 'Poker Face' at the top of my voice, and swigging from a whisky bottle constitutes 'enjoyment'.

Clare, the Croft-a-like lifestyle guru, has joined me on the desk and is performing a badly co-ordinated bump and grind dance against my leg. This brings cheers from the surrounding party-goers. She's by no means a slender girl, so the desk is now in serious danger of collapsing under our weight. I still have enough of my wits about me to know that we should get down before we have to spend hours filling out an accident report, so I help my impromptu dance partner to the ground.

'Thank you, Neo! You're my hero!' she yelps and throws her arms around my neck. 'You're very sexy in that get-up,' she adds. Any germs or bacteria that may be lurking on my face are instantly killed by her alcoholic breath.

'Thanks.' I try to come up with a return compliment that's at least half true. 'I like your ponytail.'

Clare laughs and slaps me across the face with it a couple of times. 'Naughty boy.'

I don't quite know what's naughty about commenting on someone's hair-do, but I let it slide. My blood is now sixty per cent proof, so Clare is starting to look pretty *damn good* in her little shorts . . . if you ignore the cellulite and the slightly disconcerting way her ample left boob is trying to make a break for freedom from the blue vest top she's wearing.

Yes. You're absolutely right. What you think is going to happen next is exactly what *does* happen. Some things in life are inevitable. Being stupid drunk at an office party and getting off with someone completely inappropriate is one of them.

It takes another half an hour for my blood alcohol level to reach the point where Clare is starting to look *really* sexy. There she is, over by the fax machine playing with Pete's coat hangers. She keeps throwing me little glances that speak volumes. I can tell she wants to do more than just dance on a desk with me this evening. And what would be the harm, eh? After all, I'm young, free and single!

Sure, Clare isn't the thinnest girl in the world (I'm pretty sure the guys down in Deliveries have nicknamed her 'dump truck') but she's got an attractive face and a nice ponytail . . . as we've already discussed. It's nearly six weeks since I last saw Laura, so there's no reason not to try it on with Clare. It'll be good for me to have some fun with a different woman. It might help lift the fog of depression I've been under for the past month. I miss

Laura like crazy and am getting sick of it. A bounce with Clare will be just the thing to sort me out.

Anyone who's been dumped and looked for solace elsewhere in this fashion will know that this kind of thinking is *always* constructive – and that shagging a virtual stranger mere weeks after having your heart broken is *always* the best way to get over the pain. *Hmmm.*

I saunter over to where Pete is explaining to Clare that Wolverine's claws are constructed of something called Adamantium. I give him a look that is constructed of pure GoawayPeteium and he takes the hint.

'Come back for another dance, have we?' Clare asks.

'Yeah. There's nothing wrong with a little bump and grind, eh?' I say, gyrating my hips awkwardly.

It's amazing how a copious amount of alcohol has the capacity to turn you into a complete arsehole, isn't it? I would never have come out with the above pronouncement sober. In fact, it's such an *awful* line that I'm fairly sure it causes ripples in the fabric of existence, sending shockwaves out into the universe. Strange, alien scientists on a planet across the other side of the galaxy will feel the effects of those ripples in a few thousand years and conclude that if my conversation skills were indicative of the human race as a whole, it was a good job we were all wiped out by that cold virus in 2134.

Clare doesn't appear to be bothered by it. She's well into her ninth bottle of Bacardi Breezer though, which may explain things.

'You sure that's all you want to do?' she asks and parks

her hand over my genitals. 'Or maybe we should go somewhere a bit quieter?'

'Sure,' I reply and my penis does its customary victory lap. Given the fact Clare isn't quite up to Laura's standards the lap is a lot slower and doesn't get as far as the podium celebrations.

'There's the supply cupboard,' Clare suggests. 'Or we could go to Alex's office. I would say we could go upstairs onto the roof, but they lock it at this time of night.'

Judging from her knowledge of secluded locations in these parts, this isn't the first time Clare's contemplated some extra-curricular office shenanigans.

'Cupboard's fine,' I drawl. The prospect of the Joker bursting in on me humping Lara Croft over his ergonomic keyboard isn't one I want to entertain.

The front of my coat is grabbed like a drowning man clings to life and I'm dragged towards the cupboard at the back of the office in unceremonious fashion.

Clare isn't displaying Isobel-like levels of sexual aggression, but she's not *that* far behind. I get several sympathetic looks from the other party-goers as we fly past. There are also a few chuckles. It looks like Clare's reputation precedes her. The cupboard itself is tucked out of the way down a short corridor, so there is *some* privacy, thank goodness. I can do without a herd of pissed work colleagues standing outside, listening intently and giving me marks out of ten for presentation and stamina.

Once the door is closed, Clare moves back into the recesses of the cupboard, beckoning me forward with a curled finger. I oblige. After all, what else am I supposed to do? I put my arms around her waist (which is quite a bit wider than Laura's) and move in for a kiss. Clare responds feverishly and before you know it we're sucking face like the best of them. She kisses in a firmer way than Laura, but it's not unpleasant and my johnson is soon straining for release from its denim prison.

'I want you in me,' Clare whispers breathily into my ear. I'm reminded of when Laura said much the same thing to me in bed a couple of months ago.

Clare unzips me and starts jerking me off. Her grip is quite firm and she doesn't quite have Laura's finesse, but—

I can't stop thinking about Laura.

Everything Clare does just reminds me she's not the girl I last saw standing in her doorway crying. Here I am, in a closet with a perfectly nice (if slightly chunky) girl and I can't take my mind off another woman. My penis, which has started reminiscing along with me, starts to wilt.

Stop thinking about her! She's gone! I kiss Clare harder, running my hands over her breasts, which are larger than Laura's but not as firm.

Oh for crying out loud. My hard-on is fading fast. So is my libido.

'What's the matter?' Clare asks, looking down at my rapidly deflating dick. 'Got brewer's droop have we, sweetheart? Or are you just not into Lara Croft?' She gives me a sad little smile. It's quite a cute expression, but not as cute as the one Laura makes when she's just made some sarcastic comment about—

I'm crying. God help me. I'm standing in a supply cupboard surrounded by printer cartridges, dressed as Neo from *The Matrix*, accompanied by a chubby Tomb Raider – and I'm crying.

'What's the matter?' Clare asks. 'Did I pull it too hard?'

'No. No. It's fine.' I tuck little Newman back into his hidey-hole, where he'll no doubt sulk for the rest of the night.

'You're not bloody gay, are you? Only this happened to me before with a guy. He started crying too. I was his way out of the closet.'

'Not gay, no.' I lean back against a shelving unit and wipe my eyes. 'I just split up with someone recently and I'm still not over it.'

'Aaah.'

'Didn't think I was this cut up.'

'Well, I'd say bursting into tears in front of a woman who's trying to wank you off is a sure sign that you are, Jamie.'

'Sorry.'

She sighs and rubs her eyes. 'No worries. These things happen. What's her name?'

I went into that cupboard thinking I'd get a shag. Instead I got a therapy session most people would pay good money for. I don't know why Clare writes all that lifestyle crap for the paper. She should be writing relationship advice books. They'd make a bloody fortune.

'You over-reacted,' she tells me. 'You'd only been seeing each other for a few weeks. I don't blame you for not liking it, but you should've left that night without saying anything else and then rung her a couple of days later. Slagging her off didn't accomplish anything.'

'My ego got in the way.'

'Of course it did. I'm not saying she was any more in the right than you. But you could've taken the higher ground.'

'Doesn't matter now, anyway,' I say and hang my head.

'So that's it? You're not gonna contact her again?'

'What's the point? She's probably back with this guy Mike.'

'Maybe. Maybe not.' Clare looks into my eyes. 'I've only got one question for you.'

'What?'

'Do you love her?'

Bugger, I'm going to start crying again.

'Yeah, I do.'

'Then you should do something about it.'

'What? And embarrass myself when she says her and Mikey-boy are getting married?'

'Your choice. But if you do love her, you should do something about it before it's too late. Take the risk, boy.'

'I don't know.'

'Nor do I. But it's gotta be better than blubbing like a little girl when you're getting a hand job, hasn't it?'

You can't really fault logic like that, can you? We rejoined the party just as it was winding down. I spent what was left of it sitting in a corner, thinking about what Clare had said. As I stumbled out of the main doors at midnight I saw Clare walking away with her arm round Pete. She saw me and waved.

'Good luck, Jamie!' she called and gave me a broad smile.

I looked from her to Pete. 'You too.'

'It's not me who's going to need it,' she said and grabbed Pete's arse, making him squeal.

Poor old Pete the X-Man didn't know whether to look x-cited or x-tremely scared. His evening was going to end better than mine though, that was for certain. I'm sure he'd compare favourably to Neo the lovesick idiot, even if he kept the Wolverine costume on while he was shagging her.

I was up until three in the morning thinking about Laura. It was obvious I had to do something to get her back . . . to show her how I felt. As I dropped into a fitful sleep, an idea popped into my head that I thought would do the trick.

So this morning I've got a definite plan. If Laura and I are meant to be, I'm going to do everything in my power to make it happen!

Laura's Diary
Friday, November 11th

Dear Mum,

This has been a *very* big day. So big I really don't know where to start. It's nearly midnight, but I'm still buzzing. I have to get this down now. I won't be able to sleep otherwise.

Last week I told you I was dreading my birthday. It's no fun turning twenty-nine when you're single, all your close friends are on holiday, you have no immediate family, *and* you have a meeting with your distributors at nine o'clock in the morning. A meeting where they are no doubt going to tell you wholesale prices are rising, which will cut into your profits even further.

And never mind all that – I'm turning *twenty-nine*! How the living hell did that happen? It doesn't seem like five minutes ago that I was nervous about getting into an 18-certificate movie, and here I am now old enough to look disgusted when I see someone underage sneak into a late-night performance of *Saw*.

I had to turn Radio 1 off the other day as the music was annoying me too much. To tell the truth, the music has been annoying me for the past five years, but this is the first time I've had the presence of mind to actually change stations. I now listen to Hitz FM. It's bloody awful tin-pot local radio, but they play music exclusively from the late nineties and early noughties, so I'm well happy.

I don't drink coffee with caffeine in it after six o'clock anymore, because if I do I won't get to sleep until gone 2 a.m. Do I need any more proof that I'm officially getting old?

You can imagine how *delighted* I was to hear the alarm go off this morning. The groan that escaped my lips was louder than usual.

'Happy birthday to me,' I sang into the mirror as I cleaned my teeth. 'Happy birthday to me. Happy birthday, dear loser . . . who's old, has wrinkles in her forehead and will never get laid ever, ever again unless she starts dressing like a crack whore . . . Happy birthday to me.'

Okay, so wallowing in self-pity is never attractive, but I couldn't help it. A few text messages and a doormat with five birthday cards on it improved my mood somewhat.

I rather hoped I'd hear from Jamie Newman, but there was nothing from him. Not much of a surprise, I suppose.

By the time I get to the shop the two guys from the wholesalers are already waiting for me. My heart sinks when I see one of them is Martin the Nipple King.

He has an expression on his face that makes him look like a constipated badger, so I guess he hasn't been looking forward to this meeting either.

'Morning, gentlemen,' I say as I unlock the shop. 'Sorry I'm a bit late.'

I'm not really sorry. Tim called me from his skiing trip

in France to wish me the best of the day and I wasn't going to rush such a thoughtful gesture just to get here on time.

'Not a problem,' says Aamir, the tall, pleasantly spoken salesman I've had a majority of dealings with over the past few months. Martin remains quiet. Once inside, I offer them both a coffee and we get stuck into the business they've come to discuss. Tilly has arrived and is out the front keeping the customers happy.

Negotiations tire me. I'm not the best haggler in the world and would rather be presented with a limited series of options. All this going-backwards-and-forwards business gives me heartburn. It's evident that Martin still holds a grudge after what happened back in the summer. Every time I think we're getting close to an agreement on pricing for the next twelve months, Martin chips in and tries to either raise the cash amount or lower the order number. Even Aamir is starting to give him funny looks after a while.

I'm starting to get pretty bloody angry. Angry at myself as much as at the Nipple King. His presence reminds me of how Jamie came to my rescue, which reminds me of my stupidity over Mike. When Aamir goes off to the toilet I decide to nip the problem in the bud before it festers anymore and gives me a stomach ulcer.

'Now look here, Martin,' I spit at him the second Aamir is out of earshot. 'You need to stop acting like a prick. What happened that night is in the past. I've forgotten about it, now you have to as well. You're not being fair.'

'Fuck off, bitch,' he hisses back. 'I couldn't speak

properly for days after your boyfriend grabbed me round the throat.'

'Then maybe you shouldn't have tried to molest me on a street corner then.'

'Prove it,' he says, a smug look on his face.

He's got a point. I can't prove a damn thing. Martin can cheat me as much as he likes on this deal and I have nothing to retaliate with. Time to bluff.

'Two things, Martin . . . if you keep trying to screw me over I'll go straight to your boss and tell him all about your behaviour outside the club. Proof or not, me telling everyone about how you pushed me around isn't going to go down well, is it? Oh . . . and that boyfriend of mine? He's a copper. The slightly mental kind, who likes to beat up the local criminals.' That makes his eyes widen. 'Is all that getting through your thick skull, you nipple-tweaking weirdo?'

The bluff works. Martin goes a very satisfying shade of white.

'Don't say anything, *please*,' he begs. 'I'm up for promotion and my wife will kill me if you say anything.'

'Wife?! You're fucking married?'

Martin realises he's said too much and turns even whiter. I suppose I'm not all that surprised. Of course a low-life like him would lie about being single.

'You feeling alright, Martin?' Aamir asks when he comes back. 'You look a little pale.'

'Maybe something I ate,' Martin mumbles back.

My threats appear to have worked. It's good to see that the old maxim of bullies being the biggest cowards is still true. I wish I had his wife's phone number, though. A constructive anonymous phone call may save her from years of misery – and fucking bad dancing.

The meeting concludes with a deal that won't completely cripple me financially and I bid goodbye to Aamir and the Nipple King with relief. Aamir has left a load of free samples which I hand out to the slow trickle of customers that come in over the rest of the day. By five thirty I'm knackered and ready to go home.

'Are you doing anything for your birthday this evening?' Tilly asks as we close up.

She's bought me a lovely card and a voucher for The Body Shop that I intend to waste on as many stress-relieving products as I can.

'Not tonight. My friends are around on Sunday, so we're heading out for a curry then.'

'Oh, that's a shame. It's always nice to do something on the actual day,' she says and pats me on the shoulder. 'Have a nice evening, anyway.'

Great. Pity from an eighteen-year-old.

'Night, Tilly,' I reply, sounding brighter than I feel.

The drive home doesn't improve my mood. The incessant autumnal rain has caused an accident on the main road, so I get stuck in a tailback for half an hour. This gives me plenty of time to reflect on getting a year closer to being thirty . . . which is *always* a fun thing to do.

By the time I pull up outside the house, my mood can best be described as thunderous. The birthday girl really isn't feeling the occasion, Mum.

My fingers are slippery with rain by the time I get the

door keys out of my handbag, so I fumble around trying to get them in the lock, allowing the heavy rain to drench me thoroughly. Luckily, the door opens from the inside.

'Thanks, Charlie,' I say to my flatmate. 'The keys were—'

It isn't Charlie. It's Jamie Newman. He gives me a little wave.

'Hello.'

I forget about the rain. 'What are you doing here? Where's Charlie?'

'She's out. I asked her to give us some time alone.' He peers out into the gloom. 'Er, hadn't you better come in? You're getting wet.'

Still a bit stunned, I cross the threshold. Jamie shuts the door behind me. He's got a nervous look on his face.

'What are you doing here, Jamie?' I repeat.

'Well. It's your birthday and I thought . . . look, just come through to the lounge with me, okay?'

'Okay.' I have no idea where this is going. This is the first time I've seen Jamie since our bust-up. If our genders were reversed I'd be worrying he was about to tell me he was pregnant.

I follow him through into the lounge. My jaw drops. The entire room has been turned into an Italian piazza. There's a wrought iron café table (complete with parasol) and chairs where the Ikea dining room set usually lives. On the table are two wine glasses and a bottle of top-end Pinot Grigio. An enormous free-standing photographic fresco of the Piazza Navona in Rome covers most of one wall. It's huge – easily seven feet high and fifteen feet across. Navona is considered by many to be the most beautiful piazza in the city.

There are four grapevines in a long, low planter against the other wall, giving off a pleasant leafy aroma. Smooth Italian bistro music comes from the stereo. I'm pretty sure it's Dean Martin singing.

'I know it's all a bit clichéd,' Jamie says, pulling out a chair for me to sit on, 'and I'm not completely sure the grapevines were a good idea.' He gives them a doubtful look. 'But anyway . . . happy birthday, Laura!'

I sit down, my mouth still agape.

'I brought in a cook, because, well, you know my track record. We're having pizza . . . obviously.' He pours me a glass of wine.

'Why have you done all this?' I ask in a faraway voice.

'It's your birthday!'

'But you called me a bitch.' I feel it's important to point this out.

'Yeah. I know. Went a bit overboard there. Sorry.'

'Why have you done all this?' I sound like a broken record, but I'm still in a state of shock and can't do anything about it.

'You told me about that trip you took with your mum? The one on your twenty-first birthday?' He points at the fresco. 'I know it's not quite the same thing, but you said it was the happiest weekend of your life, so . . .'

Tears prick my eyes. He remembered.

A fat man in a white apron comes into the room. I know he's going to speak in a broad Italian accent before he even opens his mouth.

'Pizza is ready, sir!' he tells Jamie and sees me. 'It's nice to meet you, Miss Laura!' he says, taking one hand and kissing it.

'Thanks Giorgio,' Jamie replies, pouring himself a glass of wine. 'You hungry?' he asks me.

'Um . . . yes?'

'Excellent. I know you don't like spicy, so you've got a four seasons.'

Giorgio returns from the kitchen and plonks two delicious-looking pizzas in front of us. I look at it. Then I look at Jamie. Then I look around the room.

'How much did all this cost?' is all I can think to say.

Jamie smiles. 'Tuck in!'

It takes most of the pizza and two glasses of the smoothest wine I've ever tasted to get my wits about me again.

'Thank you for all this, Jamie. It's lovely.'

'My pleasure.'

'I can't believe you remembered about the trip I took with my mum.'

'You sounded so happy when you told me about it. Your face really lit up. Not something I'd forget in a hurry.' He throws back a huge gulp of wine, puts the glass on the table and looks at me. 'I'm sorry about this, but I have to tell you something. I love you, Laura.'

No-one has ever apologised for being in love with me before.

'I shouldn't have stormed off the way I did when you told me about Mike—'

'No! Don't apologise,' I say, stopping him in his tracks.

'It was my fault. I . . . I was confused . . . mixed up.' A bit like how I feel right now, to be honest. 'You love me?'

Jamie flushes red. 'Yeah. I missed you so much. Knew I had to do something.' He looks round at Rome-in-Miniature. 'When Charlie told me you weren't seeing Mike, I was even more determined to get things right.'

'Charlie told you?'

'Yep. She's been dead helpful.' He grimaces. 'I did have to pay her to go to the cinema tonight, though.'

'And you love me?' There's the broken record impression again.

'Have from the first second I laid eyes on you . . . though I guess it could have been concussion from the doll's house.' The cheeky smile is back. The one I never thought I'd see again.

'I love you too.' And there it is. So easy to say, so hard to admit.

'You do?'

Tears don't just prick my eyes now. 'Yeah. Thank you for coming back.'

Jamie gets up, walks around the table and bends down to kiss me.

He hesitates. 'Are you sure you don't want Mike?' he asks uncertainly.

'Absolutely not.' That doesn't seem enough. 'I punched the arsehole in the face,' I tell Jamie matter-of-factly, before putting my arms round his neck and kissing him for all I'm worth.

Hands down, that was the most romantic thing anyone's ever done for me. Any lingering resentment I may have had about being poisoned and called a bitch was now well and truly gone. Charlie didn't come home until gone eleven, and Giorgio left shortly after dinner with a smile on his face and a large tip in his pocket, so Jamie and I had plenty of time alone to do lots of exciting things that would have got us arrested instantly if we'd actually been in a Roman piazza.

Afterwards, we lay together on the couch in an exhausted state of bliss.

'I think those vines are setting off my hay fever,' Jamie said and sniffed.

'It was a nice touch.'

'Thanks.'

'So was the fresco.'

'You should have seen the girl's face in the print shop when I told her what size I wanted it.'

'Where did the table come from?'

'Let's just say I'm glad Ryan is the assistant manager of a garden centre and leave it at that.' He frowned. 'Anyway, stop asking questions, you. You're ruining the magic.'

'Relax, Newman. Your efforts have paid off . . . *thoroughly*.'

'Thank God for that. I considered learning some Italian as well, but decided it might be going overboard.'

'I'd say you got it just about right.' I kissed him, and managed to get my head out of the blast zone just before he let out a tremendous sneeze.

And there you have it, Mum.

From a depressing, lonely birthday morning, to a

wonderful, blissful birthday evening. Who says the world can't change in a day?

Love and miss you, as always.

Your twenty-nine-year-old daughter, Laura.

xx

Jamie's Blog

Monday 26 December

If someone were to invent a time travel machine, and me from six months ago were to travel forward in time to have a chat with me from now, me from back then would probably throttle me from now after only five minutes of listening to how happy me from now is – compared to how miserable me from then was back then.

I recognise that the sentence I've just written makes little to no sense, but frankly I don't care, because I'm happier than a pig in shit right now and couldn't give a toss about such trivial things as accurate grammar and syntax. Without wanting to descend into cliché but fully aware it's going to happen whether I like it or not – the last few weeks have been a whirlwind.

From the night at Laura's house where we finally admitted our feelings for one another, to the subsequent happy days and nights we've spent together, the romance of Newman and McIntyre has reached such saccharine proportions it's a wonder we both haven't died from Type 2 diabetes.

Would you believe we went on a spa day together? Isn't that just fucking *awful*? Awful that I, Jamie Newman – born cynic and natural grumpy bastard – spent an entire afternoon having my skin exfoliated while I chatted to my new girlfriend about what kind of puppy I've always wanted? And I enjoyed every second of it! I would be consumed with self-loathing were it not for the fact that I get laid virtually every night and haven't bought an Asda Meal For One in weeks.

Recently Laura and I have embraced with gusto every hackneyed romantic pursuit you can imagine. We've had a weekend away in a country hotel that had a real log fire in every room. We've walked hand in hand along a misty shoreline. We've been to see *two* romantic comedies at the cinema. We've even been shopping together and picked out outfits for one another.

And the crowning turd in the u-bend? We bumped into Angela and Mitchell the other day – smug couple number one. After a brief chat where Laura charmed the pants off both of them, they invited us round to their house for dinner sometime in the new year . . . and I *accepted*. And I'm genuinely *looking forward to it*.

Aaaaarrrgghhh! I have become everything I despise. Some people say love is like a drug and I'm beginning to believe them. It's a powerful mind-altering one that turns you from a well-balanced individual into an utter moron devoid of all rationality. If you could get it in a bottle it would be Class A and would come with a lengthy prison sentence if you were caught in possession.

And then, so help me God, it happened. The one thing every single man in the world rails against until he meets Miss Right and gives up the battle for his mortal soul. About three weeks ago I knew in my heart that I wanted to get *married*. Knew that I wanted to spend the rest of my life with Laura and get a ring on her finger as swiftly as possible. I can barely look at my face in the mirror these days. Of course I had no idea of how to ask Laura to marry me in a way that'd begin to compete with last month's Roman extravaganza.

In an effort to do so, I decided to pop the question on Christmas Day, so spent the couple of weeks beforehand wracking my brains trying to think of a clever way to do it that'd tie in with the festive season. Nothing sprang to mind that wasn't cheesy as hell or just plain ridiculous. Hiring a sleigh and four reindeer was right out, as was getting a choir to stand outside the front door expressing my undying love in rhyming couplets. Skywriting wouldn't have been a good idea in the middle of a cloudy December day, and I couldn't take the embarrassment of being rejected at a major sporting event in front of thirty thousand people. Frankly, my girlfriend budget was more restricted than it was last month anyway. Creating Rome in someone's living room sounds like a wonderful idea, but you try telling that to my overdraft. It was going to have to be something on a much smaller scale, and therein lay the problem.

Grand gestures may cost a lot and take time to arrange, but they're usually quite easy to think up in the first place. Throw enough cash and time at a project and the chances are you'll impress *somebody* – for the effort you've gone to if nothing else. The small, subtle, heartfelt stuff is where I come a cropper. I'm a man, and therefore subtlety isn't my strong suit. Unfortunately, the one person I'd have asked for advice about this kind of thing was Laura – which would have defeated the object.

While planning the proposal stressed me out, I confess it was a problem I was actually glad to have in the first place. My gamble on Laura's birthday could have gone horribly wrong. She could have hated me for reminding her of her mother's death, and she might never have wanted to see me again after the argument we'd had. Then there was the issue of Mike.

I needn't have worried, especially about the ex-boyfriend. Laura told me about their trip to the lakes and the assault charge she'd narrowly avoided. I've made a mental note not to be standing within punching distance the next time we have an argument.

I searched the internet looking for inspiration on how to propose. This wasn't the most romantic way of going about things, but needs must when you're up against it. It wasn't helpful. The idea of putting the ring into a Christmas pudding was out the window the second I read the story of a girl who'd nearly choked to death when her boyfriend had tried much the same thing. Wrapping the ring in a present was more predictable than a Michael Bay movie, and going down on one knee dressed as Noddy the Naked Christmas Elf didn't really seem in keeping with the importance of the occasion.

On Christmas Eve I still hadn't thought of anything. Laura and I spent the evening together in her flat. Charlie had once again covered herself in glory by going away for the festivities. Laura asked me why I looked so pensive a couple of times, but I managed to brush it off, saying

I was just tired from the long days at work in the run-up to the holidays. In truth, it was the problem of the proposal putting me on edge. Before proper panic had a chance to set in, I decided to throw caution to the wind and play it by ear the next day. After all, you can plan a proposal any way you want, but ultimately it comes down to a simple question and an even simpler answer. There's no point in gilding the lily, is there?

God (or the heavenly entity of your choice) seems to agree with this train of thought as Christmas Day dawns beautifully, with soft snow falling from the sky. *Perfect!* There's a small, picturesque garden at the back of Laura's flats, which is now covered in a pristine coating of white snow. What better place could there be to ask the woman you love to marry you?

'Shall we go and play in the snow?' I say to Laura nonchalantly as she tidies away the last of the torn wrapping paper. 'It looks lovely out there.'

'That's a great idea. Let me go and throw some warm clothes on.'

By the time we walk out of the flat and along the path to the garden my heart is pounding. Is this too quick? Am I jumping the gun? What the hell do I do if she says *no*? Christmas dinner will be ruined, that's for certain. Rejection tends to put me off my pigs in blankets.

Laura sits on the small bench in the middle of the snow-covered grass. She tilts her head up to the sky and pokes out her tongue, giggling when the fresh falling snow touches it. Right then all my doubts disappear. Whether she says yes or not, I know I have to propose.

'What?' she asks, seeing my expression.

'Nothing,' I mumble as I sit down next to her.

'What's the matter, Jamie?'

This is it. This is the moment. This is the point where our lives irrevocably change.

'Laura. I just wanted to ask you . . .' I can't speak. The nerves steal my voice.

Laura takes my hand in hers. 'Ask me what?'

'I just wanted to ask you if you'd—'

'MITTENS!'

Fuck me!

Laura's Diary
Monday, December 26th

Truth be told, Mum, I had a fair idea Jamie was going to ask me to marry him. I know we've only been together a couple of months but I'm already learning to read his face and body language. I know when he's worried. In the lead-up to Christmas he seemed particularly fraught and I knew it had something to do with me. I was pretty sure he wasn't planning on dumping me, so the only other option was right at the other end of the relationship spectrum . . . so to speak.

I was going to say yes, of course. I wish I could have told Jamie that to save him fretting so much. It was evident on Christmas Eve that he was building up to popping the question. You could tell by the way his little face would crumple into a look of indecision and angst every half an hour or so.

I had no idea what he was planning, but I was hoping it wouldn't be a grand, rehearsed event. Asking someone to spend the rest of their life with you should be an intimate experience, as far as I'm concerned. I had to suppress a smile the next morning when Jamie casually suggested we go out into the snowy garden at the back of the flats. It was perfect.

I spent a good ten minutes deciding what to wear. I figured that'd give him time to rehearse. Besides, this was a momentous occasion. I wasn't about to let it pass in a pair of jogging bottoms and a parka coat three sizes too big for me. I picked out a cute ensemble of blue jeans, blue cashmere sweater and the cream Eskimo coat I'd bought from M&S a week earlier, and went back downstairs to lead my nervous boyfriend out into the crisp winter morning.

Things didn't go according to plan.

To be fair to Jamie, he managed to control his temper *fairly* well during what I'm sure we'll come to refer to as 'the second Mittens incident' in the years to come. He didn't physically assault anyone, which was a pleasant surprise, and I'm sure little Astrid's Christmas Day wasn't *completely* ruined by the crazy man next door screaming at her over the garden wall. I'm also positive she was *delighted* when the same crazy man found Mittens (having spent a good twenty minutes searching in the snow for the little blighter) and delivered him back to her doorstep with the greeting, '*There's your bloody cat. Lock him inside in the future. Otherwise I'm going to eat the little bastard.*'

It was midday before Jamie had warmed up enough to unwrap himself from the king-sized duvet and get off the couch. He looked miserable. His planned romantic proposal was ruined and he evidently wasn't happy about it. I, on the other hand, was trying my hardest not to laugh my butt off. By one o'clock I figured it was time to put him out of his misery.

'Are you okay, honey?' I ask and sit down next to him.

'Yes,' he lies, face grumpier than a Scotsman in a heat wave.

'Was there something you wanted to ask me earlier, before Mittens interrupted?'

'Doesn't matter.'

Oh dear. I'm going to have to salvage this one myself.

'Jamie?' I say, grabbing his chin and turning his head to face me. 'Yes, Jamie. I *will* marry you. Nothing would make me happier.'

Several weeks ago I was the one slack-jawed with surprise. Now it's Jamie's turn.

'You will?' he says in a disbelieving voice.

'Of course I will, you silly sod. You only had to ask.'

'Mittens wouldn't let me,' he snaps, folding his arms across his chest and making a face like a sucked lemon.

I know being doubled over with laughter is not the *typical* way you're supposed to conclude a successful marriage proposal, but my relationship with Jamie hasn't really been typical from day one, has it?

So there you go, Mum. I'm engaged! The ring sits on my finger right now and I have to stop myself looking at it every thirty seconds or so to check it's really there. We're not going to hang around. Jamie's going to book the wedding in the new year. After everything we've been through, we reckon it's best to get the wedding out the way, 'before the universe notices I'm happy and takes steps to ruin everything', as Jamie put it.

I'm feeling much more optimistic about our prospects. This is very handy, I think, as it balances out his pessimism nicely. I have a feeling this kind of dynamic is going to be the cornerstone of our relationship.

Miss you more than ever right now, Mum.

Your contented daughter, Laura.

xx

Jamie's Blog

Friday 30 December

'Oh God, I forgot about my mother.

I was so worried about whether Laura would agree to marry me, I didn't even consider what the ramifications might be if she actually said *yes*. As ramifications go, you don't get much bigger than Jane Newman. This is a woman who, had I been born female, would have had me married off to the nearest Arab prince for the price of twelve camels and all the gold you can eat before you could say 'indentured servitude'.

My two older siblings each have a failed marriage behind them, so I'm the last chance my mother has to save face with the collection of evil shrews she hangs out with at the gym. As such, she's taken an unhealthy interest in my love life over the past few years, watching with mounting disgust as I've singularly failed to land a decent relationship with a woman not suffering from severe mental problems. You can imagine how *delighted* she was when the date with rich upper-class Wendy ended in disaster earlier in the year.

'You get it from your father,' she told me. 'On our second date he set fire to his coat sleeve and we ended up in casualty all night.'

And now I'm going to tell her I'm marrying Laura. A woman she barely knows anything about. They've only met once before – a brief exchange outside my house one Sunday morning last month as Laura was leaving after having spent the night with me, and mum was arriving having decided to descend upon her youngest son to berate him for not visiting her enough. I let them exchange the usual pleasantries before ushering Laura away as swiftly as possible.

'Are you ashamed of me?' she'd asked the next day when I saw her.

'Oh God no,' I'd replied. 'It's my mother I'm ashamed of. There's no telling what she might have said to you.'

I was being completely honest. When I was eighteen I introduced Mum to Megan, the girl I'd fallen in love with at college. Within three minutes she'd ordered Megan not to dump me because 'he cried so much last time, we had to keep making him drink Lucozade so he didn't die of dehydration'. This was Mum's idea of a joke. It went down like a flotilla of exploding lead balloons and Megan finished with me soon afterwards.

I'd known Laura for six months, but had done everything I could to keep her away from my mother that entire time. Then bloody Christmas rolls around. The one time of year that you can be guaranteed your loved ones will bump into one another, whether you like it or not. Laura spent Boxing Day with her friends Tim and Dan, but when Mum and Dad told me to bring her round to meet them the day after, I couldn't come up with an excuse not to go.

'It'll be fine, Jamie,' Laura says as I turn the Mondeo into my parents' driveway. 'She can't be as bad as you say she is.'

'Oh no? Did I tell you about the time I wanted to go out at Halloween dressed as a ninja and she made me dress like a potato? Not even a Mr Potato Head, Laura . . . just a big brown fucking potato. They called me King Edward for months afterwards.'

Laura just about manages to control her giggling fit as we reach the front door of the gigantic four-bedroom detached my parents probably bought with my inheritance money. I knock, and a millisecond later Mum opens the door. She must have been standing right behind it, watching us as we pulled up.

'Hello, Jamie!' she says with a level of enthusiasm I'm not used to and throws her arms around me. My mother is not a hugger. Never has been. When I was a kid and would skin my knee or cut my finger, I would receive the appropriate treatment, followed by a pat on the head that would have made my tail wag if I'd had one. I get the feeling this upscale of affection is for Laura's benefit.

'Hi, Mum. Are you feeling alright?' I reply, gently extracting myself from the unnatural embrace.

'Of course I am. I'm just happy to see my son again.'

'I was here yesterday, Mum.'

'I know! And it's the most we've seen of you in months! Your father is always saying he thinks you're avoiding us, but I tell him it's because you're busy. Chris and Sarah are just as bad, mind you. Months go by and we don't see them either. I can't think why. Still, none of that matters now. You've all come to see us at Christmas and that's the main thing. If you can't get your family together under one roof at Christmas, when can you?'

This is officially the longest sentence I have ever heard my mother utter that didn't contain information about how much one of her friends has in the bank, or a complaint that I haven't given her any grandchildren yet. Instead of saying hello to my intended, Mum has decided to launch into a conversation with me, without so much as a glance at Laura. I'd like to think this was an accidental oversight, but I'd also like to think that politicians are honest and weathermen are accurate.

I glance at Laura, who by the looks of things is coming to much the same conclusion I have, given that her eyes have narrowed dangerously. I figure I'd better move things on swiftly.

'Mum, you remember Laura, don't you?'

She looks at Laura for the first time. 'I think so,' she says hesitantly.

Shit.

She bloody does remember Laura, because I was only talking about her to Mum *yesterday* when I broke the news about the engagement. Either she's being deliberately obtuse, or the senility has kicked in early.

'It's nice to see you again, Mrs Newman,' Laura says in a level voice. 'I hope we get more chance to talk than we did last time outside Jamie's house.' She shoots me a hard look as she says this. Great. Now I'm the bad guy here.

'You too, Laurel.'

'It's Laura.'

'Is it? I thought it was Laurel. Like the bush.'

'No, just Laura.'

'Ah. Laurel is such a pretty name, though.'

Oh good God, I'm in a lot of trouble.

'Why don't we go inside?' I interrupt. 'It's freezing out here!' In more ways than one.

'Of course, my number-one son!'

What the hell? Why is Mum talking to me like she's bloody Charlie Chan?

'Yes, oh fiancé of mine,' adds Laura. 'Let's get out of the cold, shall we?'

Oh fiancé of mine? Now Laura sounds like an extra in a bad Shakespeare play. What's going on? Understanding dawns . . . I see what's happening here. I'm being fought over. Both women are attempting – not very subtly – to lay their claims of ownership over Jamie Newman. We might as well go to the nearest field with them standing at either end, and plonk me down in the middle. They can then both call my name and whoever I run to gets to keep me. This battle of wills should be a boost to my ego, but in reality I just find the whole thing extremely creepy.

'Dad in?' I ask, hoping that the old bastard is around to take the heat off me a bit.

'No. He's playing golf. *Again.*' Mum's voice sours considerably. I can only imagine the scale of the argument that transpired this morning. 'Anyway, come in both of you,' she adds and spins on one heel.

Laura moves to follow. I chew on one knuckle briefly in the doorway, before I take an *extremely* deep breath and go in after her. The battle for Jamie Newman's soul continues in the kitchen over expensive arabica coffee. Mum launches forth into several anecdotes about my childhood – most notably ones where I have relied on her love and support. She fails to mention the pats on the head and lack of hugs.

Laura counters with an exaggerated retelling of what I now like to refer to as the 'Rome-in-a-Home' date. She makes me out to be some kind of romantic hero, attentive to every one of her needs and desires. If I really was as great to her as she's making out I'm sure I'd get more blow jobs.

I just sit in silence, sipping my coffee and watching the two of them go at it. I take great solace and pleasure in the fact the coffee has no mint in it. I'm waiting – and dreading – the mention of the 'W' word. I know it's coming, but there's still a small part of me that clings to the hope it may be forgotten in the battle of Jamie-related one-upmanship.

Nope. No such fucking luck.

'So what have you planned for the wedding?' Mum asks Laura over her third steaming mug of arabica. 'I have a few suggestions myself, if you'd like to hear them.'

Oh, I think we will be hearing them, whether we like it or not, Mother. My buttocks clench on the seat. I know what Laura's about to say – and what the fallout will be. Laura takes my hand in the time-honoured gesture.

'We're getting married on Monday, Jane.'

Luckily Mum isn't taking a mouthful of coffee at this moment, otherwise we'd both be wearing it.

'What?'

'Monday, Mum. We're going to have a simple ceremony at the register office – we booked it this morning.' I'm trying very hard not to sound apologetic. 'You, Dad, Chris and Sarah are all invited, of course.'

Laura and I discussed our planned nuptials at length last night. Neither of us enjoys pomp and circumstance, so we both agreed to keep the ceremony simple, short and sweet. The idea is to be married as quickly as possible because we love each other – not spend months and thousands of pounds planning a wedding day that everyone else might enjoy, but we'd find extremely tiresome. For us, the plan was perfect, but I knew damn well others wouldn't see it that way.

'You can't do that!' Mum exclaims. 'Weddings are supposed to be well thought out and planned far in advance!'

By *her*, in this particular case, I'm sure.

I can see the disappointment growing behind Mum's eyes and start to feel a little bad. Then I remember the potato costume and successfully shake the feeling off.

'Jamie was worried you'd feel that way, Jane. I was too. There are reasons for it that I'd like to explain if you give me the chance.'

Hang on. This is new. Laura didn't tell me she was going to say any of this. I thought I'd have to be the one to defend our plans.

'Go on,' Mum says in a cool voice.

Laura then begins a reasoned and nuanced argument that quite frankly takes my breath away. She waxes eloquently about how much we love each other, explains with clarity and purpose the reasons why we want to avoid a big ceremony, and vividly describes the wedding we are going to have in such a way that even Mum starts to look a bit glassy around the eyes before she's finished. I'm once again reminded how lucky I am to be marrying this woman. Not only does she have a fantastic rack and an arse to die for, she's also extremely intelligent and better educated than I'll ever be.

Mum still looks disappointed when Laura has finished speaking, but I can hear a grudging, new-found respect in her voice when she responds.

'You seem to have thought this through, Laura, and I can tell this is what you both want.'

'It is.'

Mum draws herself up in her chair. 'Very well. Monday it is. I'll just have to wear one of the outfits already in my wardrobe.'

'I'm sure you'll look stunning, Jane,' Laura compliments.

Mum smiles at her warmly for the first time, 'Why, thank you. Not as stunning as you, I'm sure.'

Unbelievable. Mum then looks back at me. 'Now if only we can get this son of mine into a decent suit, we'll all look the part.'

'Ha!' snorts Laura. 'That'll be a miracle. Getting Jamie to dress smartly is bloody impossible.'

'I know, my dear! I've been trying to get him to look more presentable for years. Maybe you'll have more luck than me.'

'I doubt it.'

They both stare at me with eyebrows arched in an identical fashion. I think I preferred it when they were at loggerheads with one another.

The conversation continues for another hour. I'm forced to endure barbed comments from both mother and future wife until my father comes crashing in through the kitchen door laden with golf clubs. This is a relief as the chat they've been having has descended into what can only be described as a Jamie Newman-bashing session. I'm pleased that they're finally bonding – but do they have to do it by talking about how many holes I have in my boxer shorts?

Still, at least they now have a common cause – and Mum has just about come to terms with the way we're going to get married, thanks to Laura's brilliant speech.

She continues to charm the hell out of my parents for the remaining hour or so we spend with them, and by the time we make our way back to my place I've stopped worrying about whether they'll get on with her in the long term. Now all I can think about is how eloquent my fiancée can be when she needs to be.

I've never seen anyone handle my mother so capably before. Never seen anyone manipulate her so convincingly. It's amazing.

Oh God. And this is the woman I'm *marrying*? I must be bloody mental.

Laura's Diary
Monday, January 2nd

Dear Mum,

This will be a very quick entry as I don't have much time, and have a lot to do.

I write this on the morning of my wedding day. It's early – just gone seven, but I've already been wide awake for nearly an hour. I keep trying to get my head around the fact that in just a few hours I will be Mrs Jamie Newman, but every time I think I've got a handle on it, my mind freezes up and I start to giggle like an idiot. I'm also still sporting a hangover from the weekend, which probably isn't helping matters. Tim and Dan threw a legendary New Year's Eve party at their house. It was the first one I've actually enjoyed in years, as I got to kiss a man I'm in love with on the stroke of midnight. This is an event of such rarity for most people that I had to get it down on paper for future generations to read and marvel at.

Said man then got so drunk I found him trying to pole dance against the washing line about an hour later, but we'll try to gloss over that and just remember the romantic parts of the evening, shall we? Jamie is lying next to me right now, snoring like a freight train. I'll wake him up shortly and bully him into making me a nice cup of tea – but for the moment, let's just keep it between you and me, Mum.

I'm delirious at the prospect of marrying the idiot next to me – even though he's just farted loud enough to wake the dog next door. And the wedding itself is going to be just the way we want, no matter how Jamie's mother might feel about it. It's a small affair. No bells, whistles or cans strapped to the backs of cars.

I told Jane that this was because neither Jamie nor I wanted a big wedding, but there's a little more to it than that. It's really about *you*, Mum. Jamie will have his family at the wedding, and we'll both have plenty of friends in attendance as well – but there will be a big Mum-shaped hole there for me the entire day.

That's the real reason I didn't want a huge wedding ceremony. It'll just hurt too much not to be able to see you sitting there in the crowd blubbing your eyes out as I say my vows. We could spend a hundred thousand pounds and have the most lavish wedding this side of a Kardashian sister, and I know I still wouldn't enjoy it much because my mum wouldn't be there.

If I haven't already chronicled enough reasons why I'm marrying Jamie, here's another one: I told him all of the above, fearing he'd think I was being selfish and was more concerned with your absence than his presence. He just smiled, kissed me on the forehead and said, 'We'll do it whatever way you want, baby.' I'm going to interpret that as his understanding of the way I feel, rather than him not giving a monkey's what the wedding is like, so long as he doesn't have to wear a suit for more than three hours.

If you were here, Mum, there are so many things I would say to you today. As you're not, I'm going to write them down:

All the good things I have done to this point, I owe to you. All the bad things I owe to the consumption of too much white wine. You gave me the best possible start in life a woman living on her own possibly could have done, and I thank you for everything you did to get me to this happy point. This might sound weird, but I feel like a frisbee. You threw me into the air when I was a young girl, I hovered around for a while not knowing where I was going to end up, and Jamie has now caught me – hopefully for the rest of my life. I just have to hope he doesn't trip up and send us both headfirst into the ground. He can be a clumsy bugger sometimes.

Alright, it's a fairly horrible metaphor, but it's the best I can come up with at half past seven in the morning – with a fiancé sleeping by my side who seems determined to poison me with the gas expulsions coming from his backside.

Suffice it to say, I just can't believe you won't be here to see me get married, Mum. I know you'll be watching though. Try not to think too badly of Jamie's mum, try not to throw up when you see us dancing at the reception, avert your eyes from proceedings after 11 p.m. . . . and if you see Cary Grant float past at any time during the wedding, you have my permission to leave and chat him up. Just don't do that thing where you snort when you laugh. It'll put him right off and you'll never get a second date. Trust me, I'm an expert at these things.

Right then, time to get up. And put on a gas mask.

Love you, miss you, and enjoy the wedding.

Your soon to be Newman-ised daughter, Laura.

xx

Jamie & Laura's Blog

Thursday, January 12

Okay, I'm starting this.

No doubt Miss McIntyre (sorry, I mean *Mrs Newman*) will interrupt before long with some inane comment—

Watch it, Newman.

—like that one, but for the minute the floor is mine.

So here we are in the Caribbean. You'll be entirely unsurprised to learn it's hot and sunny. This is causing my British equilibrium to be completely thrown off. It's January. I should be freezing cold and dressed in thermals right now, not strolling around in a pair of shorts and flip flops.

The locals would probably prefer it. The pasty white complexion of your legs is blinding them.

Quiet, woman. I think I look dead sexy. From the colour of my skin you might be forgiven for thinking I'm just *dead*, but I'm hoping a fortnight soaking up the rays coming from Captain Shiny Hot Ball will solve that problem. Anyway . . . we have lastminute.com to thank for our impromptu honeymoon destination. Who'd have thought you could score two weeks in paradise for less than a grand at this time of year?

Admittedly the building site next door to the hotel isn't

exactly picturesque, but when you're a freelance copywriter and your newly betrothed runs her own recession-hit chocolate business, getting value for money is your prime concern.

Thanks to the way the government is picking our pockets these days it's a miracle we could afford this at all.

Please don't start getting political. A vein pops out on your head when you rant about the government. It's not attractive.

My apologies, I'll try to curb my natural instincts. We're currently sitting by the pool, taking turns to type. This is a fairly awkward process, but there didn't seem much point in writing separate entries, given that we're in each other's pockets most of the time at the moment. Laura looks quite adorable in her big straw hat and sunglasses. Every time she leans closer to see what I'm typing I get a quick blast of the perfume she's wearing. It's a smell I'll never get tired of.

Why thank you, kind sir. You don't look so bad yourself – apart from the sunburn. The hat's on my head for a reason, dummy. I can easily provide you with the name of my perfume, and what excellent shops you can purchase it from.

Gee . . . thanks, honey.

Get on with it, Newman. It's getting bloody hot out here and I want a dip in the pool.

Alright, alright.

This is the sum-up of everything that's happened since Laura's meeting with my mother, an experience I am still trying to forget by consuming all the rum in the Caribbean.

It wasn't that bad, Newman. We just need time to get to know each other more.

When I'm at least ten miles away from now on, if you please.

Very funny.

This will be my last entry on this blog for a while. I don't feel the urge to spill my guts online anymore. This has something to do with the fact I'm happy. *Nauseatingly* happy. Misery loves company – and blogging is really good therapy if you're having a bad time of it. My life's been a rollercoaster over the past year, so there have been a lot of good reasons to post. I'm in a much better frame of mind now though (as you've probably noticed) so it's time to put a stop to things before someone justifiably murders me for writing reams and reams of sappy cobblers about my new marriage.

Oh great. They're going to blame me for ending the blog now, you idiot! It's his idea to stop, everyone. Believe me!

I agree with what Jamie says though, to be honest. My diary's probably going to get a rest for a while as well. I don't know where in the universe my poor mum is these days, but I'm taking up way too much of her time with my problems, when she could be off chatting up Cary Grant somewhere.

Why Cary Grant?

Mum loved his movies. Wherever she may be in the afterlife, there's a good chance she's pulled him

**already and is trying her best not to snort when
she laughs. I can just imagine the two of them on
a date somewhere picturesque and Heaven-y.**

Well, let's just hope you're right and she hasn't invited
him along to watch a Polish penis-slapping movie with
her.

Hilarious.

I am, aren't I? Anyway, back to the point: The wedding
was pleasurably straightforward. The weather on the day
after New Year's behaved itself and we tied the knot under
crisp, blue January skies. The ceremony at the register
office was mercifully brief – something I was very happy
about as I'm sure the collar on my shirt was at least one
size too small for me.

There was a small crowd in attendance. Just my parents,
brother and sister, Laura's best friends and a few others
who'd got wind of our nuptials. I didn't invite my middle-
class chums – they would have just spent the entire time
arguing over who'd had the bigger wedding cake at their
own nuptials. Dave and Katherine were there, though –
they looked eternally happy to be present at a wedding
they had no part in organising.

The register office staff were a bit bemused when we
requested the room be decorated with rubber plants. I
also suggested fajitas for the wedding meal. Laura didn't
think that was very funny for some reason.

**You want to be careful, pal. One day I'll get my
own back. You won't notice five-day-old beef if I
cook it for long enough.**

Gulp.

I'll take over here, thanks. You're a man, so you're not describing it properly. You're making it sound like a police report.

Tim gave me away. He ended up crying more than anyone else, bless him. Both he and Dan wore the most beautiful frocks I've ever seen. Charlie and Tilly looked adorable as well. So much so that Jamie's friend Ryan didn't stop dribbling for the entire day, much to the disgust of his terrifying girlfriend Isobel. Jane Newman looked happy . . . I think. It could just as easily have been constipation, but I'm going to give her the benefit of the doubt. The pleasure on the faces of the rest of Jamie's family looked more genuine.

That's no surprise. Any time Mum's attention is directed at me they can relax for a couple of hours. It's like the local mice when the big barn owl sods off for a fly about.

Quite. I wore a very nice strapless white silk dress. Jamie managed to stay in his suit long enough for the photos to be taken. As soon as the photographer had told us he was done, though, the jacket and tie came off so quickly you'd be forgiven for thinking they were on fire.

It's a character flaw. Sue me.

I'm not that bothered. At least I don't have to worry about you leaving me and marrying another woman. The prospect of having to wear another wedding suit would be enough to put you off.

Amen to that.

The entire service only took twenty minutes – and we were at the enormous house where Jamie's parents live for five o'clock. This was the concession we had both agreed on for Jane's benefit. We didn't let her near the wedding itself, but told her she could organise the reception afterwards.

If Hitler had been able to order the Third Reich around as effectively in one week, we'd all be speaking German now.

I won't argue with that. Say what you like about your mother, the woman works well to a deadline. She did a terrific job, all things considered. Quite how she got an entire roast pig and more decorations than you can shake a stick at organised over the Christmas holiday is beyond me.

Witchcraft. Witchcraft and thumb screws.

All in all it wasn't the most spectacular or original wedding in history, but we got the chance to spend the day with (almost) all the people we loved, which was all that mattered.

It also meant we had more money to spend on the honeymoon – hence my sunburn and her big straw hat.

That's right. A three-layered dress and a six-layered cake sound like nice ideas in principle, but give me a bikini and a Mai Tai anytime.

You'll get no argument from me on that one, Beautiful . . . particularly the bikini part.

The laptop came with us of course – despite my protestations – hence this rather convoluted entry in Jamie's blog. There is a final point we're building

**to here, I assure you – and if Newman would stop
interrupting for a minute I can get to it.**

Sorry, oh bright shining light in my otherwise cloudy,
miserable day.

**Apology accepted. Now I can't think of what to
say. The lure of the pool is breaking my concentration. You're the writer, Jamie, you have a go.**

I think what my gorgeous but absent-minded wife is
trying to say is that we've been through a lot to get to
this happy place. I've read her diary and she's seen my
blog. They both appear to be a catalogue of mistakes,
embarrassments and failures that make you wonder how
we ever managed to get to this point: in love, married
and sipping cocktails under the Caribbean sun.

There's only one explanation really, and it's as cheesy
as it is true. We love each other. Love may not conquer
all, like the songs say, but it can keep you upright and on
your feet when the cold wind is blowing hard and trying
its best to knock you on your arse. Love can bring two
people together – even when piles, sprinkler systems, food
poisoning, porn movies, microlight aircraft, sex maniacs
and annoying ex-boyfriends try to keep them apart.

When you fall in love, there's no problem that can stop
you being together, no matter how large it may seem at
the time. Whatever the issue, you just have to trust that
the way you feel about each other will overcome it.
Including when she stumbles across you taking a shit into
a pedal bin.

**And that's why I married this idiot. Not because
of the shitting into a bin, I hasten to add. There**

isn't enough alcohol in the world to blot out *that* memory.

The rest of it, though? Yeah, that about sums it up for me.

No relationship is ever perfect, but when you truly love each other . . . *it doesn't have to be.*

Laura and Jamie's adventures don't quite end there – here's a preview of the next instalment in the *Love* ... series, *Love ... And Sleepless Nights*

Laura's Diary
Monday, April 1st

Dear Mum,

Well, it's finally happened. I've achieved my life-long ambition. The one thing I knew I wanted to accomplish from an early age.

It's been many years in the making, but I can now honestly say that I, Laura Newman, have successfully thrown my guts up in front of a group of men at a crucial job interview.

It's a modest achievement in the grand scheme of things, I know. Others have sought to climb Mount Everest or cure cancer. Me? I just wanted to embarrass myself in front of important and influential people in the most spectacular way possible.

Oh my, yes. When my time on God's green earth is done, I'll have many, *many* fond memories to look back on

– including the day I attended an interview at the Hotel Chocolat central offices in London, and did the technicolor yawn all over three company senior executives.

The timing was, of course, *perfect*.

Rather than the sudden and overwhelming urge to be sick hitting me at a more opportune time – while watching *Britain's Got Talent*, or listening to another one of Jamie's office anecdotes, for instance – it happened at the precise moment I was impressing the hell out of potential employers with my unrivalled knowledge of chocolate production and marketing.

Until the time of the upchuck everything had been going quite well. The interview had come at precisely the right time for my nerves, Jamie's sanity and our joint bank account.

The stress of having to close the shop thanks to the recession was just about killing both of us, so having the chance to interview for a highly-paid role with one of the largest chocolate companies in the country was a major lifeline. Needless to say, this isn't what I'd planned for when I first opened the shop – before the downturn hit, and running your own independent business suddenly became about as sensible as juggling flaming hand grenades. To tell the truth I probably limped on for longer than I really should have. If I had been thinking purely logically I would have sold up two years ago and got out with minimal fuss. As it is though, I'd invested so much of myself in that shop that simply boarding up the windows and handing back the keys felt like a betrayal of my dreams.

Dreams don't pay the bills however, so the inevitable happened three months ago and Laura Newman's ambitious plans for chocolate-based world domination went by the wayside.

To be honest with you, by the end it was something of a relief to be free of the stress, although replacing the stress of shop ownership with the stress of finding a new job isn't the greatest of exchanges when you get right down to it. You can imagine how pleased and excited I was to find an advertisement for a senior position at Hotel Chocolat. This was a job I had the skills, experience and qualifications to do standing on my head.

So off I go to London – tottering along on my blackest, shiniest, most authoritarian high heels; wearing my most business-like black pencil skirt and jacket, my hair in the tightest, most professional ponytail you can endure without your eyes permanently watering. I'm more prepared for this interview than they were for the bloody D-Day landings. My poor, over-taxed brain is chock-a-block with every detail it can hold regarding the company's business practices and methods.

Tucked under one arm is my portfolio, which includes various new chocolate designs and flavours I've come up with, along with the receipts from the shop – right up until just before the crunch came along and ruined everything. I am *determined* to get this job. I am a modern, powerful, creative woman who will not be denied!

Sadly, I'm also feeling a wee bit queasy as I board the 8.15 to Waterloo from a drizzle-soaked Southampton. I put the unpleasant feeling down to Saturday night, and the excesses of Charlie's birthday party. It's never taken me two whole days to recover before, but I figure I'm in my thirties now, so it's probably only going to get worse.

The journey by train is spent revising and trying to ignore the two chavs at the back of the carriage. Both are clearly already drunk and one is probably mentally challenged to boot. He has that irritating song, 'Perfect', by Pink playing at full volume from his mobile phone and keeps singing along with the chorus, making a particular effort to scream the line 'You are perfect, *FUCKING* perfect to me-ee!' at the top of his lungs. There must be a class somewhere that these people join to learn how to be as annoying to other members of the public as possible. I'd imagine the first lesson is 'stopping in the middle of a busy street to hit your kids', through to a final lecture about how to most effectively drive your immediate neighbours insane with parties that go on to three in the morning, and the ownership of aggressive, smelly Pit Bull Terriers. The two I'm stuck with must have excelled in the session devoted to anti-social behaviour on public transport. Thankfully, the annoyance disappears when a muscular train guard, who looks in no mood for hijinks of this sort, stalks past my seat and neatly ejects both of the little sods at Woking before they can vandalise the train.

In London, the cab ride to the Hotel Chocolat offices costs an arm, a leg and part of my lower intestine – but I arrive good and early, ready to dazzle and wow my prospective employers to the point of them needing sunglasses.

First comes the half-an-hour wait in front of the receptionist. This seems to be a compulsory part of job interviewing these days. There must be some sort of manual for employers that suggests a good way to soften up applicants is to have them sit directly across from your receptionist in uncomfortable silence for thirty minutes.

This one is about twenty-two and wearing more make-up than the bloody Joker. I'm hoping for a loud noise off to one side, just to see if the slap she's wearing falls off her face if her head moves too quickly.

The phone on her desk rings and the clown princess of crime picks it up. 'They're ready for you now, Mrs Newman,' she tells me through her four layers of foundation.

'Thanks,' I reply, getting up and worrying at my skirt, which has inexplicably developed several large creases, despite the fact I've been sat still for half an hour. My heart is hammering in my chest like a caffeine-injected blacksmith as I pick up the portfolio beside me. I wobble past Heath Ledger towards an expensive mahogany door.

It's opened by a shiny young man in a dapper grey suit. He offers me the kind of smile I've only seen before on the face of a used car salesman.

'Good morning Mrs Newman,' he says. 'Please take a seat.' He gestures to a chair in front of an expensive mahogany desk. There must be a mahogany salesman in the city somewhere with a gold plated toilet.
  'God morning,' I reply.
  God morning? What the hell does *God morning* mean? I meant to say 'Good morning' of course, but my nerves got the better of me. He's going to think I'm some kind of weirdo, God-bothering religious fruitcake now!

'Good morning,' I say. He smiles at me again in a slightly confused fashion and walks round to join his two colleagues behind the desk. One of these is a thin, pleasant-looking black man in a crisp blue suit and the other is Christopher Biggins.

I blink a couple of times. How is this possible? Since when did Biggins – portly comedian and star of many a bawdy television romp in the 1980s – change careers and become an executive for a chocolate company?

I blink again. It's not him, thank God. He just looks uncannily *like* Christopher Biggins. Relief washes over me. I don't do well in the presence of celebrities – even minor ones. I once saw Brian from *Big Brother* in HMV and nearly peed myself. The thought of having to conduct myself professionally under the level gaze of a pantomime dame and the character Lukewarm from Ronnie Barker's *Porridge* chills me to the bone.

Hang on a minute. Isn't Christopher Biggins dead anyway? I'm sure I read that somewhere . . . *Oh God. How long have I been stood here thinking about Christopher Biggins?*

'Please sit down,' not-Christopher Biggins tells me. He's got a look on his face that suggests I was stood stock still trying to remember if Christopher Biggins is dead or not for an uncomfortably long period of time.

Stop thinking about Christopher Biggins, you mad bitch!

I sit down, grateful that the desk hides the cavernous creases in my skirt. The nausea from earlier has returned stronger than ever, but I put it down to a combination of nerves and the Saturday hangover – and do my best to ignore it.

'My name is Charles Lipman,' says the nice black man. 'These are my colleagues David Presley.' He indicates the slick car salesman. 'And Roger McDougal.' He points at not-Biggins.

'I'm very pleased to meet you all,' I say, lying through my teeth.

'As are we, Mrs Newman,' Lipman continues. 'From reading your CV, it appears you may well have the qualities we're after for the position of Southern Area creative manager.' He pulls out a copy. 'Tell us all about your previous experience.'

And with that, the interview is underway. I put thoughts of camp television stars (who may or may not be dead, the jury is still out at this point), wrinkled skirts and *Batman* villains out of my head, and begin the job of dazzling these three men with my suitability for this fabulous job.

It all goes swimmingly. For about twenty minutes. They nod their heads appreciatively as I tell them about their business. They smile approvingly as I suggest ways to increase productivity and profit margins. They even chuckle at my carefully honed jokes about running my own business in a recession-hit economy. Jamie had fed me these last night during a last minute flurry of revision. I wasn't sure about using them, but he said they'd go a long way to proving I had a sparkling personality.

It wasn't all that pleasant detailing the collapse of the shop. Nobody likes to talk about something that ends in failure. The main thing is for them to know that the shop only went under thanks to the bad economy – not because I have the business acumen of a dazed camel. They seem to readily accept my well-crafted point of view, so I move on swiftly to other matters, relieved to have got that explanation out of the way.

I'm in the middle of explaining the marketing strategy I'd like to employ for next Easter, when the nausea I've been keeping at bay all morning breaks through my carefully constructed mental dam and washes over me like a sickly tidal wave.

'Are you alright Mrs Newman?' not-Biggins asks, seeing I've suddenly gone a whiter shade of pale.

'Yes,' I squeak. I take a couple of deep breaths and continue. 'As I was saying, the campaign needs to focus on parents, so I've devised a few strap lines I believe would—'

My mouth is full of sick. One minute it's empty, the next it's full. I've never known anything like it.

In previous experience, I've usually had more warning signs: the rolling of the stomach, that horrible coppery taste, the feeling of your throat muscles constricting . . . This time though, it's like a magic trick, and not a good one like Paul Daniels used to perform with the lovely Debbie McGee, or the type David Blaine inflicts on innocent passers-by in the middle of a city street.

The vomit simply appears in my mouth in a split second. I shut my lips tight trying to prevent its exit into the world. My cheeks puff out, and I begin to resemble Alvin the bloody Chipmunk.

'My word. Are you feeling sick?' Charles Lipman asks.

Alvin can't reply. If Alvin tries to say anything, a stream of warm vomit will be the only answer. Some might say this would actually be an improvement over the high-pitched, squeaking stupidity that usually comes out of Alvin's mouth; but I'd cheerfully listen to a whole album of that crap right now rather than be sat here with a gob full of my own stomach lining.

Then horrifyingly, like a fat commuter boarding an underground train during rush hour, more sick jostles its way into my already over-filled mouth. My hand flies up to cover my lips, but the inevitable is already happening. My gob can't take anymore. The barrier is breached. The walls of Jericho have well and truly fallen.

From between my fingers, a fountain of vomit sprays forth, happy to be free of its enforced imprisonment. It's like putting your hand over a hose – only smellier and involving more dry cleaning.

All three of my interviewers back away in horror. Charles Lipman and David Presley are out of their chairs in an instant, but poor old portly not-Biggins is less limber, and instead of jumping out of his chair to avoid my upchuck, he simply falls backward in a slapstick tumble his famous döppelganger would have been proud to execute in any matinée performance of *Jack and the Beanstalk*.

I'm up out of my seat as well, one hand still clasped to my face. With the other I try to indicate that I need the nearest toilet. I waggle my finger around feverishly while skipping backwards out of range. It looks like I've invented a new dance, some kind of finger waggling, puffy-cheeked update on the Charleston . . . with added stomach broth.

Thankfully, Charles Lipman divines the import of my interpretive dance. 'There's a bathroom through that door!' he screeches, pointing maniacally at another expensive mahogany door to my right.

I rush towards it and bang the door open. Inside is one of those executive washrooms that I have no doubt no-one has thrown up in previously. It's just not designed for that kind of thing. This washroom has seen many rich hairy men's arses in its time, but I bet I'm the first woman in history to come in here and lose her giblets. I happily christen the facilities in the toilet stall at one end of the room.

Most of the sick has already made its way up from my stomach, so I'm spared the hideous dry heaves. These are always the worst part of being sick. You sound like a power-lifter trying to get four hundred pounds over their head, and look like dog trying to bring up a stuck bone.

After only a couple of minutes I'm able to move away from the toilet bowl to clean myself up. There are some flecks of vomit on my jacket, but on the whole things could be worse. My face is that of a heroin-addled prostitute, but my clothes are in a fairly respectable state of repair considering what's just happened.

Of course, I can never leave this bathroom again. This is my home now. They will have to send in food, drink and other supplies. I'm glad my mobile phone is in my pocket so I can still communicate with loved ones. They'll miss me no doubt, but perhaps the people at Hotel Chocolat can arrange visiting hours. I'll have to bed down in the toilet stall and I'll need some books to while away the coming decades, but on the whole staying in here is far better than opening the door and facing the three men I've just been sick in front of.

'Mrs Newman?'

It's fucking not-Biggins. He wants me out. He wants to bask in my shame, to delight in my embarrassment, the bastard. I *hate* you, not-Christopher Biggins, and everything you stand for.

'Are you alright, Mrs Newman?' Presley also pipes up.

Of course I'm not alright you colossal pillock. I've just completely ruined my chances of getting a job with your company.

'Yes, I'm fine!' I shout through the door a little too loudly. 'I'm going to come out now.'

The door swings open and I'm greeted by three worried faces. Not-Biggins looks the most concerned, to his credit.

'I do apologise gentlemen. I can't explain how that happened. I assume I must be sick.'

Charles Lipman's eyes narrow. 'You're not . . . *pregnant* are you?' he asks tentatively.

Me? Pregnant? Don't be so flaming silly!

'Oh, I very much doubt it, Mr Lipman. My husband and I are always careful with our contraception.'

And there we have it. I'm now discussing my sexual health with three men I met less than half an hour ago. The bright red of shame flushes my face.

'Oh.' Lipman looks horrified. Presley looks like a deer in the headlights. McDougal continues to inexplicably look like Christopher Biggins.

'Well Mrs Newman,' Lipman carries on, 'perhaps we should end the interview there, given what's just happened? We wouldn't want you to have to continue in your present state.'

You mean the feeling of bloated nausea? Or the drying vomit now forming an unsightly crust on my lapel?

'Perhaps you're right Mr Lipman.' My face takes on its most hang-dog expression. 'Thank you for seeing me today. I apologise for the sickness.'

'That's quite alright, Mrs Newman. My wife suffered with morning sickness with our first child,' not-Biggins points out.

I'm not pregnant. Fuck you, Widow Twanky!

I go over and pick up my portfolio.

'You're welcome to leave that here if you like, Mrs Newman, I'd like to read through it,' Charles Lipman says. A glimmer of hope breaks through the clouds of abject mortification.

'Thank you Mr Lipman, I will.' I'm surprised by the way my voice is shaking. With sudden unvarnished terror I realise I'm close to tears. Lipman's simple offer to read my portfolio is about to make me cry like a five-year-old girl.

What the hell is the matter with me?

With shining eye and trembling lip, I go to shake hands with Charlie-boy. He looks down at the hand I proffer, no doubt examining it for signs of my stomach contents. I smile like an arsonist holding a match and withdraw the hand, swallowing the hard lump I've got in my throat.

'Well goodbye gentlemen,' I say in a rush. 'I hope you all have a very pleasant day.'

All three offer me an equally polite farewell.

For an instant not-Biggins looks like he's going to hug me. I don't think I could stand that. If he tries it I will burst into tears. How could I not? He has the friendly, open face of a pantomime legend. Thankfully he doesn't go for an embarrassing clinch, and without another word I scurry out of the room. As I pass the Joker, I can hear her on the phone asking for a cleaner to come up to Mr Lipman's office as quickly as possible. I couldn't feel worse about myself right now if you told me I had dengue fever . . .

Of course, there is no way I'm actually *pregnant*. No way in hell! It's just the result of the hangover from Saturday – and probably the Thai takeaway we had last night. Yes, that must be it! Just a combination of too many vodkas and some bad chicken Pad Thai.

The visit I make to a nearby Boots on my way back to the train station is *entirely* coincidental. I merely go in to purchase some Rennies to settle my stomach. Quite how the pregnancy test finds its way onto the counter in front of the sales assistant is beyond me, but for some reason I buy it anyway and stick it in my jacket pocket. I may – or may not! – take the test later, just out of idle curiosity. Only because I've never taken one before, and am interested on a purely academic level as to how they work.

After all, there's no way I'm pregnant. Oh goodness gracious me no!

Oh good God, I'm pregnant. Knocked up. Up the duff. In the first blossom of motherhood. Carrying the first few cells of an unborn human being that will one day soon expect to squeeze itself out of my vagina . . . which can't happen of course. It's *impossible*. Squeeze a human being from my prim, healthy lady garden? Don't be so ridiculous!

Oh Mum, I really wish you were here. I'm *terrified*.

Love and miss you,

Your soon to be enormous daughter, Laura.

xxx

Jamie's Blog
Tuesday 2 April

'Don't worry, I'll pull it out before I come and finish up on your back.'

As far as I can tell, with the above words my life as I knew it came to an end. Not the most apocalyptic, erudite or quote-worthy of statements to mark the end of existence itself, I admit. Nevertheless, this was indeed the utterance that signalled the death knell of Jamie Newman's carefree and frolicsome existence. I've put a lot of thought into this, and I'm sure I'm right.

It was a month ago.

No . . . let's go back a bit further than that, to last autumn, when Laura had to come off the pill because it was giving her migraines. That was fine though, the family planning clinic wasn't far from the office so I was happy to pop down and pick up a free supply of condoms, until such time as she found another pill to take – one that wouldn't leave her needing a darkened room for the rest of the day. Either that, or until we agreed on an alternative form of contraception.

It was only supposed to be for a few weeks, but if there's one criticism you could level at Laura and I as a couple, it's that we can procrastinate to absurd lengths if we want to. Testament to this fact is the eight-year-old couch we're still sitting on. No matter how many times that bloody DFS advert comes on the TV, we still can't get our arses in gear to go and have a look at their latest collection of sofas in their never-ending sale.

Anyway, fast forward to a few weeks ago – and a mesmerisingly dull Sunday evening in March. Frankly, I'm going to blame Simon Cowell for this entire thing. If the selection of lunatics on *Britain's Got Talent* had been of a higher standard they might have held our attention for longer and I wouldn't have suggested a quick screw before *Top Gear* started.

I'm aware that sounds about as romantic as herpes, but it's not actually so bad. Laura and I have a very healthy sex life – where long, sensual and romantic love-making sessions are very much in evidence. But the universe thrives on variation, and as such, we also enjoy the occasional quickie when we have a spare bit of time. As two people with long work hours, these quickies have sadly become more common than the sweaty, lengthy, candle-lit sessions – a big drawback to living in twenty-first century Britain if ever there was one.

We've really perfected it over the past few months. We can have sex in the morning before work, in the evening while the chicken is defrosting, in the bathroom just before heading out to Tesco – and on one memorable occasion, when we were both feeling uncommonly horny, in the disabled lift *at* Tesco. Don't worry, we felt awful about it afterwards.

Suffice it to say, if there was a speed-shagging championships, we'd make a good showing.

And thus it was that Jamie Newman positioned his lovely, graceful and inordinately beautiful wife on her knees on the aforementioned eight-year-old couch and prepared to administer a good, hard, quick pounding.

But, *disaster*!

'Oh shit. I haven't got any johnnies,' I tell her, pumping little Jamie rapidly in order to maintain an erect state while we consider this dilemma.

'Really?' my gorgeous wife replies, bum aloft and arms gripping the sofa cushions. 'I haven't got any either!'

'Stay right there,' I order. 'I'll go have a look in my bedside cabinet.'

Off I trot, penis waggling gaily in front of me like a divining rod, leaving Laura to rest her head in her hands – the perfect globe of her peachy little behind still pointing upwards, making her back arch in that way I find so irresistible.

Sadly, there are no condoms in evidence in the bedside cupboard. I move on to the bathroom to check the cabinet in there, still pumping away at little Jamie to ensure that should I find any of the little rubber lifesavers, I will be standing proud and ready. Thus begins a five-minute search of every cupboard and drawer I can think of – all conducted with one hand. I resemble some kind of sex pervert with a fetish for household storage facilities.

'Come on Jamie!' Laura shouts, the impatience in her voice unmistakeable.

'Sorry! Just er . . . play with yourself for a while. I'll be there as soon as I can!' Yes indeed, the romance is well and truly alive on this very special night.

So there we are, me frantically pulling drawers with one hand and penis with the other, while Laura is left to her own devices with Ant and Dec in the background, chatting to a contestant who's just sung 'Camptown Races' at Amanda Holden in full scuba gear. (The contestant is the one in scuba gear, by the way.)

'It's no good,' I say, wandering back into the lounge. 'There's none in the house.'

'Shit,' Laura replies. 'We'll have to leave it then.'

She's right, we should stop. It's the sensible course of action. But here's my problem: my wife is a *very* attractive woman, and right now she's kneeling on the couch, her legs apart and her bum in the air. This was the time for Jamie Newman to utter the words that would seal his fate:

'Don't worry, I'll pull it out before I come and finish up on your back.'

There's a part of Laura – the romantic, soft demure lady inside her – that is no doubt disgusted by this pronouncement. Fatally, the part of Laura firmly in charge of her faculties right now is the animalistic, filthy sex kitten that every woman *also* has inside her – if you look hard enough and poke her in the right places.

'Okay, but make sure you do it right,' she breathes in a husky voice.

I do indeed *do it right*, in my defence. I exhibit what at the time I believe to be *superhuman* levels of self control, and succeed in not arriving at my destination until I've successfully made Laura's toes curl and removed myself from the equation.

The aim with which I dispatch my manly exuberance at the conclusion of events isn't particularly good, so at least we now have a *very* good reason to get off our arses and buy another couch.

The problem is that particular method of ad-hoc contraception isn't good enough. Pulling out early *doesn't* mean you're safe even if you think you are. This is something that teenagers with no common sense whatsoever know, but was a fact we had both conveniently chosen to forget until yesterday: April Fool's Day.

And what a crappy April 1st it had been for me already, before I even walked in the door at 6 p.m. I'd spent the entire day arguing with a sub-editor over the advertising space at the rear of the paper. I say *arguing*, but it had mostly been a series of passive-aggressive emails, culminating in a testy five minute 'chat' outside the reprographics department.

This isn't the kind of fun-filled day at work I'd envisaged when I'd struck out on my career as a writer. I thought it would be all about sitting in a whirlwind of creativity, knocking out brilliant and insightful articles about whatever important topic I felt needed Newman's expert opinion. It was my destiny to write the best press releases, news articles and advertising copy that had ever been committed to paper.

Sadly the universe hasn't humoured me thus far, so I find myself killing time at the local paper, arguing over an extremely trivial three inches of column space. It was an argument I'd lost so my mood was blacker than the soul of an adult Justin Bieber fan by the time I got home.

'Evening baby,' I say morosely to my wife when I see her standing in the kitchen.
'Evening,' she replies in a very small voice, after I administer my usual hello kiss.

Had my mood not been quite so bad I would have noticed the signs right there. As it was, I pulled off my tie, ambled into the lounge and parked myself on the semen stained sofa cushion (turned upside down), intent on watching people less fortunate than myself on *Sky News* for half an hour or so. This is an aspect of human nature I've never really liked, but when you've had a shitty day at work, it does often make you feel better to come home and find out all about somebody who's day has been so bad they've wound up talking to Jeremy Thompson about it. I'm completely oblivious to the emotional state of my nervous, fidgety wife as she comes and sits next to me.

'Good day?' I ask her, hoping she'll just say yes, and then ask me how mine went so I can launch into an epic diatribe on how much of a wanker Colin Forbes the sub-editor is.

'Umm. Not . . . not so great, I suppose.' She picks at one corner of a cushion.

'Really? That sucks,' I reply, eager to use this point in the conversation to steer it towards my own woes. 'I can sympathise. I've had a ball-ache of a day. You know that twat Forbes? The one with the squinty eye? Yeah, well he's been a right prick today. I had to get an extra half page spread sorted for the Easter promo, but *oh no* . . . he says he needs it to run the rugby report. Bloody rugby report. Who cares about rugby, eh? Stupid sport. I tell you baby, sometimes this job does my head in. I really wish I could leave it, but I can't be arsed to look for anything else at the moment. Going through all that interviewing rubbish makes my blood run – *oh shit.*'

My blood runs cold. I've forgotten about Laura's job interview. Today was the day she went to London to see the Hotel Chocolat people. (It's chocolate with an 'e' by the way. This is Britain, for crying out loud. The day I start spelling things in French is the day they can come and lock me up for general insanity.) How could I bloody forget such an important thing? I even wished her good luck this morning before I left for the coal face. Nine hours later and I've forgotten about it completely. I'm going to blame Colin Forbes and the dry chicken sandwich I had for lunch.

A tiny mewl escapes my lips as I try to get my head around the utter catastrophe I've just brought on my own head. I know that the next few minutes of my life are going to be *awful*. I also know I'm likely to be sleeping on the spunky couch tonight.

I begin to apologise . . . and stop. I simply cannot think of an adequate way to express my sheer, unbridled regret. There aren't enough words to appease the wrath that I know is coming my way – like a dark harbinger of the Jamie Newman apocalypse. If I thought hacking off one hand might do the trick, I'd do it. Hell, I'd gnaw the bloody thing off.

I look at Laura. It's even worse than I thought.

I was expecting a vicious scowl – a vision of pent-up female fury, ready to be unleashed on my stupid, forgetful man-face. But no, this is far, far worse. She just looks pale, upset and very, very confused.

Oh God! The raging animal I can deal with. But Laura just looks deeply hurt by my oversight. This makes me feel a million times worse. I haven't made her angry, just sad. I wish I could kill myself by choking on a sofa cushion.

'I'm so sorry, honey,' I say and take her hand. 'Tell me how the job interview went.' I look at her downcast face. 'Did it go well?'

Which is about as silly as asking a Jewish person in 1939 if they're going to vote for Hitler at the next election. She looks at me with those glorious blue eyes, her mouth trembling. I gird my loins and start mentally compiling a shopping list of Häagen Dazs ice cream, flowers – and possibly a brand new car. Her hand squeezes mine. I take a deep breath and prepare myself for whatever she has to say.

'I'm pregnant.'

'Well, never mind,' I begin. 'I'm sure something else will come up, and this won't—'

Hmmm. Something's wrong. My brain is sure Laura just told me the interview didn't go well, but my ears are insisting she said something completely different. Best to rewind the last few seconds and re-evaluate . . .

Nope, she definitely didn't say anything about the job interview.

But what was the strange and alien sentence she *did* come out with? It sounded like 'I'm pregnant' . . . but that is of course *impossible*. That is a sentence Laura must *never* utter, at least not for the next six or seven years, while we're still building our careers and there are far-off holiday destinations to be visited. It's probably a good time to ask her to repeat herself so we can put to rest the silly idea that she said something about being pregnant.

'Sorry? What did you say?'
  'I said I'm pregnant.'
  Oh my—

My ears don't appear to be functioning properly at all today. It still sounds like she's saying she's pregnant. I'd better ask one more time just to get to the bottom of it once and for all.

'What?'
  'I said I'm bloody pregnant, Jamie. Are you deaf?'
  I try to respond. 'Blurben hurmen?'

It now sounds like the speech centre of my brain has short circuited. I am no longer able to form proper words, and will spend the rest of my days communicating in a way that only Mr Blobby and the people of Sweden will understand.

'What?' Laura says.

This time I can only produce a sound like a tyre deflating. My mind is going a hundred miles a second – yet is inexplicably also frozen solid. How can this be happening? How can today have started with me straining to release last night's Thai (I really need to cut down on the unhealthy takeaways), continue with a terrible chicken sandwich at lunch, peak during an afternoon argument with Colin Forbes, and end with my wife telling me she's pregnant? How can this happen today? On the first day of Apri—

Aha! Now I get it! It all becomes abundantly clear. It's the first of April! Laura – the little scamp that she is – is playing an April Fool's joke on me. How very clever and funny my wife is!

I love a good April Fool. I've been on the receiving end of a few crackers in my time. For instance, there was the one back in university when my course mate Carlo changed the submission date on my creative writing assignment to April the second. Oh how he laughed as I spent the next six hours working at the keyboard like a chimp on amphetamines, trying to knock out three thousand words before his fake deadline. It was my fault really. He knew how bad I was at paying attention to deadline dates and exploited my lack of concentration in expert fashion.

Then there was Superglue Thursday. I was eleven, my brother Chris was thirteen and he thought it an excellent idea to coat the inside of my Spock ears with UHU. How he laughed as I spent the afternoon in casualty with mum while the acetone gently melted the glue and slightly burned the tops of my ears. He wasn't laughing by the time we got home and he found himself grounded for the next two months. I took great delight in wearing my brand new set of Spock ears as I cycled past his bedroom window whenever I had the chance.

Laura's particular choice of April Fool on this occasion is more prosaic and required less thought behind it, but I have to give her props for the commitment she's putting into the performance.

'Yeah . . . good one Laura!' I exclaim happily.

I'm so pleased I've managed to work out the joke. She had the wool pulled over my eyes for a while there, but now I've seen the light!

'What?!'

That's funny, she should be smiling now, happy in the know-ledge that her little ruse has been discovered. I jump out of my chair, releasing some of that pent-up nervous tension.

'I said good one! You really had me going there baby. You . . . pregnant! *Brilliant*!'

For some reason she still isn't smiling. My feet, having a far better grasp on the reality of the situation that my mind, take me swiftly out into the kitchen to make a cup of tea. Laura follows me. She stands and watches me banging cups and the kettle around for a moment before speaking.

'Jamie, this isn't an April Fool. I'm being serious. I'm pregnant!'

See, this is the problem with my wife: she never knows when to let a joke go. It's all about the timing and I've seen through her duplicity, so there's no real reason to keep it up.

'Come on baby, you can stop now. I know you're mucking about.'

Her face like thunder, Laura stamps over to me and pulls the tea towel out of my hand. She hits me with it. Twice.

'I'm not bloody joking, you idiot!' She hits me with the towel again to emphasise her point. 'I' – *whack*! – 'AM' – *whack*! – 'PREGNANT!' *Whack*! *Whack*! *Whack*!
　'Please stop assaulting me with the bloody tea towel!' I wail.

Her arm drops. I put the cup I'm holding back onto the counter with trembling fingers. Silence . . . terrible, terrible silence descends.

I look at my wife's exhausted face. 'How?' I ask.
　The look of exhaustion turns to disgust. 'It might have

had something to do with you humping me like sex-starved rhinoceros. That's generally the way these things happen.'

'But . . . but we're *careful*.'

It will be a couple of hours before I remember the night of the frantic wank-search for condoms.

'Not careful enough.'

I breathe in and out a few times. I can't think of anything to say, but I *must* say something. I can't spend the rest of this marriage communicating via clicks and grunts.

Unable to utter anything more about the pregnancy, I give her a half-hearted smile and say, 'So, how did the job interview go?'

She gives me a look of pure, unadulterated misery, her eyes welling with tears. 'I was sick all over Christopher Biggins!'

'Isn't Christopher Biggins dead?'

Laura starts to cry in great hitching sobs and I throw my arms around her. I have to as my legs are about to give out on me.

An hour later, I've consumed two beers and am feeling a touch calmer. Laura went to pour herself a glass of wine, but remembered the reason why she needed a glass of wine in the first place and put the bottle back. Instead she nurses a cup of sweet tea – because that's what you do when you've had a shock: drink sweet tea. Quite how a sugar rush and caffeine injection is supposed to calm your nerves is beyond me, but what do I know? I can't even screw my missus without putting a baby in her belly.

'What are we going to do, Jamie?' Laura asks, staring at the television, where *Sky News* reporter Joey Jones is standing outside Number Ten, telling us all about the new tax breaks for working families. The coincidence is eye-watering.

'I don't know, baby. I really don't.'

Now, there is *one* suggestion I could put forward . . . but it is a *horrible* suggestion. The kind of suggestion you hope to never make in all the days of your life. Sometimes though, necessity trumps all other considerations – and this is one of those times.

'Do you . . . do you want to have it?' I ask. 'Because, you know, you don't have to.' The words are like ashes in my mouth. I can't believe I even said it.

'Do you mean a . . . a . . .'

'Yes,' I say, cutting her off. 'It is an option.' An awful, *awful* option.

'I don't know. What do you think?'

The logical, sensible part of me says: *Yes, oh God yes. We don't have enough money, or time, or money to have a baby right now.* But looking at Laura, her beautiful blue eyes glistening with tears, I just can't imagine ever putting her through that kind of . . . *procedure.*

This is the woman I love. The reason why she's now pregnant is because I love her. Because I *made* love to her. This baby is a product of that love. Alright, it wasn't the most romantic bunk-up in history, but it wasn't a casual, meaningless shag either.

'No,' I say emphatically. 'I don't want that.' I take her hand. 'I love you baby, no matter what, and if you're going to have my baby, then you *are* going to have my baby.' I sit back a bit. 'Unless you don't want to have it of course.'

She laughs. It's a short, brittle sound, but a laugh none the less. 'I hadn't even thought about not having it, to be honest. All I've been thinking about is how big my arse is going to get.'

'Don't forget your tits,' I say, smiling for the first time in what feels like a century. 'They're going to be *massive.*' I waggle my eyebrows at my tired wife and make obscene grabbing gestures with my hands, making her giggle.

She wipes her eyes and sniffs. 'It's going to be bloody hard, honey,' she says. 'Me without a job, I mean. The money from the sell-off isn't going to last long.'

I put my arm around her. 'We'll be alright. I can grab some extra freelance stuff. Maybe you could find some too.'

She gives me a withering look. 'What? Like a freelance chocolate maker?'

'Yeah! Why not? That kind of thing exists, yeah?'

Of course things like that don't bloody exist. I'm clutching at straws, but I'll say anything right now to keep the mood away from abject misery.

'Maybe,' she replies, and giggles again, 'I could go to people's houses and cook a shit-load of chocolate for them.'

'There you go then! I could do the marketing for you.' I put a hand out. 'Laura Newman: She'll cook you a shit-load of chocolate.'

This makes her collapse with laughter, which makes me laugh too. I guess if you can get the shock of your life and be laughing your arse off an hour later, it must mean the situation can't be all *that* bad.

Right?